i

Now You're Someone Else

William Baruch

Characters in Alphabetical Order of First Names.

Abraham	Cardozo	Son of Cardozo and Mendez
Anwar	Anwar	Ari's Palestinian cousin
Ari	Geffen	David and Ayelet's Israeli son
Atsuko	Atsuko	Marty's Japanese girlfriend
Avril	Keighley	Moishe's partner
Ayelet	Geffen	Ari's Israeli mother
Beelzebub	MacAllister	Maria's cat
Daanya	Mohammed	Ari's biological sister-means
David	Geffen	Ari's Israeli father
Gillian	Mendez	Avril's friend and doctor
Hadassah	Cardozo	Ari's Jewish girlfriend
Hannah	Geffen	Ari's little sister
Hiba	Hiba	Nadeem's girlfriend
James	Roth	Supervisor, lead programmer
John	Cardozo	Host doctor at dinner
Maria	MacAllister	Ari's Catholic girlfriend
Marty	McCann	Maria's work friend
Moishe	Maxwell	Brooklyn artist.
Nadeem	Mohammed	Ari's Palestinian brother
Norman	Bates	Lead programmer
Rafik	Mohammed	Ari's biological father
Saarah	Mohammed	Ari's biological mother
Sebastian	Beatty	Architect
Shona	Cohen	Ha'Aretz journalist
Spiros	Spiros	Greek Cypriot retiree.
Walter	Wilson	Journalist

Table of Contents

Chapter 1 - I came to America - Ari

I came to America one fine day in May equipped with paperwork that would grant me permanent resident status. The reason for coming was not the usual stuff about wanting a better life and opportunities. No question that I wanted all that, but I wasn't tired or poor or huddled or yearning to breathe free. Well, yearning to breathe free? Maybe.

Mostly, life had been pretty good for me up to this moment. I came from a prosperous family, lived in a comfortable home, had friends, and was enjoying my education at the University of Tel Aviv, Blavatnik School of Computer Science.

Compulsory military service came and went after finishing high school, and that, thankfully, is now behind me. But it was the same for everybody in Israel, and frankly I thought it was right to do my duty for my country, and I never questioned it openly. I served my two years and eight months with mild distinction, but without ambition, and most fortunately, without fighting in one of our all too frequent wars. I served without protest or rebellion against boredom, or even discipline. I admired and respected some of my commanders, others I held in contempt, but kept my feelings to myself as far as was possible.

What counted for action in my case, was manning checkpoints on the West Bank. I'll explain what the West Bank's all about later, but for now, just know that manning a checkpoint there was a dreary job that came with much human contact. Passing through the checkpoint near Jericho, at which I served for most of my army time, were a constant stream of women with children, women in groups, women in fancy cars, women sitting in the backs of trucks being taken to olive groves to harvest the fruit. There were families of Jewish settlers in beat up sport utility vehicles. There were men with donkeys and mules and camels and goats and sheep. There were men in Mercedes and BMWs and Land Rovers wearing designer sunglasses. And there were service busses, trucks of all kinds and Israeli soldiers, and so on.

I found I could converse well enough with the Palestinian people, although somewhat haltingly at first. I owed my skill in Arabic to the days when my dad hired an elderly Palestinian gardener, who turned out to be a cheerful, sociable, and kindly man. Sam was his name, short for Sameer. He used to be a farmer that my dad had met years earlier when working in Galilee, and by coincidence had met again in the town of Jaffa which adjoins the southern end of Tel Aviv. In conversation Sam told my dad he was retired and bored, at which my dad asked if he would like to tame the jungle, which at the time passed for our garden. The answer was yes, and he came and bumbled around the yard performing miracles without, apparently, much effort. He wasn't paid much, I understand, but he worked at his own pace and helped himself to anything that the garden produced as long as he left something for our family.

When there were no kids around to play with, I would hang out with him while he worked in our unusually large lot. His Hebrew was minimal, so he spoke Arabic to me all the time, and some of it stuck. When my parents went out, he would even babysit my sister and me from time to time. This experience, together with my high school Arabic gave me a passing competence in the language, sufficient, I gathered, to be promoted to corporal only four months after I'd completed my basic training.

I casually continued to learn the language, sometimes from a textbook to fill time in the dreary hot days at the checkpoint when things were slow, but also by listening to Arabic radio stations and reading Arabic newspapers. The speech I heard most of the time was in the local dialect of the Levant, like that of our old gardener. As my competence in the language improved, the fewer were my moments of confusion and embarrassment when trying to untangle some excited protest. The people passing each way were often aggrieved at the inconveniences of showing IDs and passes merely to be allowed to move along a road that they and their parents and grandparents had moved along without hindrance in years past.

But all of that was in what now feels like a different era. My life had been turned upside down and I had to get away and stay away from where I was in Israel, and the obvious place for me to go to was America. That's what this is all about, written, some by me, but most of it by my good friend Maria who seems to know me better than I know myself. I'll say at the beginning of each chapter who the narrator is as part of the title, as I did in this chapter.

Before coming to America, I had to fill out endless forms and wait for what felt like eternity. The expectation was that I would be successful in my application, since I had applied and been accepted at New York University in Manhattan, to continue my computer science graduate studies. But the visa I applied for was for permanent residence not just a student visa. My life was on hold while I waited for a definite yes. I had to attend an interview and answer some mind-numbing questions at the US Embassy on 71 HaYarkon Street in Tel Aviv, not once, but twice.

The style of the embassy building is, I believe, called "brutalist", and on this occasion for good reason. Externally the ground floor where normal buildings have windows, this has solid concrete panels, and what I presume to be courtyard or garden is surrounded by a tall opaque fence with spikes on top of it. I know how important security must have been in its design but walking into its secure innards seemed to suck all the joy out of the day. Perhaps that was my response to the realization of its ultimate meaning for me? Namely, this is the reality of leaving my family and my friends and my life as I knew it; this is the start of the process that's really going to make it happen, probably forever.

Some of the questions they asked seemed funny and in more normal circumstances would have invited funny answers but the rigid non-smiling middle-aged female face across the desk exuded power and brooked no humor. When she goes home to a husband or family, that face must change for the better, mustn't it? It has to, and I tried to think of that

4

when I mumbled my replies just loud enough to be heard. I reminded myself that she's just a person doing her job, maybe trying to cope with work burnout, or a shitty boss or too long hours.

Anyway, all those English language video games I played as a kid came in especially useful after all. Imagine that! I learned something inadvertently, and useful, while having fun. I suppose they have Hebrew speakers at the embassy, but my interview was in English. English was a required class at school but certainly playing English language video games since barely more than a toddler had helped.

I was warned about, but did not quite believe, I would be asked the old saw of the question "Are you now or have you ever been a member of the Communist Party… bla bla?" or something like it, but when it was actually asked it I felt a giggle bubbling up inside me. I suppressed the giggle, but only just, and felt a little better after that.

And before we go any further, no matter what you may have heard to the contrary, no I'm not a member of…, nor have I ever been. I suppose the curiosity I felt about exotic ideologies led me to acquaint myself with some charming, dedicated lefty whackos. Israel has its share of them, tell you about that sometime, maybe, but for now the focus was on the short-term goal of getting a visa in the bag.

In total I thought the interview process cold and unwelcoming, but I suppose that's understandable given how routine and mind-numbingly boring it must be for the interviewer. How many millions like me there must be with their millions of reasons that they want to leave behind the life they live now and take their chances across an ocean in a different and strange land? How many millions were turned away even before they had the chance of an interview? And how many deserving interviewees failed to get an entry visa for reasons they never understood?

Be that as it may, it appears that the U.S. Immigration and Naturalization Service looked kindly on my application for permanent residence. I'd had some unwelcome celebrity in Israel for which I was not responsible in any way. For some committed religious folks, the celebrity was more like notoriety, though not officially, of course. In Israel I became a mild security risk for military service, for government employment, and even for private sector employment, and worst of all an embarrassment to have for a friend. Well, some friends, not all my friends. It doesn't take long to find out who your real friends are when something like this happens. The eventual arrival of the US entry, and permanent resident's visas came as a welcome relief, strangely mixed with the terrifying prospect of leaving behind my parents, good friends and all that was familiar to me, possibly forever.

So, the momentous day came when my parents and little sister Hannah came to Ben-Gurion Airport to see me off. I had a seat on an El Al flight to JFK airport in New York City. My excitement was tempered with a deep sadness that we all shared, Hannah, my little sister most of all. She kept saying to my dad:

"I think it's stupid daddy, it's nonsense, nonsense, nonsense," saying nonsense louder each time she said it. "He doesn't have to go, he doesn't have to go, why does he have to go? Why does he have to go" building up to a crescendo. The poor child was distraught, as was I, but I tried not to show it. I couldn't speak and wouldn't try, knowing how my voice would betray my feelings if I did. Then she was quiet, as were we all in the sure gloomy knowledge of separation for a long, long time.

She hugged me, and I hugged her and the feeling of how much I really loved this bright little jewel of mischief and fun of a sister was welling up inside me. "You come to visit me sometime, right?" I asked her, and she nodded mutely and tearfully at me. My parents too, nodded. We were all crying. We were all in a deep funk.

So, we parted. I got my boarding pass from the departures desk and went to the security line, dumped my bags on the conveyor and answered all the penetrating whys, whats, and hows that the airport questioners at Ben-Gurion International Airport know how to ask. I answered with a peculiar gravity which is not usually part of my nature. Given the security risks of flying from this part of the world, I was willing to cooperate.

The flight took about 12 hours which seemed like an eternity. I felt exhausted with stress and boredom, but the local time of arrival was barely any later than when I set off. At JFK I was pulled aside by a friendly immigration official who needed to check out my visa and generally piddle around on his computer, take a photo, print a slip of paper for me to keep inside my passport and other inscrutable bureaucratic things. I was too tired to care about what he was doing. He was middle aged with a black and gray anarchic mustache. His demeanor was calm and routine-like. He bulged slightly out of a dark blue uniform looking very Italian.

In my travel-fatigue stupor I felt my eyelids drooping and I pictured him on the stage at La Scala in Milan, still in his dark blue uniform singing some tragic aria while surrounded by a cast dressed in Renaissance costume. Our family had vacationed in Italy the previous year where my dad and I had been to the opera. My mom, who hates opera, went shopping at Mercato di Via Fauche with my little sister Hannah, and felt sure that they had had a whole lot more fun. Anyway, this silly micro-dream had the effect of relaxing me. Now I had to find my way in a new strange enormous city, but I'd had time and help preparing for this.

My dad, David Geffen, had a friend who had moved years ago to New York City. We called him uncle Moishe. He and my dad had first met sometime in the late nineteen sixties in northern Israel, specifically at Kibbutz Sasa in Galilee. My dad was born at Kibbutz Hatsor, near Ashdod, somewhere south of Tel Aviv, and went to Sasa in 1965 because they were short manned. There he met Moishe, a migrant originally from London, with whom he developed a life-long friendship. Both left Sasa in about 1975. This would have been about two years after the 1973 war and eight years after the 1967 war in which both had served together, forming a bond with each other, unbroken and unaffected no matter where they went to live subsequently.

I mention all that because I was an unwitting beneficiary of that bond. Uncle Moishe is an artist, (of course he isn't really my uncle). He set up a studio in Tel Aviv and barely made a living at painting. Many of the paintings he did manage to sell were to American visitors. So, he moved to America where he found a lot more customers for his artwork in than he ever had in Israel. His apartment-cum-studio in Brooklyn was where I was headed until I could find a place and an income. My parents said they'd help too. Moishe said if I'd come on any other flight, he would have met me, but he was opening an exhibition in Manhattan that same evening. His email told me to take a cab and find a key in the lock box by the apartment door.

Chapter 2 - In America for The First Time - Ari

So, I ditched the cab idea and took the subway. Our family vacations in Europe gave me a love for travel and getting to know how countries worked for everyday people. I won't bore you with all the details except to say I figured out how to take the AirTran to Howard Beach JFK subway station, then catch the "A" train to Broadway Junction.

This station was a delicious shock introduction to a vigorous and work-a-day side of New York. There were staircases, bridges of dirty green and black ironwork, and tunnels under and over a spaghetti of subway lines from beneath the ground to high above it. Crowds streamed along pedestrian tunnels, filled moving and still staircases and filled platforms to their edges before embarking and disembarking in great waves. All the while trains are stopping and starting and screeching and clattering around in different directions. There I caught the L train, alighting at Bedford Avenue in Williamsburg, and walked the last half mile closely following emailed written directions, dragging my large, wheeled suitcase, and carrying an overstuffed backpack.

The apartment house where Uncle Moishe lives looks like an old, converted warehouse on North 10th Street. It has a formidable, locked oak double door at the side of which is a keypad. My emailed directions gave me the entry code. I took the elevator to the 6th floor and found my way to the apartment in the northwest corner of the floor, I think. I rang the apartment buzzer several times but there was no answer but beside the door was a lock box containing a door key to which I had the code, also per my emailed directions. I let myself in, dropped my luggage and yelled hello, but there was still no answer.

I walked straight over to a large window opposite the apartment door because my first instinct was to orient myself in the city. I could see a patch of dark gray blue, which I figured would be the East River and bits of the Manhattan skyline. The setting sun was just touching the tips of the towers, their sides now dark gray and merging into one another, devoid of sunlight that so sharply defined their profiles. So, I knew then I was looking to the West.

The apartment was a penthouse with a high ceiling. It had two roof lights in a studio section with windows on the North wall and a sort of partition wall just long enough to block the bright evening glare from the setting sun, but not separate from the large and generous, gigantic actually,

11

living area. As you would expect in an artist's studio there were frames of all sizes and paintings in various stages of completion, and of various subjects, and paints, brushes and bric-a-brac tools and several easels, and an ambient but not unpleasant aroma of turpentine and linseed oil. Some works were arranged carefully, in a way that suggested they were displayed for visiting customers.

The large open living and kitchen area was not what you'd call ostentatious or even luxurious, but it was very adequate, and very comfortable; the kitchen was well equipped. Two doors near the entrance passageway were the only completely walled off rooms and turned out, thankfully, to be bedrooms, a large one and a small one each with its own bathroom. Clearly uncle Moishe was not doing too badly in the good ole USA.

This was a relief to me. It seemed that his resources would not be too stretched if I were to stick around for a few weeks or months if that's what it took for me to find and afford a place of my own. So, I dumped my suitcase and backpack in the smaller of the two bedrooms, kicked off my shoes and felt a gravitational-strength force pulling me towards the refrigerator, my hunger having been suppressed by nervousness and excitement up until that moment. There I found an Aladdin's cave for a foodie. I grabbed some hummus and pita bread and followed that with some toast and peanut butter to satisfy my immediate need, eschewing the epicurean delights within. There wasn't any soda, so I took some apple juice and added water the better to quench my thirst.

Then I stood in silence. The hum of traffic below in the street was barely audible. The relaxed untidiness of books and papers on a sofa, bottles of wine on the kitchen counter, photos on the walls were calming to me. There was even a photo of my parents and myself as a baby and a few which looked like kibbutz life. I think one of them, of light honey-colored small stone houses dotted on a hillside, was Sasa, where my dad and Moishe met and lived for a while. Then there were pictures of uncle Moishe, in one he was getting an award of some kind. I was startled because I didn't know he had a beard! He never used to. He doesn't have one in our photos back home. Oh wait, this is my home now. What a strange feeling Looking round again there were two other photos that were head and shoulder portraits of him with a woman. A woman!? Huh!

Also, in the living room there was a large screen Mac computer on a desk in a corner office-type area. I went to look more closely at it, noting that it looked like a powerful machine. I guess Moishe must do graphics and possibly videos, I wondered if he'd let me use it? I had an Israeli cell phone and found out that it didn't work here. That was back in 2004. I heard they do now though.

I didn't have much time to reflect on my situation, and in any case, I didn't intend to. Uncle Moishe was likely to appear at any time, as too, it now seemed possible, was the woman in the photograph, I'll call her his partner for now, that I'd never met and never even knew existed.

Of course, relaxed untidiness is one thing, masculine total chaos is quite another. There has to be a woman here, I thought. I looked around again and this time noticed flowers on windowsills, a calendar with two handwriting styles in the date squares. Cosmopolitan magazine and Forbes on the sofa. Then I went to look in the larger of the two bedrooms. There was no doubt. A king size bed, men's and women's shoes in two walk-in closets, and a few casual clothes, both men's and women's left on the bed as if the wearers had hurriedly discarded them to dress in something more formal for an outing.

It was deadly quiet in the apartment which amplified noise going on in my head. There was so much to do and think about. I needed to sign up for classes at NYU (New York University), and actually attend them. There would be assignments to do, so I was going to be busy. Too busy I hope to think about my predicament. I had to think about earning some money. Then I thought of my parents and Hanna so I wandered back to the computer and sat down without thinking much about it, logged in as a guest user and wrote the following email to my mom and dad:

Dear Mom and Dad, I arrived safely about five minutes ago at Uncle Moishe's place. It's really very nice. It's a bright airy light apartment on the 6th floor, the top one. I haven't seen Moishe yet because I guess he's out at an exhibition he's holding that he told me about in his email. There are signs in his apartment that he's either married or has a longtime girlfriend which I didn't know about. He didn't mention in his email to me, and I haven't met her yet. Maybe she's with Moishe now? Or not? If/when she comes, I'll tell you all about her.

Anyway, I just wanted to say I've arrived safe and well. I raided the fridge, so I've eaten, and I love you both and Hannah very, very, very much.

Ari.

Then I looked again at the photos with the woman in them. She had strong but regular facial features. I guessed she was younger than Moishe, but she was no child. Her face was handsome and feminine rather than pretty, with a lively smile that showed slightly irregular teeth.

She was plainly not self-conscious, at least she didn't appear so in the photos. She was totally good looking, having a straight nose, full lips and a regular chin. She laughed with her eyes which curved downwards with heavy-ish lids suggesting she might be Asian or part Asian. Although the photos were monochrome, I figured she had fair, not Asian hair, which in a shade of gray matched a semi casual jacket with wide lapels, covered partly by that hair, as were her shoulders. The jacket looked open perhaps to the waist, but the photo did not cover that far down her body.

As for Uncle Moishe, do you know how hard it is to describe someone you've known forever, almost for as long as your parents and whose photo is on the wall of your childhood home? Of course you do. OK I'll look at the photo and pretend I don't know him, here goes. Well, he's just sort of medium height, medium build, not fat not thin, he has a beard, I said that already. The beard looks whitish or grey on these photos. I guess you could say he's well preserved, his brown eyes (that's from memory) are intense, piercing even.

His nose is a bit crooked from knocks he took during his early years as a stevedore on the London docks.

I don't think stevedores exist anymore, now that everything comes in a shipping container, but I'm told stevedores used to be the guys that loaded and unloaded the ships. Usually, nets made of rope full of stuff used to be lifted from the ships' holds with a crane. Placement of the goods on the dockside was guided by a stevedore, which sometimes hit him in the face if the crane operator was not paying attention, and sometimes even if he was. That's the official reason. Dad hinted that he used to get into fist fights with other stevedores for the diminishing number of jobs on the docks, a common union membership notwithstanding. The introduction of shipping containers to load and unload the ships needed many fewer workers. So, I digress; in short, he had a history of fighting and his face showed it.

It was eight years ago since I'd seen him. That was when he last visited with us in Israel. The memory of a pleasant vivacious guy was very clear. I was eager and a little anxious to renew my friendship with him. Anxious because in the past it was not a peer-to-peer friendship but that of a child, make that a boy, in his early teens, to an adult. Not being a teenager anymore, this had to change for both of us.

And as I thought of meeting him and his partner, I realized that I may not be too pleasant a person to stand close to, having accrued many hours of travel dirt and sweat. I made for the shower in what I presumed to be my room, the smaller one, and treated myself to a long hot soaking and a change of clothes, finding the least crumpled jeans and shirt in my suitcase that I could. Coming out of the room having descended into a stupor of travel fatigue and lack of sleep, halfheartedly drying my hair I stumbled back into the living room. Two people on the sofa turned their heads towards me.

Chapter 3 - Hello My Boy - Ari

Hello my boy, shalom, shalom, God it's good to see you! God how you've grown!" Uncle Moishe got up and hugged me.

"God! You're taller than me" he added, "How are your mom and dad and your baby sister? not a baby anymore I expect?" As he gripped me in his hug, I saw over his shoulder his partner get up with a bemused grin.

"Don't want to interrupt this love fest but are you going to introduce me?" she asked.

"My dear, this is Ari, David and Ayelet's son, Ari, this is Avril, my...." Moishe was struggling to describe his relationship.

"Partner," she interrupted helpfully, raising her eyebrows, and grinning a full grin while she looked at him.

"So good to finally meet you, I've heard so much about you," she said turning to me without pausing, and speaking through her friendly grin.

I reflexively returned her very welcoming smile, thanking her for letting me share their home and expressed a hope that I would not be getting in the way for too long. I did not say, but wished, that Moishe had told me at least something about her, I guess it was not a big deal to him. No, that can't be right. Obviously, it's a big deal to him.

She acknowledged my thanks by saying: "That's alright luv, where else are you going to go in this town?"

"Luv", she called me in a peculiar accent, a sort of English accent but not a bit like the London Cockney accent which I hear when Moishe talks. His accent is so strong you can hear his Cockney when he speaks his poor Hebrew. As a kid I used to find this funny, and I would try to imitate his peculiar way of speaking.

I learned over the next few days and weeks that Moishe's partner was just that, his partner. She is what is sometimes called his common law wife. In other words, they had been husband and wife in all respects for the last six months and had progressed to that state in stages over about three years. They started with casual dates, then a divorce of one of them from a previous spouse, then a steady relationship but having different apartments. Lastly an architect assisted renovation of this penthouse, customized to their lifestyles and Moishe's occupation. Except for having a government piece of paper that states it, they were man and wife.

Avril told me she hails from a town that I'd never heard of in Northern England called Bradford, in a part of that country called Yorkshire. Up until that time I would not have been able to find it on a map, and of which I'd only ever heard in the context of terriers and puddings. I liked her

19

accent, and she made no attempt to hide it or moderate it. She told me that on her home turf it was considered very much moderated, and devoid of local dialect. She had forced herself to eliminate dialect words and phrases from her speech in order to be understood in foreign parts like New York.

Moishe then broke back into the conversation. "Make yourself comfortable my boy, Ari, I should say, you must be dog tired. Have you eaten?"

"I...I, raided your fridge, took some hummus and peanut butter."

"Is that all? You must be starving."

"Not really, I'm mostly tired".

"Of course, of course," he continued kindly, "your body clock must be telling you we are in the wee hours of the morning. I see you found your room. Have you told your mom you have arrived safely? There's a computer over there. Does your phone work over here? Mine didn't a few years back when I came, I had to get a new one"

"I don't know about my phone, but I logged on to your computer as a guest user and told everyone at home that I'm here".

"Good, good, now tell me…"

"Leave the lad alone, let him get some sleep" interrupted Avril.

"Of course, of course…" Moishe mumbled something. I don't know what, because I turned around and went straight to my room to a comfortable bed and slid between soft, clean sheets that must have been Avril's doing. I thanked her mutely while lying awake waiting for sleep which came, I can't say how, except that it was quick. I don't remember anything until I awoke, you won't believe unless you've been on one of those flights which cross many time zones. It was at about 4am New York time. I dozed until about eight and it took me about three days to get completely over the time difference.

You may have noticed, as I have, that sometimes I refer to uncle Moishe and sometimes I just called him Moishe. I felt that our friendship moved quite quickly to a peer-to-peer relationship, and it no longer made sense to call him "Uncle", so I dropped it - sometimes and forgot at other times.

The following day I planned to go to NYU to sign up for classes which I did the following week, to my satisfaction. When I'd finished the paperwork, I joined an orientation tour. One of the passageways we walked through had paper notices of all kinds pinned to notice boards. There were several cards pinned to it that were job advertisements looking for coders or programmers, part time and flexible hours. I couldn't phone immediately because my old Israeli phone didn't work here, so I wrote down a few names and phone numbers and reminded myself to get a new cell phone soon, which I did a few days later. In the meantime, I called the numbers on the landline from Moishe's place and struck gold.

To cut a long story short a large finance company wanted someone familiar with Cobol, Sybase, C++, JavaScript, HTML; plenty of those coders around, but they also wanted someone who knew a language called SAS. It stands for Statistical Analysis System, which I think is cool, and if you'll pardon the nerdiness, I think statistics are cool and I have thought so ever since I saw my first bell curve.

My phone conversation with the company person that answered the phone went like a dream, I was bubbling with enthusiasm. The HR person I spoke to didn't understand much of what I said but she asked me to come in for an interview. I did. This time I spoke to a lead programmer, and it didn't take long to convince him I knew what I was talking about. He stared at me as I talked, and I stared back. As my mouth moved, spouting the arcane vocabulary of our trade, I noticed so did his; his brain was following the same path as mine as if he couldn't help himself. It could have looked comical if you weren't 'in the zone' with us.

In short, I was to come into the office when available, and work on an hourly basis on whatever project they assigned to me for $35 an hour. No, I'm not kidding, I could hardly believe it. I started the following day. What a place, what a beautiful friendly place is NYU and NYC. I really felt like I'd landed on my feet in this town, in this country. Some things about America I thought were very odd, but I can handle it.

About four, maybe five months passed in this happy state of affairs. I could cope well enough with summer temperatures and sweaty subway stations and crowded Manhattan streets. When winter came, the icy wind down some of its canyon-like streets felt like it would cut off your ears. How could a place which in summer is as warm as Tel Aviv be so incomprehensibly cold on winter days?

My first attempts at shopping for winter clothes were mixed, some, with the benefit of hindsight now look ridiculous. Other things I bought were less so. For the first winter there I equipped myself with waterproof warm shoes, thermal underwear, and a puffy down jacket. I walked cheerfully among sidewalk crowds and felt like a seasoned New Yorker even though I had so far only two seasons to my name. Anyway, back in September, though Moishe and Avril had been wonderful, I felt sometimes I might be getting under their feet. They needed their privacy in their place as did I, in mine.

My daily routine was pretty much like this: As my class schedule allowed, before or after class each day I went to work at 42nd Street Finance Corporation. For the most part the lead programmer would give me specs or parameters for algorithms and blocks of code that needed fixing. At first, I felt my lips moving in sync with his but stopped myself feeling a bit silly, or worse, letting him suspect I was mocking him?

Sometimes they'd ask me to write new code that they needed for specific tasks. I'd work on it and when finished, give them to the QA (quality assurance) people, who would check and test it all ways up to make sure the code did what it was supposed to do. If there was a problem, or if requirements had changed, they'd give it back to me for corrections. I'd work on it some more, then re-submit it to QA and we'd push it back and forth like ping pong until everybody was happy.

The thing was, that after QA had validated my code, I'd ask the lead programmer if they'd like me to stick around or if I should leave, keeping in mind that I was being paid hourly. They'd usually ask me to stay even though they often didn't have another project ready for me to work on. So, I stayed and worked on my school assignments which sometimes ran into hours, and they didn't seem to care. I always asked to make sure it was OK, and I'd put my schoolwork aside when there was work for the firm to do.

From what I could gather, 42nd Street Finance had plenty of cash; the corporate office was deluxe. The most worrying thing for them was a computer problem in some way associated with stock trading in which every minute of downtime cost them thousands and possibly millions of dollars. Compared to that, having me around at $35 an hour wasn't such a bad deal for them. It turned out I'd inadvertently made myself into a bit of a hero by solving what appeared to me to be quite routine problems, but for them catastrophes in the making.

This gave value, simply to my presence. $35 an hour soon became $55 an hour and bonuses put icing on the cake. I'd heard that if things seem like they're too good to be true they probably are.

Chapter 4 - An Offer Refused - Ari

I came to regard Moishe and Avril's place as their studio in the sky and I loved it. I think they liked that I was around. The art on their walls came from all corners of the planet. Japan, China, Africa, Russia etc. It was entirely secular except for a Buddha statue and Hindu Vishnu. There was too, a print which showed an endless plane of grass bathed in pink evening sunshine. In the far distance was a Russian church, drawing the eye upward out of the plane through its onion-shaped domes, outlined in a darkening sky. On its right, trees and small houses trailed off to infinity, the whole, evocative of the vast Russian Steppe.

"You like that?" I heard Avril ask.

"Yes, it sort of takes me there, I'd never have thought to leave so much grass in a photo."

Avril continued, "Thanks, I took the photo, developed it and printed it, actually not that print on the wall, other smaller ones though. That one's too big for the equipment I had at the time. I'd attended a service there at the church in the distance. Didn't understand a word of the service, but what an experience! What theatre! I don't even use that camera any more by the way, it's that one, the Hasselblad on the shelf. I miss using it. After the service I walked towards the setting sun, so when I turned around to look at the building it was an incandescent claret color. Pressing the shutter at that time gave me a deep feeling of satisfaction. Photography is too time consuming any more, now that I spend all my working hours healing the sick. I take some digital snaps now and again. Not the same, but I love the convenience of it"

"Did you say working hours?" joined in Moishe. "You could have said waking hours. Sometimes you leave so early and are home so late. It's like I open my eyes in the morning and a second later the door slams as you leave. I close my eyes at night and a second later the door slams as you return."

"Poor baby" she said, coming over to console him with a kiss. "Spending all that time working leaves me no time to spend all that money I'm making. So, when I do get a spare second with you, we can buy some luxury without worrying."

Thus, I learned that Avril used to be a photographer, is now a doctor, and horror of horrors, is possibly not Jewish. No, I jest. Knowing Moishe's background I was just a little surprised that he should have become the partner of a non-Jewish woman, but I was certainly not horrified. This may explain why Moishe didn't share his situation with my parents, but I don't think they would have cared. Even if she were Jewish, a person like Avril might have attended a Christian service anyway. But she is not Jewish. I asked her.

"I was brought up in the Church of England." she answered. "It's called Episcopalian in America. And quite honestly, I don't miss it much. Except maybe at Christmas. Nobody does Christmas like they do in Bradford. It wasn't so much the grandeur of the occasion, more like the modesty of it. We'd go caroling in windswept icy wet streets. The weather was so bad at that time of year that decorative lights had to be indoors only. They were arranged around the windows so you could see them from the outside. At times I'd go to hospitals with my school choir to entertain the patients. It was really heartwarming."

"C'mon, I heard you were boozing Christmas Eve. When they kicked you out of the pubs you went to midnight mass to keep dry and warm," added Moishe. "How spiritual is that? Then you went home to sleep it off."

"Not every night…" she responded, and so it went on back and forth and I learnt much about them. I learnt about Moishe's youth too in the working-class East End of London, at a time redolent with change as its bombed-out core stirred back to life.

I was not at all shocked by their secular lifestyles. Just interested. Neither of my parents practiced Judaism any more by attending regular services at a synagogue, although they both did as children, and talked about it sometimes. They did, however, celebrate the Jewish holidays and the traditions and food and paraphernalia that goes with them at Passover, Purim, Rosh Hashanah, Hanukkah, Yom Kippur etc. My dad made a big deal of Yom Ha-Shoah, Holocaust Remembrance Day, which was the only one he took seriously, really seriously.

"What do you do during end-of-year Jewish holidays? Except for the odd bottle of wine and slightly different food we haven't done much about any holiday so far. Do you really celebrate them at all?" I asked Avril late one evening emphasizing 'really' when she and Moishe were relaxing with a glass of wine. That would have been when Rosh Hashanah was coming up in late September.

"I celebrate Rosh Hashanah with Moshe and friends, some Jewish, some not."

"What about your Christian holidays then, like Christmas? Doesn't it clash with Hanukkah?"

"We celebrate those too, and far from clashing with Hanukkah, it fits right in. We're inclined to call it Chrismukkah or Hanuchris, which one is it Moishe?" She saw that Moishe was listening to our conversation.

"Both", said Moishe without looking up from his magazine.

"Are you going to celebrate Rosh Hashanah here? Are friends coming over?"

"Glad you asked", answered Avril, "no we're not because we have been invited to celebrate it with some Jewish friends of ours. She is a doctor that works with me at the same hospital. Her husband is also a doctor but at a different hospital. I told her that you're here with us, so she invited you too. Oh, and by the way they have a daughter about your age. I hear she's rather pretty, and," she paused, "and very smart."

She too, like Moishe, was looking down at her magazine and trying not to smile.

"What did you tell them about me?" I asked.

"Just that you're a student at NYU and making some good money for yourself at 42nd Street Finance."

"So, nothing about why I'm really here? Nothing about what forced the decision for me to come here?"

"No, nothing, and quite honestly, it's nobody's business but yours. I don't care what's in your DNA, I find you are a decent, kind, clever young man." Avril sounded quite passionate, and I liked her for what she said, and the way she said it.

"Let's face it," she continued, "that's what this is all about isn't it, DNA? If the human genome hadn't been mapped, or even mapped just fifteen years later there'd be no question about your patronage, and you'd still be in Tel Aviv. Having you here is our gain and their loss and if some people over there are too stupid or blind not to see our common humanity, more fools them. I feel so sorry for your parents, I know they love you and I also know that the love is returned. The irony is that the people who made life difficult for you over there are clueless about the science which now underwrites their bigotry."

"Whew!" I gasped "I just write code, I don't get into this stuff, but thanks for saying that; it makes me feel better"

"Don't you ever...!" It looked like she was working up to something. Then she stopped. Moishe got up and gave me a friendly pat on the back, went over to Avril, kissed her full on the lips and said "c'mon luv, let's get some sleep, you've got surgery tomorrow and I have some potential customers coming over".

They walked into their bedroom arm in arm. I sat there thinking about what I'd heard trying to imagine their early lives somewhere on that mysterious island off the northwest coast of Europe, while I stared mutely through a west facing window at the distant glitter of the Manhattan skyline.

I went to my early class the following morning called "Economics, Macro and Micro", oh it doesn't matter what it's called, it's not important. Then I went to work, dumped my books on my desk, logged on to check what projects had been lined up for me. It seemed there was something strange going on. I thought one of the secretaries looked up at me then back to her computer as I caught her eye, then another looked down quickly as I looked around. I shrugged and opened my email.

OK, some routine code to write, should be finished in an hour, possibly two, then I can get to my schoolwork if nothing else crops up, I was thinking. At that moment Norman, the lead programmer came over to me. He's a tall man, stoops slightly as he walks. When he talks, he looks directly at you and enunciates every consonant in well-constructed sentences. He's also polite, avuncular, and calm, and appears to have the confidence of his subordinates. That may be in part because of his age. He looks over 60 and acts like it, but he is at the same time, sharp as a tack.

"Morning Ari, Mr. Roth would like a word with you if you wouldn't mind walking over to his office with me"

Oh shit, what now? I thought. I've got too much schoolwork for a big project. Mr. Roth is the IT (information technology) manager. He was another jacket wearing smart guy, plumpish fortyish with thinning straight fair hair and watery blue eyes which dart all over the place while he speaks to you, as if other thoughts are going on in his head at the same time. When he walks through the office, he really is thinking several things like "Sue, call IBM about their cloud, Eddie, check the mail, see if we got a check from Exxon, how's it coming along Fred...," and so on all the while barely stopping except to contort and twitch his face nervously. The older people here call him James or Jimmy, but we kids call him Mr. Roth. It's a corporate culture thing,

"OK, sure." I replied to Norman, "Let me get my notepad and pencil".

My notebook was a must for me, when asked verbally to do something, that is to say, not in writing. I would take notes to aid my memory of the assignment, and to confirm with the requester by restating it to them, to be sure that I'd understood correctly. No matter how simple and straightforward it appeared at first, it never was entirely so.

"You won't need your notebook, not this time"

I looked at him. There must have been some alarm in my expression.

"It's OK, it's not an assignment and you're not in trouble. We just need to talk about something."

So, I got up and followed him, after quickly slipping a notepad and pencil into my back pocket just in case.

Norman knocked softly on Mr. Roth's office door before the pair of us walked in. "Hi Norman, come in Ari, take a seat, oh just a mo', what time is it? Have you had coffee yet this morning? Maybe we can go down to the cafeteria on the first floor and chat. I'm going stir crazy in this glass cage"

I was glad he suggested that; I was just ready for coffee which was usually fresh at this time. The cafeteria was a shared space by many of the tenant companies in this typical office tower. I picked up a coffee and an egg sandwich at the cafeteria. When I got to the checkout Mr. Roth was waiting.

"I'll get that," he said.

He paid and the three of us sat down. Mr. Roth looked down at his coffee while he stirred it slowly. Strands of his thinning hair flopped down over his forehead exposing a shiny top. Then he quickly grasped his glasses to prevent them falling into his coffee, looked up at me, fixing his gaze and stilled briefly his wandering eyes.

"This company prides itself on recognizing and rewarding talent and keeping it when it sees it." he started. "I'll come straight to the point. In you we see talent that we would not like to lose. In fact, some of your suggestions that you tell us are just common sense, have made a significant difference to some of our operations. It's more than just common sense. Your hourly paid status is not consistent with what we regard as your inadvertent but welcome addition to our company's intellectual core. In short, we'd like to offer you a permanent position here, complete with benefits and health insurance."

I sat there and stared. My jaw dropped and felt slack. Anybody that saw me at that exact moment would not have thought me part of anybody's "intellectual core".

"Oh, of course, I should have said," he added hastily, "your salary will be well in excess of what we're paying you now, although I'd have to check with HR before I can give you the exact figure."

This was all very nice, but it was also quite embarrassing. I swallowed a mouth full of egg sandwich and took a quick gulp of coffee, and as gracefully as I could, explained that I had to refuse the offer "because, b, b, b, because" I stammered, "I am determined to finish my post grad studies at NYU. That would mean attending classes at times when a permanent employee would be expected to be present. I would be studying for exams, and actually taking exams all of which, with my full study schedule would necessitate absences. And all of this before taking any time off for vacations or sickness."

He looked at me, making his eyes still again. "That's final? He asked."

"I'm afraid so. Yes" I answered. "I really don't want to leave, I like it here and I'll help you all I can, but I'd think you would come to resent my frequent absences, or if not you, then other employees might."

"OK, I hear you, I understand." Mr. Roth looked thoughtful. "Will you be here tomorrow?"

"Er, yes, I have another early class, I'll be here at about 10:30."

"OK" he said, then turned to Norman and said in a completely informal tone "How 'bout them Yankees then, huh, huh?"

"Ugh, too stuck up." He answered.

It was an average day after that. I completed a few straightforward assignments and left about 5pm. Crowds on the subway were thick at that time. It was late September, and the Rosh Hashanah started that evening at sundown, so I needed to get back to Brooklyn to get ready. At Avril's prodding, Moishe had taken me the previous week to a menswear store to get fitted for a suit. I wasn't sure I needed one, but I went along with it and Moishe paid. At least I think it was him that paid, I didn't see the name on the credit card but one part of me suspected it might have been Avril. I went to pick it up a couple of days later and it fitted perfectly. I got some formal black shoes too and a medium dark colored tie and a dress shirt. I felt awkward in it, like someone I didn't know when I looked in the mirror. Moishe said I looked like a million dollars.

When home I took a shower and emerged 10 minutes later in my new outfit to nods of approval from my stand in parents. That's right, they were just like parents in a way, well not really, but not as bossy. Avril looked absolutely stunning in a beige sheer long dress, dignified, formal and not too revealing, but just a slight tease of reveal. Moishe had abandoned his arty relaxed style and turned formal too. Perhaps this doctor they were going to visit was Avril's boss? Oh no, wait, she said he worked at a different hospital. I guess he wanted to appear business like and not too worn or working class or, how shall I say it? He wanted to look like a compliment to Avril's choice of a partner. He really looked pretty good in a suit just like mine. I suppose we could have been mistaken for father and son and the three of us, for a family.

Chapter 5 - Introductions - Ari

It had been a cloudy day, and dusk was closing in early. Avril called for a cab which arrived outside the front door in about five minutes, and ten minutes after that we were on Cranberry Street in Brooklyn Heights. The homes there are posh-looking brownstones. The cab stopped outside a very handsome brick house with brownstone window ledges and lintels. It had broad steps up to a double front door. There was a chill in the air. Avril had a black sweater around her shoulders as she pinched her long dress above the knee to lift it slightly and held Moishe's arm to negotiate the steps. The door opened as we approached it and there to greet us were the host family, the middle-aged Dr. John Cardozo and Dr. Gillian Mendez, and an elegant young woman in her early twenties called Hadassah and a boy about nine called Abraham. Gillian Mendez was Avril's friend and colleague who had invited us.

The two doctors John and Gillian were man and wife, Hadassah their daughter and the boy, Abraham, their son. They introduced themselves at the door. I forgot all their names immediately except for, oddly enough, Hadassah's. Conversation later refreshed my memory when they addressed one another. One more medical couple arrived with their two children, slightly younger than Abraham making a total of eleven.

In the large formal dining room, the table was set out in festive style, covered with fruits of all kinds, the usual egg bread or challah, salads, cold vegetables and apples in honey.

Conversation ran easily among those that knew each other. I thought about this holiday in years past back home in Tel Aviv which was often colorful and fun and an opportunity to get together with family and friends from near and far. My dad would make jokes incessantly and about everything including religion. Since Judaism is the only one of significance in the Tel Aviv area, it was the butt of his jokes. The more he drank, the more he would excoriate adherents of ultra-orthodox denominations that wear medieval clothes and study mostly the Torah to the expense of science and mathematics and other useful things. All the while my mother would try to restrain him.

I was not much involved with the conversation as I sat looking at each talker in turn and trying to appear as if I was listening, but my head was full of nostalgia. I thought more of my dad who would occasionally say something funny and follow it up with something not quite so funny or even something inappropriate. Then he would apologize, stay quiet for a few minutes then start up again like nothing had happened.

I smiled broadly at the thought which happened to coincide with something funny that someone else said here at the Mendoza table. I've no idea what, but it must have looked like I was enjoying the joke. It crossed my mind that one thing which made my dad angry and embarrassed for his country was the shameless expansion of illegal settlements on land in the West Bank, sometimes stolen, and justified by self-serving interpretations of the Talmud. I could see them in my mind's eye back home with talk lurching from jokes to politics to religion and science and food and books and work and back to jokes again. The children would sing or play an instrument they'd been learning and tell us about school and their friends. I imagined a friendly chaotic roll of conversation, getting more chaotic as the wine bottles emptied.

It was not like that here at the Cardozo-Mendez table. Five of the eleven attendees having in common the medical profession, inevitably medicine was discussed. Avril brought Moishe into the conversation several times which was a relief. One of his contributions had the table listening quite intently. He said that his less satisfying work found more customers than work he regarded as superior. "My customers value visual shock and decoration above all else. I can do that," he continued, "and as a component of art as I understand it, I believe it is valid. Lasting and profound visual expression requires more than shock; it needs to hint at diverse interpretations and needs paradox and composition and passion to invoke those interpretations."

I liked listening to Moishe's cornbread cockney. His occasional grammatical slip was somehow incongruous with his obvious intelligence. And I liked Avril's proud beaming face as he spoke.

Hadassah sat opposite me, demure, poised and beautiful. A brief pause in the conversation gave her mother the opportunity to call attention to her. "Hadassah wishes to study medicine as her parents did. She's done some of the foundation courses at community college already, but is now thinking of a gap year, is that not so dear?" It reminded me of the old Jewish mother joke who tells her children: "Of course you can and should do anything you want, dear, just as soon as you've finished medical school."

"It is so my dear mother" she answered with a hint of mockery, and continued in that formal tone, "however the gap year could be extended if I find satisfaction in that which I happen to be doing at the end of that year."

It was one of those moments where I could not possibly suppress a smile. While the gentle rebuff may have been a little tense, how could I not commend a proud mother for calling attention to her darling beautiful daughter? And for that matter how could I not comply with that intent and give her the attention which she so deserved? I looked at her again. She had straight black hair cut in a rounded bob which softened her slim regular face. The eyes were deep brown to black. The skin on her face, neck, and shoulders, perfect with the slightest olive tint. A thin gold chain bore a heart shaped gold locket about an inch across and sat high on her chest, the bottom of the heart describing the line of the neck of her straight black dress.

Banter with her mother continued a little longer but Hadassah would not be drawn about her plans or thoughts or intentions or anything. The more her mother probed, the more Hadassah pushed back. I had a feeling that out of curiosity and politeness our hosts would soon attempt to draw me into the dinner conversation.

To forestall an unwanted question, I blurted as calmly as I could: "I think a gap year could be a good thing. After all, Avril was a much-travelled photographer before she became a doctor." I could have said more about a rounded personality resulting from varied experiences, but I stopped, realizing that by so doing I was criticizing her parents.

I looked up again at Hadassah and this time it was her turn to smile as she came to my rescue, filling the brief silence that followed my comment.

"Quite so Ari, there are more things in life than medicine even though it is an honorable profession and can be a satisfying career. So what brings you here Ari, to America I mean, not just to our dinner party?" She smiled as she said it.

So, the question I didn't really want to deal with came in any case so I tried my best:

"W... well, I came to study. I'm a grad student at NYU and have a part time job at a finance company. So far, it's been good. I've been here about four months and I love NYU. I guess you figured out I'm living with Moishe and Avril now. Much as I love them, I don't intend to depend on their kindness indefinitely. Sooner or later, I'll get my own place. I don't really know anybody yet except as classmates and colleagues at work but that will change in time. I love the cafés in Brooklyn. I go out for brunch at weekends, and I've spoken to people from time to time there. I'm not at all confident making conversation with people of my own age and I'm a little self-conscious about my accent. I think I'm having what you call culture shock. I don't know what's going on in popular music and movies and that sort of thing. Most of the time I'm doing work projects or school projects or sitting in lectures. I'm not complaining, on the contrary I love it, especially NYU, but I think there will be more to enjoy in time."

"Do you have a favorite café?" she asked.

"I have a few that I like. I go to…" and I told her about the ones I liked and why.

"Oh really! I like those too; I may see you there some time."

"That would be ni...I hope…" I couldn't quite get out all of my reply because the good Dr. Cardozo had put on his Yarmulke and wanted to pray but I think I got the message back to Hadassah. Her mother, who, judging from her concentrated gaze, was following every word of our conversation; she looked daggers at her husband.

Dr. Cardozo raised his head to look around the table in the expectation of silence but the three children at the table who sat together were comparing the Victorian gothic grandness of the room with Hogwarts, a castle turned into a school for witches and wizards in a popular children's book. They pretended to cast spells on one another using silverware as wands. When finally coaxed to silence by their parents Dr. Cardozo commenced in Hebrew, familiar to me

41

but gibberish to two of the children who squirmed and giggled.

I noticed the little girl surreptitiously wave a finger wand and mouthed "obliviate" at Dr. Cardozo, a spell which inflicted immediate forgetfulness to its victim. I tried not to smile but I don't know if I succeeded. I think Dr. Cardozo smiled too but he carried on, preserving his dignity. Other adults who knew the prayer answered the ritual Hebrew questions spoken by the annunciator. The sudden coordinated replies by the adults in the know caught the children by surprise. I'd been watching them, waiting for this moment which I found flat out funny. I looked at Hadassah who caught my eye, but it didn't seem so funny to her.

When the prayers were over Avril called for a cab, briefly explaining she had to be at work early. Her friend Dr. Gillian Mendez said she concurred; she too had to be at work early and thanked us all for coming. Friendly goodbyes continued until the cab arrived. The three of us talked all the way home about the wonderful food avoiding a continuation of dinnertime conversation. It was true what I had said though, at the table, about cafés and music and movies.

Having money to spend freely helped a lot, but weekends were especially lonely at first. That began to change after getting out for brunch on Saturday mornings. No city is as good as Tel Aviv for sidewalk café life, in my opinion, but Brooklyn is not bad at all. It was one of those Saturday morning brunches that a quite trivial incident became the starting point of meeting friends and other events in which one thing led to another.

Chapter 6 - The Apartment - Ari

I don't think I'd ever worked or been to school during Rosh Hashanah before; quite a few people in NYC take the day off I discovered, but not NYU and not 42nd Street Finance. So, the following day I went to school, and later to work where I was deep into an assignment when Norman came over to me as he had the previous day.

"Good morning Ari, would you mind walking over to see Mr. Roth with me, notebook not necessary." He smiled as he said it. "He asked that we should join him in the cafeteria. He's already down there."

I suspected they might be wanting to sweeten the offer to try to persuade me to go full time at 42nd Street Finance. I was fortunate that it would not be difficult to refuse, having a good place to live and good people to live with. Not only that, but the NYU course was deeply interesting, covering matters that were regarded as cutting edge. After earning a higher degree, I had research in mind and a possible PhD. So, I was preparing myself to decline an expected offer as graciously as I could.

Mr. Roth looked at me without expression except that he stilled his eyes as in our earlier meeting.

"Ari, as you probably have guessed I have another proposition to make to you. However, it is not to ask you to start full time and does not involve money at all except indirectly. Quite recently our company installed an entire system of our proprietary software for a large NY real estate company." This company had involved itself in a development at Long Island City in Queens...

"Wait, wait, wait...," I interrupted, "I'm not going out to Queens to work, it's too far from NYU, and too far from my home in Brooklyn."

"Let me finish." He stopped me holding his palms up to me in a defensive posture. "As I was saying, the development turned out to be on land seriously polluted from previous industrial activity. The company had hired contractors to clean and prepare the land for building, but the more the contractors attempted to make it safe for housing, the more they found heavy metal contamination which made completion of the project impossible."

'Why on earth was he telling me this?' I wondered. 'He's hardly stopped for breath.' I was frustrated and impatient and shuffled my feet, but Mr. Roth continued. He held up his hands again, seeing I was about to interrupt him again.

"We sued them immediately, anticipating that the bank would call its construction loan and they'd face bankruptcy. So we took action to get paid for our work. They had no cash but they did have an unsold apartment in a tower block near the water's edge in Brooklyn, just south of

East River Park. Its value on the market was only about 75% of our bill. Our attorney advised to take it fast or be left with nothing but litigation and frustration."

I was feeling pissed off. This made no sense and had nothing to do with me at all, I breathed out, folded my arms, resigned to sitting this out: "OK, OK," I said, nodding as politely as I could but still confused.

"We took it," Mr. Roth continued. "We talked about selling it, of course, but now have in mind to keep it, with the intention of hosting or housing recruits to our company temporarily if/when they move to the city from afar, to work for us. No matter what we do with it, it's going to be a good investment, certain to increase in value at that location."

"Excuse me once again sir," I interrupted. "I just don't understand why you're telling me all this."

"We're offering it to you for up to two years," he continued at a fast clip, "or until you graduate with your higher degree, whichever comes first. Obviously, your tenancy is contingent on you continuing to work for us.

"Come on," I said, getting up from my chair, "I don't know that much about tax law, but I know that an apartment at your expense would be seen as income by the IRS. I don't think I could afford the Federal income tax on it, let alone the real estate tax in New York City, and the condo maintenance fees whatever they're called which I don't have to pay at the moment, but from what I overhear in conversations are very steep."

"Our company accountant will assist you with the tax implications as, yes, you're right, the Internal Revenue

Service is likely to regard this as income," he continued speaking so quickly he could scarcely draw breath. "In your case, as you say, on your income you will have difficulty paying the rent, real estate tax and fees of such a place without taking full advantage of what tax law may allow."

"What tax law may allow?" I repeated back to him, trying to keep the sarcasm out of my voice.

"Our company maintains a tax lawyer. He'll figure it out so that we can reimburse you in such a way that it can be paid by us and written off as a company expense to us, incurred by our client's collapsed real estate project."

The whole thing seemed farfetched and unlikely so I played for time.

"Can I see it, and can I think about it?" I asked.

"Yes, you can think about it," he answered, "but don't think too long, the directors may change their minds."

Thinking about it, for me, meant talking to Moishe and Avril. I went to the accountant's office to get a key and that evening asked M & A (forgive the abbreviation, you know it means Moishe and Avril by now, right?) if they'd like to come with me to look at it. It was quite close to the studio. Fortunately, Avril came home early that evening and the three of us walked over to see it after dinner and after sunset. Moishe thought it was great and said, "Obviously you should take it." Avril agreed with him, but cautiously, and I couldn't help feeling there was a touch of maternal sadness in her endorsement.

Moishe's final words on the subject were: "If you get kicked out come on back to our place, we have room."

Meanwhile, as I had hoped and anticipated, I did meet beautiful Hadassah several times at weekends for brunch. I wouldn't like to say we were dating, but I think that in her mind we were. I really quite liked seeing her, at the cafés that is, but I didn't feel all that close to her. Our conversations were cordial enough but somehow formal at the same time. She wanted to know more about me than I was ready to tell. 'She'll get to know in good time and then what?' I asked myself. I was not ready to go to movies or dancing with her and had adequate excuses related to my workload which was considerable.

But she was beautiful, there's no question of that. We became regulars at a few cafés and known by the wait staff who expected us and greeted us by our first names after a while. We talked of many things, on her part her studies and ambitions and parents and a dread of being channeled into medical studies before having the chance to explore and travel. I talked about Israel and work and studies, but I didn't tell her about my new apartment. It was comforting though, to be accepted by her in such a way and to enjoy cafe life. I was starting to feel more settled and at home.

"You never talked about kal?" she said to me out of the blue at one of our restaurant meetings.

It was a pleasant restaurant just off Bedford Avenue in Williamsburg. There was a buzz about the place. We were shown a table in a backyard extension to the old tenement building, covered with a greenhouse-like glass roof. It was busy without being excessively so. Decorative plants kissed up against the glass walls from the outside. Small indoor plants between some of the tables were spaced far enough away from each other and carefully modulated background music allowed for conversation. You didn't have to shout and wouldn't be overheard at the next table. And there was this scattering of intermittent aromas of coffee, fresh baked bread and vanilla that wafted gently around. And I was feeling happy.

"That's because I have nothing to say about kal, is that what you call it? You meant beit knesset, or schul, right?" I answered, hoping to close down this line of conversation, and feeling much less happy quite suddenly.

She smiled. "Yea, Yea, I know, neither do I. Yea, that's what we call it in our community, we're talking about the synagogue, right? Anyway, I know you work a lot, but your schedule seems pretty flexible on Saturdays even though you can't spare much of your time."

Not yet having succeeded in closing down this line of questioning, I figured that the best way to do it would be to face facts, or at least some facts, and state them.

"I don't go to kal," I said blandly. "At all," I added, "and I don't intend to."

That should do the trick, I thought, Nothing ambiguous about that. She won't raise that subject again and I looked into her beautiful deep brown sparkling eyes. They were slightly wet, as if a tear was forming as I gazed at her beautiful face. What am I doing? I thought. If I had half the sense I was born with, I should sweep her off her feet. But something held me back. No, I'm not - I know what you're thinking, no I'm not gay.

"Well, maybe I'll come sometime, if it's important to you," I softened. I couldn't stand the thought that I may have upset her. She cheered up a lot after that. Unfortunately, it had the opposite effect on me. I really thought I'd left all that stuff behind. Moishe and Avril were cool and secular. They didn't need a priest or a rabbi to tell them what's right and what's wrong. They just knew.

I had a sickly feeling. My chin fell on my chest; my head drooped so I picked up a menu and held it to my stomach so that I might appear to be reading it rather than falling into the deep deep funk that suddenly overwhelmed me. It was a kind of nightmare but in the middle of the day. I couldn't say it was a daydream because they're usually thought of as pleasant. But all that I could see in my mind's eye were hostile faces intoning insults and barbs and threats that were confusing and hurtful. I could see my friends too, coming to my aid, surrounding me, protecting me. "You're insulting a man who served our country with distinction!" my friend Yanni yelled back at them. They shrugged and walked away while letting me overhear derogatory expressions for Arabs and Muslims, as if I were one."

"I'm not Jewish!" I blurted.

"Yeah right," she smiled, as if I was making some kind of joke. "Israeli born, Israeli educated, distinguished Israeli soldier."

"No no, I mean it, that's all in the past, I have to go. It's complicated." I really didn't want to hurt Hadassah, but I couldn't help myself.

And for all that good news I've been talking about, I guess you know by now there's something going on in my life that I can't quite describe and can't even at times comprehend. It's the same problem that made me want to leave Israel and come to the US to live.

I felt there may have been an element of danger and another one of romance or love in the not too distant future, maybe? I don't feel confident trying to explain it, so I'm going to have my good friend Maria write it all down. You will meet her in the next chapter, and she is very talkative. She will explain the whole thing about me and our mutual group of friends, but from her point of view. I may chip in later or along the way if I think she hasn't got it right or if I feel I need to add something.

OK Maria you're up.

Chapter 7 - Brooklyn Café - Maria

Well, I'm a Catholic; the name's Maria, as Ari told you earlier. I'm picking up the story where Ari left off because, well, it'll give you a different perspective about what happened. Added to that, Ari is shy about expressing personal things, and frankly some of this gets personal. And one more thing, Ari can tell you all about his work and interests and classes, and very little about himself, so I'm going to try to help out with that too. But first at little about myself:

In Catholic terms I'm a good girl mostly. Not that it means much anymore to be a good girl, not even to me, but to know that may help you, and especially other Catholics, to understand who I am.

I'm moderately slim and pretty. I don't want to brag; I'm not what you'd call beautiful, but I want you to get an idea of what I look like. It means so much to me and how I feel, and how confident I am, that you wouldn't be understanding me completely if I didn't try to put you in the picture, as it were. So, I'm tallish, about 5′ 8″ and have mousy brown straight hair which shines nicely after I wash it. I found a single gray hair a few days ago and I'm only twenty-two, eek! But I don't want to talk about that. My eyes are greenish gray, my nose smallish and straight, my chin regular and my lips - ah my lips are full, naturally. Thank you, mom, for my lips.

I'm shy with strangers, which for much of the time gives me a severe, and some think sophisticated expression. I don't feel sophisticated or severe, but I can feel myself take on those airs, like I can't help it, when I think I'm perceived as such. Another reason I think I may be mistaken for sophisticated is because I'm careful about my posture. I know tallish women are often sometimes embarrassed about their height and tend to stoop. Well, I'm not one of those, not since I left my teens behind.

I'm completely unable to flirt. I'm sure there are a lot of good shy men who I will never get to meet because they'll be too shy to talk to me, and I to them. I guess I'll be doomed only ever to meet the bold, the garrulous and the stupid. Or so I thought until a few weeks ago.

As I was saying, three weeks two days four hours and ten, no eleven, minutes ago I met this guy who was neither garrulous nor stupid, just a little bold, perhaps, maybe not even that. I went to a popular restaurant on Bedford Avenue, a good half mile walk from my cool but small apartment in the Williamsburg area of Brooklyn. It's called Harriet's. It was a Saturday morning in the Fall, a long time in coming after a blazing hot summer. As I walked, the sycamore trees in the park were scattering their seeds and rustling their brown-red leaves in the cool welcome breezes. The strong morning sun noticeably lower in the sky than two months earlier dressed the apartment houses with color while casting shade onto the sidewalks.

The clatter of trucks along Metropolitan Avenue was unabated, weekend notwithstanding, as was the endless roar of traffic along the Brooklyn-Queens expressway which doomed any chance of neighborly peace across a wide swathe of the borough. Once past it though the gentle downhill to Bedford and beyond it the East River beckoned. The meal I went to enjoy was a late breakfast or brunch. I just wanted to see people and be seen, even if I didn't talk to anyone. But you never know, I thought, I might just get drawn into a conversation somehow. That may sound quaint but it's really true. I was not looking for close company, nor as the weekend was still opening its broadening arms, was I trying to avoid company.

Since the restaurant was busy when I arrived, the waitress asked if I wouldn't mind sharing a table and of course I didn't mind when she gestured to where a young man was seated, reading a tightly folded newspaper. As I sat down, opening a novel on my tablet, he acknowledged my presence with a quick faint smile, which I returned just as quickly and faintly as he went back to reading. He was absorbed in some news item which was written in Hebrew characters, just as I was absorbed watching him.

Across the table from me the man bent his head towards his paper, so I watched his curls move in the morning sunshine. They were dark but so delicate they seemed to become a few shades lighter as his head moved slightly. I could just see his eyes moving back and forth behind his frameless glasses, which from where I sat at an angle to him, were a pale green-brown color. He stopped reading, looked up at me, somehow not seeing me, absorbed as he was, in his thoughts.

"What are you reading about?" I heard myself asking him.

"About a comedian who died recently", he replied in clear fluent but slightly accented English.

"Anybody famous?" I asked.

"No, not famous, not here at least, he's not an American. I don't think he ever visited America."

I was quiet for a while. He returned to his food and his reading as I returned to my reading, and after a few minutes a waitress showed up to take my order.

"Are you a comedian?" I blurted as if you had to be a comedian merely if you read about one. I was sure he wasn't; he just didn't look or act like he could be. But I was curious to know what he did for a living even though I was ninety percent sure he was a student, a graduate student perhaps. In any case it was a way of re-starting the conversation.

"No, but I'd like to be. I'm thinking of becoming one"

"You're thinking of becoming a comedian?" I asked, feeling surprised as I said it and stupid after I'd finished saying it, causing, an awkward pause.

But he sensed my discomfort and replied cheerfully enough and seemed to talk as much to himself as to me, putting me at ease again.

"Yes, you see I have some unusual inner conflicts and some anger," he answered in a light-hearted way at odds with what he said. "I guess I feel the need to express it. Have you noticed, the very funniest comedians can project a demeanor that's partly pathetic and in part defiant? They are often to some degree unfortunate or victimized. I feel myself to be the victim of circumstances beyond my control. What better way to handle it than to turn it to advantage as a comic?"

I was thinking, as he spoke, that he was articulate and interesting. He spoke in well-constructed sentences such as you'd find with intelligent foreigners who have studied our language carefully but not had much practice at colloquial speech. He just didn't seem all that funny.

I was going to say something bland like: 'But surely, to be a successful comedian it takes more than anger?' Instead, I said: "I don't believe you," and stared straight at him as I said it. But he continued with his silly monologue:

"Yes, no-one believes me, and I know it takes timing, empathy with your audience, a lot of hard work writing and rehearsing your act, a desire to perform, and large doses of insanity, determination, humility and luck. Most of all it takes a hide as thick as a rhino. Oh, and you have to be able to take endless rejection and disappointment."

"And you have all that?" I asked.

"I have the anger and the insanity, the rest I need to find out. That's enough about me, what about you, what's your name, may I ask?

"I still don't believe you," I persisted, "have you ever been to a comedy club and listened to the stand ups there?"

His manner changed and he seemed like he was trying not to laugh when he asked me: "Are you picking a fight with me, a perfect stranger?

I shot back: "Do you know what these standup guys are like? Do you know what they say? How they say it? How they interact with their audience? And most difficult of all how they deal with hecklers? You're not a bit like them, I just can't see you doing it."

"You are picking a fight," he said, smiling, "and we're still strangers."

In response I smiled back and held out my hand for him to shake, more confidently than is usual for me saying: "The name's Maria" as the waitress accidentally put down a hot plate of omelet atop my suddenly outstretched hand. Some of the omelet landed on the floor, some on the table and some on the young man's newspaper. A scene of competing apologies followed. The waitress was gracious; she cleaned up and went to order a replacement omelet. The young man was gracious too. He busied himself cleaning up silently and expressionlessly while I wondered if he would speak to me when he'd finished.

When he had finished cleaning up his half of the table with the help of the waitress, "Nice to meet you Maria," he said holding out his hand as if mine were still there to shake, and it was there soon enough, "my name's Ari," he said, "are you a student?" There was just enough movement in his face to see that inwardly he seemed to be laughing at me, but not cruelly, just gently teasing. I was returning to my previous train of thought about the necessary qualities of a comedian. He didn't mention a sense of humor as one of them. But that was beginning to be evident.

Then he continued: "And before you tell me about you, my real day job is being a student. My other real day job is working for a finance company, writing, and fixing code, computer code, that is. The comedian thing is just about a compulsion I have. I guess there may be some cash in it too, but I have this yearning to stand on a stage and scream something stupid, but not quite so stupid that people don't understand why. That's what happens at a comedy club. Well, I think it does. It's a sort of mix at the clubs, I find. Some give me the impression that they're just yelling obscenities because they're not allowed to do it elsewhere. Some are crying from the heart and are looking for empathy. All of them are excited to hear laughter that they made happen, who knows why?"

I thought for a while and looked down at my book pretending not to have heard him, but he knew I had.

"So, you're not going to tell me anything about yourself?" he said, returning to his earlier unanswered question. I looked up and there he was looking at me and I heard myself mumbling: "Nothing very cool really, nothing interesting, I just sorta' work. It pays the bills." He was still looking at me as if waiting for an answer but then he said, sounding disappointed, bored perhaps, "well I suppose it's not important," and returned to reading his paper.

I didn't answer that I was a budget analyst although I'm not ashamed of what I do. Experience tells me it doesn't generate much more than "oh" in the average conversation which fades soon after I say it. But now the conversation had faded anyway so I asked:

"What are you studying, like, what's your major?" I don't know why I have to say "like" in the middle of a sentence. I felt dumb after I said it.

"I'm doing my master's in computer science with a special interest in statistics and graphics."

"Where"

"NYU"

"And you're thinking of becoming a comedian?" I said in such a way to make it obvious that I still didn't believe him.

"I told you it's just about an emotional release," he said while he looked at me without seeing me. But reading his face I could see something was going on in his head. I had meant the comment to be light-hearted but perhaps he was really thinking about reconciling computer science with standup comedy.

"What did you say you do?" He asked again.

"I didn't say".

I must have been concentrating hard on his face at that time because I didn't notice a young woman until she arrived at our table and sat down. I looked at her and she looked at both of us in turn. Then she turned to Ari without another glance at me.

"Is this your new girlfriend?" she asked him tensely.

"I was eating here, a server brought her to my table because there were no empty ones, we talked," he replied in a flat artificially bland voice.

"My name's Maria" I interjected but she ignored me. She was pretty, very pretty, intense, and intelligent looking. She was carefully and expensively dressed in a pale blue blouse and cardigan and matching culottes. Her straight pretty chin nestled in a color keyed paisley scarf.

She relaxed somewhat and continued in a tone half petulant half sad:

"You can convert." Her short vibrant hair glinted as she nodded to emphasize her point.

I looked down out of a sense of embarrassment for me and for them and I focused on her matching shoes, comfortable and stylish but not exactly in sync with laid back Saturday morning Brooklyn. Plainly they knew each other well. They were in each other's zone where a minimum of words carried mutually understood expansive meanings and just as plainly it was a difficult subject for them. I should have left but I glanced up at them again unable to stop myself.

Ari held his hands apart, palms facing upward in a despairing gesture.

"I am already as Jewish as anybody could be. What's to convert to?" But he appeared to know she wouldn't be satisfied with that answer. And she wasn't, and he seemed painfully determined to stick to it.

They stared at one another for what seemed like an eternity. I could see tears forming in corners of the woman's eyes and a growing smudge on discretely applied makeup. I averted my glance, this time involuntarily looking at Ari. Tears were forming in his eyes too.

I was starting to get my things together to leave or ask for another table if there was one, but at that moment my omelet came, and the server put it down in front of me. Oblivious to what was going on she asked the young woman in blue if she'd like a coffee or to place an order.

"I'm just leaving," she answered in a dull monotone. Rising with precise swift movements she was gone.

So, there we were again, strangely alone together in a crowded restaurant and I knew, I thought, some quite personal things about this stranger. And, of course, there was a lot I didn't know. We ate for a while in silence; he read his paper, I, reading but not absorbing a single word of my book and unable to speak.

Eventually it was he who broke the silence.

"What did you say you do?"

"I didn't say," I replied, smiling slightly in spite of myself, at the repetition of the question, which he must have known he'd asked already, and my answer, as if nothing had just happened. That was just slightly funny and was a clever way of defusing the situation I thought.

"I'm a budget analyst." Being really boring about my job felt like a soft landing for conversation after flights of emotion.

He nodded and looked at me without expression, which was a relief. After all, what could he say? It's not impressive and he wasn't impressed. Silence again. If he'd praised me excessively it would have been patronizing; if he'd been amused, it would have been insulting. I saw his eyes wandering away from his newspaper. I think he was trying to disguise that he was not yet calm after his brief exchange of words with his ex, and to this end he restarted the conversation with me.

"A budget analyst?" he said slowly and deliberately because, I guessed, he needed time to think about what on earth to say that is interesting about a budget analyst. There just isn't, so he resorted to:

"So, who do you work for?"

"I work for Catholic Charities," I replied.

"Here in Brooklyn?"

"Of course, where else?"

"Do you like working for Catholic Charities?"

"It's a job, pays the bills."

"But you believe in what you're doing? I mean it's a good and socially valuable organization and you can feel good about it. I guess you're Catholic?"

"Yes, I am, sort of. I mean my family's Catholic, so I was born Catholic and confirmed Catholic and all my friends going back to school and college are Catholic and everybody I work with is Catholic. It's rare I talk to anybody who's not. And yes, I do believe in what I do. There are much worse jobs than mine."

I stopped abruptly and was feeling a little irritated. I didn't come out to talk about work and my religion, it seemed so heavy duty for the weekend, and it must have been evident in my voice.

"That is such a pretty necklace, was it a present?" He'd changed the subject and was smiling faintly.

"Yes, my mom brought it back from Ireland. And now since you know everything there is to know about me, I have a few more questions I'd like to ask you."

"Right, thought you might. I don't promise to answer them, but ask away."

"OK," I said, "I'm guessing your girlfriend or ex-girlfriend now, it seems, who was here a few minutes ago meant you can convert to Judaism when she said: 'You can convert?' Right?"

"Right."

"So, either the question, or your reply, or both, were weird. If you're already Jewish, why does she want you to convert? If you're not Jewish, how can you be as 'Jewish as anybody can be?'"

He paused, drew breath slowly and answered:

"Well, whether or not I'm Jewish depends on who you ask."

I can be direct and said directly:

"So make sure you ask the right person and get on with your life. What's the big deal? You are what you say you are. If you love that beautiful woman that was here a few moments ago you wouldn't be splitting hairs about what religion you are."

I was starting to feel exasperated.

"She is beautiful isn't she? I do love her, I wish it was that simple." he said mournfully, pathetically.

I was starting to get my Irish up. This was too much. I stood up spilling my omelet yet again but rescuing it this time and more ostentatiously than the situation demanded:

"You simpleton," and suddenly feeling a fool for getting involved with something that had nothing to do with me, I sat down and continued in a harsh whisper that made me an even bigger fool: "get after her now, tell her you love her and that you'll convert."

He didn't move but sat there with a mournful expression until he said,

"I'm not Jewish."

"You just said you were, but never mind that, if you love her, you can convert and get used to being Jewish and a Jewish God, whatever that is - like she said."

He didn't answer and I was getting up a head of steam. "People do it all the time when they're not Catholic and they want to marry a Catholic. Sometimes they don't even convert, they just get married and say the heck with it. I'm not saying you should do that, though.

He laughed out loud. I didn't know it was so funny.

"Maybe you're right." he said, but he said it without any conviction. I knew he didn't really mean it; he just wanted me to shut up. He hesitated then added:

"Trouble is I'm an Arab".

"Who cares, just convert. This is New York; baggage like that melts away like snow on a summer's day. I paused and caught my breath, "Oh, oh wait, Arab you said? They're the ones who are always picking fights with Israel - or the other way round - I don't know, and, well weren't they the ones that - Oh my God - flew airplanes into the World Trade Center? Not all of them of course you can't blame them all, or yourself for that matter just because a few whackoes were on a mission to prove who knows what? OK well. . . OK maybe it's not quite so easy for you."

I sat back in my chair and looked him in the eye. I wasn't being brave; it's just that I can only stand shenanigans for so long. He returned my stare looking bemused and sheepish.

I continued, more calmly this time: "OK, maybe I've assumed the wrong thing all along. When I see people around here in Brooklyn reading stuff that looks like what you're reading, they're Jewish. I think they're reading Yiddish or Hebrew or something, so I assumed you are Jewish. Your girlfriend was Jewish, she made that plain enough. You said yourself you're as Jewish as anybody could be. I don't mean to be rude but just cut the crap or I'm leaving, and not too soon."

"Please don't go; wait a minute Maria," his demeanor had changed to serious. "Give me your phone number and your email address. I have to leave right now, and on the way out I'll be paying for your brunch, plus some, in case you want to order some more, and a tip. I can't say how thankful I am that I've met you. I'll be in touch, I promise.

Chapter 8 - Side Trip to Ground Zero - Maria

Sure enough, I got an email from Ari the following Wednesday. It was a wishy-washy invitation to dinner at his apartment. He was going to have a couple of friends over a week from Sunday. One part of me said forget it. This guy was too deep and complicated for simple little me. Oh, I don't really mean I'm simple. Straight forward would be a better way of saying it. If I see a solution to a problem, then I like to just grab it and deal with it; ha! like a good budget analyst should. Maybe I'm suited for that job. I'd had a sample of his moping in a very brief acquaintance at Harriet's Cafe. What if a longer acquaintance just meant a longer period of moping?

Another side of me though was bubbling with curiosity about what Ari's place (that is Ari Geffen's place; I learned his last name from the email) would be like, and if he could cook, or if dinner meant pizza home delivery and a few bottles of beer. And what were his friends like? And yes, what was this weird Jewish-non-Jewish thing all about? Maybe the friends would be two cute Catholic guys, although then I guessed not. It had to be a couple and he invited me to make it a foursome of two couples? We'll see. So, after I'd agonized for a full 15 seconds about whether to go or not, I looked again at the date of the dinner: an endless week and a half away on Sunday! I wanted to answer: "What's wrong with tomorrow", but I didn't, I answered like this:

Dear Ari,

It was kind of you to pay for my brunch on Saturday; I owe you one. Seems like even before I got up to leave, they regarded me as some kind of home wrecker. They wanted to give my table to a waiting couple - the nerve! They were just two degrees short of rude. They must know you and your girlfriend at that place. I gave them an extra over-generous tip to help straighten out their attitude.

Anyway, thanks for your invitation to dinner. I'm not doing anything that night. I'd like to come but only if you promise not to sulk about what religion you are, or are not, and I promise not to ask.

I don't see this as a date kind of date. You made it quite plain on Saturday where your real affections are. Just the same, it will be nice to see you again and meet your friends. Thanks for asking if I'm veggie or not. I'm not, but I'm quite happy to eat veggie if that's what you'll serve.

Best,

Maria.

It was about six months since I'd been invited anywhere by a young guy, but the same day I got the dinner invite from Ari, a guy at work asked me out and that occasion was moderately pleasant and slightly interesting. I'll tell you about that too sometime. No I won't, I'll tell you about it now since in a peculiar way it affected my expectations of dinner at Ari's while I waited a whole freekin' week and a half for that non-date.

This guy, called Marty by the way, works in the office where I work in some kind of community relations role. He asked me if I wanted to go into the city on Saturday, take a look at Ground Zero and later find a cool restaurant down the East Village. 'Hmm? not a bad idea,' I thought, 'low key, could be fun.'

And so it was that on Saturday Marty came to my apartment at exactly 10:00 AM as arranged. I was ready, well, nearly ready. I took a quick shower, did my makeup while some coffee brewed, fed my cat Beelzebub, scoffed a quick bowl of cereal, made a last minute change to my outfit, tied my hair in a ponytail to fit through the back of my NY Yankees hat and unearthed some sunglasses. "You'll need flats," he said flatly looking at my heels."

"Nobody tells me what to wear." I mumbled under my breath as I kicked off the heels and pulled on a pair of comfortable sneakers. He and I were out the door not a minute after 10:45. Marty had emptied the rather large coffee pot by then and you could tell by the quickness of his steps that either he was a little wired on caffeine. It was just possible he was irritated by my lateness.

We didn't speak much, that is we didn't speak at all on the way to - "Where the heck are you taking me?" I yelled as we passed the street that would have taken us directly to the Bedford Avenue subway station. That would have been the obvious way to get across the river to Manhattan and on to Ground Zero via the L Subway line then changing at 14th Street.

"Just a minute," he said as he dashed into the bathroom at Harriet's café as we passed it. Must have been all that coffee I plied him with. I gawped through the window into a bubbling crowd, bumping into a guy walking the opposite way playing with his phone. Gawp as I might, there was no-one in the café that I knew and no Ari. Marty reappeared after several minutes looking more relaxed.

"Are you good for a hike?" he asked, taking off again at a fast clip South along Driggs Ave, leaving the Subway station behind. He nodded in the direction we were going.

"What do you mean?" I burst out. All I could see was this vast blue-gray steel structure crossing above the street which I knew to be the Williamsburg Bridge.

We found steps up to the bridge cycle path and walkway. I had to admit it made for a different kind of date. Was it a date? On a clear mild sunny day, which it was, it's difficult not to smile at the classic urban landscape as we tracked westwards past the ever-present street art into the middle of the East River. The autumn sun still East of South, illuminated the Eastern side of the metropolis. A clear view was at times chopped up by steel beams of the bridge which framed the buildings behind it into angular and unusual poses.

Half the population of the planet could name the rock which supports a forest of towers and whose image is burned onto a million photos and movies. I felt a little flushed and happy with the exercise, the view, and the fresh mild breeze. Though the traffic over the bridge caused a consistent roar, when a subway train passed us road traffic was barely audible over the colossal clatter of the train. Then it passed and the mere roar of traffic was a relief. But there was no relief from bicyclists in a hurry. If you stepped into their lane, they had all the patience of a NYC cab driver with an angry fare.

The Bridge lets out at Delancey Street on the Manhattan side, mercifully near to the Subway station of that name. While waiting for a train on the Z line to Fulton Street I was tempted to tease Marty by asking him why we hadn't simply taken the subway all the way from Bedford Avenue, but having caused him considerable annoyance earlier that morning, I reconsidered and said, "Interesting hike Marty, good idea, thanks." It did wonders for his mood, and he explained that a foundation stone had recently been laid at Ground Zero which he'd like to see, and to pay homage to those who lost their lives there. After leaving the Subway it was a short walk along John Street to our destination.

As we drew near it was quite evident that damage and destruction was far more than just the two targeted iconic buildings. Scarred dirty walls and boarded windows surrounded a gigantic rubble filled pit. It was as large as a whole city block which holds so much tragedy and defiant optimism. We stared mutely at earthmovers and construction gear with their endlessly grumbling engines and clanking tracks, all the louder seeming because of the respectful hush of the tourist crowds.

An Asian tourist came up to me, Japanese I thought, holding out a camera and pointing first to herself, then to her three friends and said:

"Would you mind?"

"Of course." I replied.

I took the camera and framed the group in several poses with several backgrounds. We got to talking as we followed Marty who walked slowly East, back to Broadway. There he turned left and continued a little way North to Saint Paul's chapel, a fittingly beautiful Georgian treasure which served as a refuge and recovery center for the emergency workers of September 11th. 2001, and in the days following.

As we walked, Atsuko wanted to know if I lived in New York; she told me how exciting and beautiful it all is. She and her friends were having a "gap year" after finishing high school before starting University, which was very unusual in Japan, firstly because everybody is very ambitious to get into a career as soon as possible, and secondly because they were women. So, there we were, five women enjoying each other's company making all sorts of silly comparisons between America and Japan. I liked them; I complimented them on their English.

After admiring the church, we continued northwards, and the mood of our group grew lighter. Atsuko, the one with the camera thanked me and said: "We want to be fluent by the time we go back to Japan." Then she asked me "Is he your boyfriend? He's very cute, what's his name

Me: "He's not really. . .er my b... ., anyway, look...."

But Marty jumped right back into the conversation: "This is our first date, I'm Marty, nice to meet you."

"Oooo Hi Marti," the girls said in sing-song coy unison, each introducing herself. They knew a few things about American humor, and they had a few teases to serve to us in a giddy inoffensive way. Our moods lightened further by relaxed weekend traffic and crowds, the sublime scenery and perfect weather.

You must have gathered by now, although I liked him as a colleague I was not especially awed by Marty. Looking back on it now, I must have seemed to him, at times quite rude. As Atsuko had said, he was cute. He had fair hair, blue eyes behind gold-rimmed glasses and was a little taller than me in my flats. He was also nicely dressed, not too fat, and he was quiet. It was not the kind of quiet where your intuition tells you there is something brewing in the mind. It was just a bland quiet, residing in a bland regular face which occasionally spoke bland sentences. I could see why his work was in community relations, there was just no edginess or even animation in his face; it was calming, and to me boring, just to look at him. That was his defining feature, calming. I shouldn't say boring, I'm sure he's interesting to somebody.

"Aaahhh . . ., first date, how romantic, have you held hands yet, shall we be your chaperones?" Atsuko asked playfully, followed by mock censure and more giggles from the other three girls Emi, Hana, and Mari, while accusing Atsuko of embarrassing their new friends.

Since it was now way past lunch time we parted from the Japanese girls after exchanging email addresses with them. They headed to another Manhattan tourist site while Marty took me to a small unpretentious French restaurant, somewhere in the general area I'm not quite sure where now, I just followed along. I had to hand it to him; it was perfect. It was busy but not crowded, the decor was French, of course, with lovely monochrome prints of chateaux. Among them I recognized Chenonceau and Françoise Hardy was streaming discreetly through the p.a. system. Marty suggested a croque monsieur; the waiter nodded in approval, so I followed suit. It came with a simple salad called assiètte de crudités and a carafe of red vin ordinaire.

As you would expect the restaurant's small wrought iron table and chairs made an intimate seating arrangement well suited to conversation. We had by now shared the pleasant company of the Japanese girls and talked quite naturally about our morning. My concentration waxed and waned as Marty re-hashed something we'd seen at Ground Zero. Of course, my mood, the wine and the ambience helped a little I suppose, but I found myself passing dreamily into a state where Ari's head would appear and disappear in place of Marty's, like the Cheshire cat in Alice's Adventures in Wonderland. One minor difference was the Cheshire cat, I think, was in control of whether it appeared or not. But to the best of my knowledge, on this occasion Ari had no active part in it.

Marty asked: "What are you smiling at? I don't think I said anything funny."

I let my docile idiot smile fade gently, answering:

"I was just thinking of the Japanese girls. They were such fun. I guess just thinking of them makes me smile. I had such a lovely time. By the way, don't forget I told you I'm going to my parents' place for dinner. I need to go home now."

"Yeah, the girls were fun" he said with enough conviction to make me remember the enthusiasm he showed when exchanging email addresses with Atsuko.

We took the subway back to Brooklyn needing only one change of trains at 6th and 14th Street. We both live somewhere near L route stations, so we travelled together most of the journey. In the long tunnel under the East River, he was sitting opposite me. The train clattered along with its stupefying rhythm as heads bobbed around in time with the rocking carriage. I was sitting directly opposite Marty and once again I found myself substituting Ari's head for Marty's as I looked at him. I was thinking this time, as Alice had in Wonderland, I've seen a face without a smile before but never a smile without a face, because sure enough Ari's wan smile remained suspended above Marty's shoulders after all else had disappeared from his face. Marty stared back at me uncomprehendingly. What could my stare possible mean to him?

I got out at Graham Ave., he a few stops further down the line, I'm not sure where.

On the whole excursion there was no spark of romance between Marty and me, at least from my side. That much must have been obvious to him, but save where he made a bathroom stop on our way to the bridge hike, he'd shown little sign of irritation. After that we were both distracted by the Japanese girls until lunch. On the other hand, I had discovered myself to be in some way captivated by Ari after only a brief time with him the previous Saturday. It was a little frightening since there was no common sense about it. Just animal feelings, curiosity maybe? nothing more, but powerful and disconcerting just the same.

Later when I went to my parents' for dinner, they asked me about my day.

"How lovely," my mom said when I told her about the French restaurant.

"Is he Catholic?" asked my dad.

"I don't know. What difference does it make?" I replied.

"Right, no difference" said my dad, "and he works at Catholic Charities with you?"

"Right"

"And his name's Marty. . .?" the inflection in his voice told me he was waiting for me to complete his sentence. I obliged"

"McCann".

My parents looked at each other trying not to be obvious about their ever so brief smiles and nods.

Me: "Don't get any ideas. We're just friends."

My Mom: "Yes dear. And you have a dinner date next Saturday. Is that with Marty too?" She sounded perky, no doubt a result of her perception of my improving prospects for a long-term relationship.

Me: "No this is a different guy and it's not just the two of us, it's a foursome"

My Mom: "Is he Catholic too, I mean do you work with him too, or does he work at the office where you are?"

Me: "No no I don't work with him and I'm pretty sure he's not Catholic"

My Dad: "What's his name?"

Me: "Ari Geffen." I didn't wait for my dad to say "Ari what?"

My Mom: "Sounds Jewish?" She said it with a guilty look.

Me: "Well he's not Jewish. I know that for sure because I overheard his Jewish girlfriend say to him: 'You can convert'.

My Mom: "Oh, he has a girlfriend already and you have a date with him?"

Me: "It's not a date kind of date. Oh, never mind. What's Robbie up to?" I changed the subject. It worked. There's always time to talk about Robbie, my brother, and his new girlfriend. When he's not out boozing, he's working on his master's degree in history at Notre Dame University.

I was busy at work the following week. Traveling back and forth to work on the subway I thought about Marty sometimes. I felt a little guilty about the way I'd treated him and thought that maybe there's more to him than I allowed, but that Atsuko had seen in him.

As for Ari, I thought about him all the time and shot him a couple of emails. The first was to ask unnecessarily if dinner arrangements were still in place, and the second, just as unnecessarily about how I should dress, would his friends be formal or casual? To the first he replied 'Yes, regards' and to the second: 'Casual, regards.'

Despite my eagerness for time to pass quickly to Saturday I was apprehensive about it too. I said to myself as an analyst should:

1. He's in love with somebody else.

2. By his own admission he's in love with somebody else who also appears to love him, but he hasn't got the gumption to do what it takes to claim her for his own.

3. I hardly know him.

4. He's insecure.

5. He doesn't know what religion he is.

6. I have irrational feelings for him which could spell the kind of trouble I don't want to get into.

Added all together that makes for a complicated set of baggage.

Chapter 9 - Dinner at Ari's - Maria

Saturday evening came. I took the Subway to Bedford Avenue and walked to Ari's address in a new apartment house by the East River. Five floors up I stepped out of the elevator where Ari greeted me with relaxed charm and consideration. He took my coat and led me into the dining room of his three-room apartment. It overlooked the river. To the South the sturdy lines of the Williamsburg, Manhattan and Brooklyn bridges stood out as did the Queensboro to the North. In the far distance the Triborough was just visible.

Right across the river barely a mile away was Manhattan in all its incandescent glory. Eastern profiles of the buildings had darkened in contrast to the glorious pink bloom of sunset behind them, but like a thousand bright stars on a clear night their windows twinkled in defiance of the gathering dusk. I don't usually stand in awe of scenery, but this was extraordinary, so much so that when I should have been paying attention to the two guests that had already arrived, I was standing open-mouthed by the floor to ceiling window.

I didn't realize Ari was standing right by my side until he said: "It has that effect on people; pretty, isn't it? I want you to meet my friends Wilson and Beatty." He gestured to two guys, yes guys, I was expecting a boy/girl type couple not guys, seated by a coffee table in the adjoining living room.

"Nice to meet you Wilson, nice to meet you Beatty, I'm Maria. I was so awed by the view; I didn't see you sitting there.

Wilson: "Nice to meet you too, Maria, Ari told us all about you."

Me: "Really? He must have made it all up because he hardly knows me"

Wilson: "He knows you're a budget analyst, he knows you're a Catholic, he knows you throw omelets at strangers in restaurants then lecture them about their love lives and religion."

Me: "I was the inadvertent witness of a tense scene between Ari and his girlfriend. I kinda let myself get sucked in."

Wilson, smiling: "Of course, unavoidable, I'm sure."

Me: "There's a nice smell of cooking and I came hungry, glad you didn't order in pizza."

Ari was listening to all this but was quiet. The situation felt a little peculiar to me. There was no 'official' romantic attachment between Ari and me and I wasn't quite sure what the two guys were all about. It all seemed a bit artificial and too much attention was being paid to me. Really, I didn't feel I could start a conversation or laugh too much when I just didn't know these people. I went quiet, deliberately so. I didn't feel I had to be the life and soul. I just listened, then walked over to the window to admire the view again and waited for the others to talk.

Ari was quite relaxed about cooking dinner, I don't know how much help he got, not much, I think. He prepared what he knew, which was Israeli. Yes, he's Israeli, did I tell you about that? I'll tell you more about it later. Oh, excuse me, I think he told you that already. The fish was interesting and different. He called it St Peter's Fish which is, he told me, "actually tilapia". Actually, I knew that, but I didn't let on. I nodded like I was learning something. It wasn't the kind of tilapia you'd find at the average American grocery store but a whole baked fish on a plate. Now, I admit I hadn't seen it prepared like that before. He'd fried four of them with only salt and pepper and put one before each of us as we sat down to eat.

On the table was a smorgasbord of various salads, chopped veggies, some runny yogurt, hummus, baba ghanoush, mashed up eggplant garnished with I'm not sure what and stuffed vine leaves. There were other things too, like capers and olives but it's not important for the story. You get the idea. If you think tilapia has no bones, think again. These fish, though very tasty, still had their heads, tails and fishy skeletons which I gradually exposed as I picked carefully at the flesh with my fork. I want to call it rustic eating though that's probably not the right word for it but getting some scales and the occasional bone can soon tangle with fancy eating etiquette.

Thinking back about it, if Ari's goal was to break the ice socially between the four of us, he could not have made a better choice of food. Everything on the table begged sharing and questions starting with how and what.

Ari: "This is called St Peter's fish, did you know?"

Me: "Who calls it that?"

Ari: "You call it that, I call it moosht. It's Israeli"

Me: "No kidding, actually I know, and I know why. Where did you get it, Israel?"

Ari: "At the Chinese grocery store."

Me: "So is moosht the Chinese name for it?

Ari: "No it's the Hebrew name."

"So why is it called St. Peter's fish, Maria?" asked Wilson. "Was it involved in some kind of miracle?" He said this with a hint of mockery in his voice and I wasn't about to let that pass.

"It reads as a miracle in the bible but with further study it's entirely credible," I said, not quite believing what I heard myself saying, hoping I didn't sound hysterical. There was an embarrassed silence.

"You see," I continued, softening my tone, "Peter needed cash to pay his temple tax and Jesus told him to go and catch a fish in the Sea of Galilee. He said he would find a coin in the fish's mouth to cover the tax. Tilapia is one of the species that live in the lake. The mother fish take their eggs into their mouths to hatch and to nurture the fry. When the growing fry have outstayed their welcome, she often puts a pebble in her mouth to make life uncomfortable for them, so they'll leave. The mother fish, it's believed, mistook the coin for a pebble."

The conversation revived slowly about food trivia with Wilson and Beatty joining in until I was feeling a little bored and a little emboldened, with the wine helping perhaps, I said:

"So, Beatty what do you do, are you a student?" somehow I didn't think he was. He looked much older and mature and quite carefully groomed.

"I'm an architect," he replied.

"Look through the window with binoculars here at Ari's place and a 3-D textbook opens up before you." I said somewhat mechanically. He nodded approvingly while he extracted a fish bone from between his teeth.

"Did you design anything that we can see from here?" I continued.

If you imagine the towers of Manhattan as a mountain range, then its foothills would be the seeming castellated acre upon acre of apartment houses just beyond the far shore. Among them there was a little block that he identified by some blueish filigree around its top. "Wow", I said blandly, thinking that if this conversation were written, wow would be without its usual exclamation mark.

He smiled. He didn't seem to mind my directness. I think he thought me funny and refused to be intimidated. I liked that in him

"Actually," broke in Ari, "I invited my friends, Beatty and Wilson here to help me explain why I'm so vague about my religion."

"I don't really care what religion you are Ari. That's the sort of thing my mom and dad care about, and your girlfriend or your ex-girlfriend whatever she is, but not me," I answered. "I'd rather talk about movies." Although that sounded disingenuous given my earlier and acute curiosity and my dreary little fish monologue, but at that very moment it was true. I would have preferred at that instant to dance or sing and drink a whole lot more. So we talked about movies for a while. Wilson was quite knowledgeable and animated talking about them. He'd seen just about everything I'd seen and a whole lot more.

"What do you do Wilson?" I asked.

Wilson: "I'm a journalist."

Me: "You write about movies, I bet?"

Wilson: "Sometimes, I'm freelance, I write just about anything, mostly for the magazines based here in town. Sometimes I need to travel for my stories. If I see an obscure foreign story, there are times when I can just about smell there's something interesting going on that begs investigation and that will support an interesting magazine piece."

Me: "You didn't happen to meet Ari when you were abroad did you?"

Wilson: "No I met his brother, he looked exactly like Ari."

Me: "So what was interesting about his brother?"

Wilson: "Well, his name for starters; it was Mohammed."

Me: "Oh wait, that's not a Jewish sounding name, is it? It's an Arab name, right? Like a Muslim name? That's weird, one brother has a Jewish name and the other an Arab name. I don't know much about those religions, but I know they don't like each other too well. I think one parent must have been Arab and the other Jewish?

Wilson: "No that's not it. . ."

Then Ari joined in: "He was not my real brother; I just call him that.

Me: Why? Is it because he looks exactly like you?

There followed a silence so tense and awkward from the guys you could feel it. Then Ari said: "Why don't we just leave it alone. What was I thinking when I brought everybody here to talk about my problems with religion?" The question was rhetorical of course. He was holding his head as if in pain. "I'm so damned self-centered."

The atmosphere in the room had suddenly gotten very heavy. It's not like there was any animus flying around, there was just a four-way embarrassment. "Let's go out to a bar," said Beatty; the suggestion met with immediate approval. Our party of four emerged from the apartment tower into a refreshing breeze blowing off the river and headed a few blocks East to an Irish bar. The prospect of oppressive conversation about religion evaporated in the cheerful atmosphere. Moreover, the volume of Irish singing with its boisterous rebel lyrics curiously intermingling with loud good-natured laughter overwhelmed any attempt at conversation.

As for me, liberated from shyness by a few glasses of wine, I flirted shamelessly with Wilson and Beatty enjoying myself, secure in the assumption that these two guys just had to be gay, and therefore risk free. That is to say, I didn't need to worry that I might have successfully hit on either and then needed to switch to a back-away mode. So, I strutted my stuff more blatantly than I care to admit, but as I sipped my vermouth it began to dawn on me that maybe they were not gay after all. The guys played along and seemed to be enjoying themselves too. Then there was Ari, he was quietly watching me, the guys, the band, the decor then me again. He was in another zone. He was thinking about something and suddenly I wanted to know what about.

And at that very moment he looked at me and said: "Come on I'll walk you home, we can talk, it's too loud here."

Chapter 10 - The Void - Maria

I t was a relief to be outside again in the relative peace of a busy street. Ari had rescued me from any inadvertent consequences of my shameless flirting, and it pleased me to think he might have done it for selfish reasons. Since Ari didn't know where my apartment was, by way of showing him the route I linked arms. He passively let me keep this contact when it was no longer necessary. I basked contentedly in this mild intimacy as we strolled slowly along one of Brooklyn's wider leafy sidewalks, enjoying the fall evening.

Thinking back, I suppose I was not totally content because I was not quite able to squash the thought of Ari's girlfriend seeing us and making a scene. This, irrationally, caused me to look behind me several times as if she might be following us. She was not. Unfortunately, it appeared someone else might be. There were three young men who seemed to be quickening their step to catch us. Surely not! 'Just my imagination,' I thought as I poked Ari gently with my finger and said: "Hey, look behind us. Anyone you know?"

Ari turned around and simultaneously his posture seemed a little stiff. "I'll take that as a yes," I said trying to sound lighthearted and unconcerned. My wrist was squeezed by Ari's frozen arm. I wiggled it to free it as he collected himself and he waited with a cool and what I thought was a determined gaze at the approaching group. The three men looked just as cool and determined as they came face to face. One held out a hand to shake, which Ari took, as he did with the other two, but you could tell that while there was no real warmth there was little overt hostility either. All ignored me.

A conversation followed in a foreign language which at first, I assumed must be Hebrew. When I started to tune in to get hints of what it was all about it sounded more like Arabic. Why did I think so? Well, when I had a vacation in Jordan early last year, I heard a lot of it. Arabic consonants seem to me to be very strongly articulated with staccato breaks between them. And there was something else, if it was Arabic, Ari was speaking it too, but slightly differently. He was speaking more slowly and deliberately as if it were not his mother tongue. Then I heard the word I thought was "shiksa" spoken by one of the three and noticed quick furtive glances towards me. I know shiksa is some kind of Jewish slang for non-Jewish women, so now I was puzzled. I was starting to feel a little scared.

There was a tall, bearded stout one wearing a black leather jacket who seemed a little older than the other two who started speaking. There were no introductions, so I'll call him Big-beard. He was slow and loud and had an aggressive posture and continued for about 30 seconds. Ari's head drooped and then there was a silence. After a few seconds he looked up and an animated conversation burst into life. Then another of the three joined in. He acted like a referee. He was beaded, aloof, small, and wiry and kind of 'in command'. I'll call him little-beard. He held up his hand to the Big-beard to stop what appeared to be threats. You could tell by the inflections in his voice that, unlike Big-beard, he was meeting Ari's replies with carefully considered explanations and counter questions, but tinged with exasperation and repetition. It appeared the two of them had different roles to play. Big-beard emphasized his arguments by punching his left hand with his right fist.

The third, who was short, thin and wiry appeared mild and apologetic in his manner, as if he was reaching out to be friendly. He was clean shaven and therefore, no-beard.

After about five minutes of to and from No-beard turned to me and said in a gentler voice and very poor English: "Ari want come with us, I walk you see you safe home. My name Anwar." Ah! at last, a name, so forget No-beard he was Anwar.

"The hell you will. Ari what's going on? What are you doing with these men, who are these men?" I was angry now as well as scared.

Ari's mouth moved but nothing came out.

"We Ari cousins," said Anwar, "this about family, about brother. Ari come with us."

"Ari, is this true, are these men your cousins? Is this a family problem? Do you have a brother? What do they need you for?"

He turned to me wearing a lame expression, nodded then turned to walk away between Big-beard and little-beard, almost shoulder to shoulder as if they needed to prevent him from running away.

Then he stopped and turned back to me saying, "I...I'm so sorry, I just have to go, I'll get back to you. I promise. Thanks for coming to my place, I love to be with you."

He turned again and walked in what looked like the direction of his apartment.

I just stared in disbelief at what I had just seen. What was going on? How could he just leave like that?

Anwar was still standing beside me pleading with me to let him take me home. I was almost crying by that time, shaking with anger, and thinking 'what am I going to do now?' all at once.

"Go fuck yourself," I said without looking at him and took off at a fast clip back towards the Irish bar where I figured Wilson and Beatty might still be. And so they were, just as I'd left them talking amicably above the din with a couple of girls. I burst into the conversation and spilled my story somewhat breathlessly. Grabbing the guys' attention caused the girls to float away. I watched the guys' eyes follow them, then switch back to me.

"Wait", said Beatty, gradually refocusing on me and what I had to say, "start again I'm not sure I follow; are you saying Ari was kidnapped?"

"No, he wasn't exactly kidnapped, he... he... well, he seemed to be under some kind of pressure to go with some guys who said they were his cousins."

"Some kind of pressure...?" repeated Beatty slowly with a questioning inflection in his voice.

I began to realize, feeling rather stupid, that going somewhere with your cousins voluntarily does not, usually, constitute something to get alarmed about. I looked away in confusion and there to my right I was surprised to see Anwar, the little guy who attempted to be friendly, standing with us making a kind of foursome. I didn't know what to say but I needn't have worried because Anwar took it upon himself to explain. I glanced at Wilson and Beatty whose attention was fully engaged now, but their expressions, if I read them correctly, barely seemed to register concern. I reflexively put a bit more personal space between myself and Anwar but when he started talking with a soft throaty nervous voice, I had to move in closer again to catch what he said.

"His brother by Palestine, Israel, he not with us, he gone, disappeared." Anwar kept repeating in his very limited English, unable to hold back tears and becoming incoherent. Of course, we were stunned into silence. Wilson and Beatty were no longer smiling. I sort of put two and two together and assumed Ari would be going to Palestine/Israel to search in some way for his brother.

Why else would he go with his 'cousins?' But it was all so abrupt. If they'd come in a friendly manner, explained what was going on, talked about flights and so on, it would

89

at least have made some kind of sense to me. There may have been talk of a return flight. There was something going on, spoken in a foreign language, Arabic, I think. But Anwar was not telling me or Wilson or Beatty the whole story, I was sure. Even if he wanted to, his English would have fallen short.

So, it seemed like there was nothing more to do. I felt deflated and helpless. I just murmured something more like a groan, turned around and walked slowly home retracing the steps I had walked only thirty minutes ago. Once there I put on my favorite Queen CD, slumped in a chair, and thought I may have to start smoking again, even though it had been two and half years since I stopped. But of course, I hadn't any cigarettes and by the time I could have collected myself and walked to the store to buy some, my mood would have changed. I knew I was fooling only myself. There's no question though that I was unhappy. I hummed along with the music to some defiant lyrics. Not only had I lost company with Ari in circumstances bordering on weird, but what I'd hoped would be a fun and interesting evening out, had just fizzled. Then my apartment door buzzer buzzed.

"It's Wilson, you know, Beatty's friend, hi."

"Yes," I replied through the intercom, followed by silence. I recognized his voice and was relieved that it wasn't Anwar, but I wasn't sure what to do.

"I thought you may like to hear more about Ari?" I heard.

"I guess," I replied, feeling like a zombie. I pressed the button to open the door.

Up the stairs he came. I opened my door still in zombie mode, let him in, pointed to a chair with a weary

90

gesture and sat down opposite him. He sat too. He had a polite manner and an economy of movement such that he blended into the room unostentatiously. Other than that, I don't remember anything about his appearance that evening. I may have seemed rude, but I forgave myself for that, considering what I'd been through. And compounding my rude mood I just stared at him and said: "Well? how do you know where I live"

"Here's the deal", he said.

"OK," I said, but I don't know why I said it. I probably would have said OK no matter what he said. He didn't say how he knew where I lived, and I forgot to press the matter.

After a few more awkward pauses I heard Wilson exhale, then inhale as if in readiness to commence a monologue, which he did, fluently, barely pausing, almost as if he was reading it from a prepared text. He was a journalist, of course, and he could have written this all down before now and be simply recalling what he'd written. To test this thought I interrupted him several times, but his monologue followed where my question had led him. Thus, I had to believe he was speaking spontaneously with a full knowledge of his subject matter.

"I'll start at the beginning", Wilson said.

"Yes do, please", I replied blankly. "And what's this 'cousins' bullshit all about?"

"I'm not sure, but here's what I think," he answered then continued after a pause. Firstly, one of them really is a blood relative, the guy who introduced himself as Anwar.

I'm pretty sure the other two guys are not, and it seems to me they have another agenda. All three of them are broke, they have an airline ticket home and that's about it. They want to hole up at Ari's place while they work on persuading him to go to God knows where? Cyprus was mentioned. They have some family loyalty leverage over Ari which is really very complicated. I called him. He said the guys have nowhere to sleep. He sounded really depressed."

"I'm listening," I said wearily.

Chapter 11 - Horrible Incident - Maria

About twenty-three years ago...."
"Hold on, twenty-three years? Is there a short version?"
"Well, I just need to tell you about an incident that happened back then. Then I'll fast forward through the other stuff. I don't mean to be too obvious, but twenty-three years ago is around the time Ari was born.

"Here's the incident: Two heavily pregnant women of similar appearance, one Jewish, one Palestinian, got on a bus in Tel Aviv that was bound for Jerusalem. A suicide bomber got on too and positioned himself at the center of the bus. The bomb he was carrying exploded soon after the bus started off. Many on the bus died, some immediately, some later in hospital from their injuries. But the two women escaped with their lives - just. There were a few other survivors, most having very serious burns, gashes, broken limbs, and torn & burnt clothes."

"Jesus Christ, holy shit and holy...", I blurted several more holy this and thats, sounding like my dad after he hit his thumb with a hammer. Wilson resumed gravely:

"Ambulances arrived and whisked them away to hospitals; the two women were taken to the same one. In the emergency rooms doctors decide that the women's injuries are too severe for them to carry their babies to term. Both give birth to baby boys by cesarean section. Their clothes had been mostly burnt away. In the absence of personal possessions from which they had been separated by the bomb blast, their names and ethnicities or anything else about them are not known.

"Jesus Christ, holy moth...," I put my hand to my mouth; I couldn't finish, and he kept going.

"The emergency nature of the operations dictated that the child births were not in maternity wards, and keeping that in mind, and given that both women were under anesthetic, after two healthy babies had been delivered there was no time or immediate tagging method to tie the identity of each baby to each mother."

"No way, no way," I interrupted, "you're saying one of the babies was Ari? That would never happen here," I babbled."

"Look," he said, "there was urgent life-saving surgery being performed in different rooms on both women. Both were literally at death's door, their skins blackened with terrible burns and lacerated with flying glass and debris. The medical teams surrounding them were covered in blood. In the midst of all that, the surgeon in charge did have the presence of mind to specifically instruct verbally which recovery room each baby and mother should be assigned to, after procedures had been completed."

"How do you know?" I asked.

"It was in my journalist friend Shona's account which I read in full, every word of it. She traced and asked every surviving member of the medical team. Her reputation depended on it. It was a big story in Israel and in many other parts of the world. It was bound to be examined and cross checked in every detail."

"Well even without tags to attach to each baby they would still have taken some quick reckoning to associate each with the right mother," I insisted.

"Well, yes, and in fact they did just that; and here's where the slipup occurred according to Shona's research. After many hours of toil, the hospital teams had stabilized the conditions of the fifteen or so survivors, having failed to save ten of them. They handed over the patients gradually and wearily to a new shift, following standard protocols, explaining verbally and with notes, the progress of each. Pediatric nurses assumed the care of the babies.

"While in recovery about ten days later the mothers were introduced to, slowly bonded with and eventually breast fed their babies. After about another week they took home the wrong babies, the Jewish woman with the Arab baby and vice versa."

"Really? But how could that have happened? You said the mothers and babies were reunited in their assigned rooms." I interrupted again. It seemed Wilson was so emotionally engaged he felt he was actually there during some part of the story. Then I asked again: "But if I'm going to believe you, I need to know one thing. How, exactly could such a thing have happened, and how was the mistake discovered? I'm straining to believe you."

"That's two questions, but it is difficult to answer the first with certainty. It took more than twenty years for the mistake to be discovered that an investigation could not uncover with any certainty what happened. But it goes something like this:

"The first mother to come out of surgery was placed in a recovery room. A different physician in charge of recovery realized she needed equipment that was temporarily not available there and moved her somewhere else to stabilize her. Immediately following that the second mother came out of a different operating room and was placed in that same recovery room which had just been vacated by the first of them, and by staff that had not been briefed. A pediatric nurse busy swaddling and attending to the baby simply was not told of the switch and tagged the baby with the wrong mother.

"She'd been moved, so what? Why didn't the nurse just find her when she saw the room was empty - oh wait, it wasn't empty you say?" I said, then hesitated. It began to dawn on me what had happened. "Oh no, so they'd brought mother number two to the room where mother number one had been?"

"You got it," Wilson Answered.

"Don't tell me, baby number one was placed into the arms of mother number two" I said.

"No, not at all," Wilson continued, "both women were so heavily sedated they were in no condition to even hold a baby or for that matter be aware of which room they were in. Each was shown a baby as a brief humane gesture in the hope that through the fog of anesthesia some happiness might be brought. They were reintroduced the next morning when the anesthetic was wearing off. They both continued to be under heavy sedation and pain medication, some of which continued for weeks. Mothers and babies got erroneous ID wristbands, of course. As fast as their recoveries would allow each mother bonded with her child, or should I say, 'a child'.

The mothers had been standing close to each other on the bus and their injuries were similar. They suffered serious burns and lacerations on the left legs, left sides and breasts and necks. On one side their clothes were entirely burned away, and their hair singed off on that same side almost completely. Their faces were burned only moderately. Skin grafts restored them to a point where time and makeup achieved an approximation of their former looks. How shall I say it? They were pretty women when they got onto the bus and several months later, they were not hideous."

"You damn them with faint praise," I said disgustedly. "So, they all go home, and then what happens?"

"Nothing much really, at least not for a long time. Shona, my journalist friend was impressed by the support of their respective communities, starting, thankfully, with supportive and affectionate husbands in both cases. That bye itself is another story."

"Nobody suspected anything was wrong. The surgical teams were praised for their dedication and skill. Funerals of those who died in the incident became the news stories of the following days" Wilson answered, then continued:

"As for the boys, two parallel and entirely separate upbringings followed, each steeped in the culture, religion and propaganda of Palestinian and Jewish communities. Each boy to each family's pleasure, and in a kind of bizarre symmetry, widening his contacts in his community and deepening his commitment to his ethnic traditions. And so might that have been the end of the story."

"However, when each man was 23 a horrible politically motivated knife murder occurred in Jerusalem.

"Oh boy," I said, resigned to hearing about further complications." I wanted to say what's that got to do with anything, but I had a feeling it had a lot to do with everything. Then Wilson got a bit mystical:

"I'll come back to the young men and what happened to them but to understand this better let me try to explain some background. To know this city, Jerusalem, is to be aware of its moods. Yes, moods, I think, is the right word. When there's a lull in the tension between the communities, the city relaxes. You can feel it, you can see it and hear it in the street vendor's displays and calls and even smell it in the street food barrows and stalls. Thousands of excited tourists of all kinds inhale the aromas with the special atmosphere and very special spirituality. They merge with thousands of locals of all the disparate communities in the narrow alleyways inside the Old City walls and spill out to its tree lined hilly boulevards into the new, well, at least more recent part of the city."

"Ok, well I think I've absorbed about as much as I can in one evening," and feeling confused and exhausted, with a lot of questions still unanswered, and without thinking twice added, "Hey, look, I'm just not up for a tourism pitch right now. Do you want to come over to my place sometime and finish the story?"

I never asked guys I don't know well to come to my place but this time I didn't hesitate. "I want to know the whole thing, beginning to end. I want to know what happened to Ari's so-called 'brother,' born to the Palestinian women and how the boys got to know one another and call each other brothers. Do you know all this?'

"I'll tell you what I know", Wilson replied.

"Not now, not now, not now", I said tiredly, my voice fading away as I talked, "But soon! call me" I said, suddenly becoming animated surprising myself as well as him. It may seem peculiar that I make no secret of wanting to hear the whole story, yet I wanted to get rid of Wilson at the same time and then I wanted him back to finish the story.

I felt a little woozy as I glanced at the empty bottle of Merlot plonk. My attitude must have been confusing for Wilson. It reflected my conflicted state of mind though.

In my quiet apartment after he left, I began to realize, in spite of myself, I'd been drawn to Ari from the first moment I met him. I wanted to know more about him and spend more time with him. But at the same time, I wanted to pull away. The more I learned about this complicated mess of Israel and Palestine and clashing religions, and the people mixed up in it, the more I wanted to run away and resume my pre-Ari life. I thought about his girlfriend whom I saw briefly venting her frustration at Ari in that Brooklyn café and began to understand a little bit how she felt. Even so, I understood the seriousness of what happened to his 'brother,' and in all conscience how he could act and comply with the requests of his 'cousins.' I still felt irritated, though, that he just left me cold.

The following evening, I went to see my parents thinking that their presence and the familiar surroundings of my childhood home would get my feet back on the ground, that is, would help me reconnect with the comforting easy routine of my life as it had been until about several weeks ago. But it was not to be. My parents' innocent assumptions about my 'relationships' were more irritating than soothing. I smiled as I realized not long after I arrived there, that I was yearning to be re-ensconced in my lonely angst back at my own apartment. The smile was inadvertent but of course it was seen, and must have been interpreted, as a response to something my dad said. I often smiled at his naive optimism.

The truth was that while he was saying whatever he was saying, I was lost in my thoughts. I don't know what he'd said. I smiled again at this thought and started to giggle as I imagined myself once again as Alice in Wonderland, unable to make sense of the conversation in which I was taking part. And still wearing a smile I got up to go, hugged my mom and then my Dad and kissed him affectionately, looked into his puzzled anxious eyes and said: "o mio babbino caro", oh my dear daddy.

I know he loves opera and this aria from Puccini's Gianni Schicchi in particular. It seemed so much in keeping with what I think of him, these pure lyrics of love interjected between the complications that precede it and follow it.

Ah the street again, the friendly street, cool, never judging. I welcomed back my thoughts which only two hours ago I so urgently needed to leave behind and strolled idiotically carefree humming Puccini's aria imagining myself as Maria Callas at the Met.

Back at work the next day I was bumbling around trying to unjam some paper from our routinely jammed printer when Marty showed up looking for his print-out. We looked at each other, awkwardly at first but in the course of opening the various printer doors and drawers for the offending sheets, fell into conversation.

"You seen the Japanese girls again?" I asked.

His presence seemed like a link to my newly minted alter ego as worrier-in-chief about Ari's welfare while I waited for Wilson's phone call, as if waiting for Godot. Perhaps I exaggerate. It had been two days, just two days, but when something's on my mind that I need cleared up, time slows down to taunt me. It was odd how Marty was conflated in my mind with the whole Ari experience of the last couple of weeks but in reality, when I think about that time, he had nothing to do with it, he was just a diversion. Perhaps I needed another diversion?

That evening, unable to wait for Wilson's call any longer I called him and told him somewhat crudely to get his "ass over to my place this evening and spill the beans, all the beans about Ari and his disappeared brother." He agreed and he came, promptly at seven o'clock. He seemed to have dressed more carefully than I remembered at our last meeting, but truth be known, I hardly remembered anything about how he looked at our last meeting.

He was wearing skinny jeans, sneakers, a blue shirt and tan jacket. It all seemed to match his light brown hair and hazel eyes. He was cute, about 5' 10". I took it all in as he looked round at my apartment. I saw his eyes rest on photos of my parents, of fondly remembered beach shenanigans in Florida, of my grandparents, my brother with his former girlfriend and a few of me with a college sweetheart from whom I parted tearfully after college and never saw and barely thought of again. His movements were deliberate and calm, externally at least. He was probably stressed at our previous meeting and taking his time to calm himself before he had to deal with crazy me. I let him be.

He asked for nothing, but I had bought a large bottle of Merlot, again on the way home, looked out a recipe my mom once gave me and made us a chicken pot pie to share.

"Should have been a white wine with chicken," I heard myself saying to Wilson who had picked up the bottle and corkscrew I'd placed in front of him on the table.

"Works for me," he replied as he filled our glasses and proceeded then to slice the pie, serve it and start eating almost without a pause. I took the hint that he was hungry and started without enthusiasm to pick at my slice of pie, feeling a knot in my stomach.

Chapter 12 - Murder and Exoneration - Maria

You'd think Wilson was trying to sell me on a vacation the way he described Jerusalem. it sounded nice, at least when, by Wilson's perception of the city, it was in a good mood. My mood though, was one of impatience to move the story along and I prompted him to do so: "You had just started to tell me about a murder in Jerusalem."

"Yes, I was coming to that," he answered, "It's a lovely city when it's relaxed, but when there's tension you can feel that too…"

"The murder?" I interrupted, but he just continued with his train of thought:

"Tension engulfs the city in a wave of angst and mistrust, almost palpable. Violence committed by any individual or group causes an unequal reaction and escalation that lasts for months, years sometimes, until exhaustion and sheer boredom with the excesses of caution relaxes the mood like a tired muscle relaxes after a workout."

"So, if I want to go there, I'll ask you first what's the mood of the city, right?" I asked, not quite getting why he was telling me about the city's moods.

Wilson just smiled, then continued "Anyway, as I was saying, when this murder took place, it was a time of tension. The perpetrators escaped into crowded East Jerusalem. Ari's counterpart, the second baby born 22 years ago and raised a Muslim, called Nadeem by the way, is near to the scene of the crime at the time. He saw a large contingent of police approaching, ran in fright, but was chased and caught. His denial of involvement was not believed and this, plus his involvement with Palestinian nationalist causes, and the unseen escape of the real perpetrator, converge to implicate him."

"Well, there has to be more to a prosecution than what you've said so far… and I'm guessing that this Nadeem, is the one that has disappeared recently?" I added.

"Yes".

"Ok, ok, ok, God, I think I get it, this is truly weird, I'm sorry," I replied, "let me sit down."

But I was already sitting down so I stood up and flopped on my sofa.

"What am I saying? No, of course I don't get it. Is there more, there has to be more?" I asked after a pause during which Wilson was politely silent. Then collecting my thoughts and mostly mumbling to myself I continued, "I don't mean to digress but they're not really brothers, are they? In fact, they're not connected in any way at all except by their coincident birthdays and birthplaces."

I looked at Wilson and he looked at me and I said: "OK, well before you go any further let me tell you in the simplest of terms what I understand so far: A long time ago a hospital switched the moms of two baby boys accidentally, and twenty-three years later one of them is implicated in a murder. Right?"

"Right."

"Is this what you planned to tell me when we were at Ari's for dinner? ...it must be, why didn't you tell me then?" I asked. "It doesn't seem like anyone has to feel bad or guilty about anything" I continued, "they were just caught up in something they had no control over."

"Well, it all just seemed too awkward, we couldn't bring it up," said Wilson. None of us could. We were just sort of happy and normal, in large part because of your happy and normal presence."

I must have beamed at that, "My presence made you happy and normal? That's funny, I felt nervous and awkward," I said, but I still don't understand why you didn't bring it up."

"It's difficult to explain, in some places religions and the cultures associated with them have such a strong hold on their believers that any discussion of them becomes somehow charged with emotion and even guilt. Like if you don't buy into it completely, you're somehow an enemy" Wilson answered. "For example, if you say anything negative about the prophet Mohammed you are guilty of the crime of 'blasphemy' in some Muslim countries."

"Pheeueh blasphemy? I do it all the time. And if you ever heard my dad when he's working on a DIY project...well, I don't know, it's definitely not something my church would approve of. But a crime? Gimme a break."

"Exactly!" he answered. "Trivial in our culture, a serious offense somewhere else, punishable even by death in some places."

"And guilt you say? I don't get it. I'm a Catholic, it's a strong culture and plenty of other things too. But I don't have any guilt about anything. I confess my sins and poof! They're all gone. It's just what I am," I said rather awkwardly trying to stop my face cracking into a smile.

"Right," he answered with a straight face, "but it's not the same. There's a lot of hostility between the Jewish and Palestinian cultures In Israel. Poor Ari doesn't know what the hell he is." He looked at my blank uncomprehending expression then tried again:

"Look at it this way," he continued, "When you're among other Catholics I'm sure you criticize the church and the priests and other Catholics to your heart's content. But if a non-Catholic does it in your hearing, it begins to sound like anti-Catholic bigotry."

"OK", I said, tilting my head, first to one side then the other acknowledging without agreeing and he continued:

"I believe that for many people, especially young people that have acquired an education or profession, all that political and adversarial religious baggage gets left behind when they come to America. I don't mean the core Faith or whatever cultural meme you associate with your identity, that's not really the focus of assimilating. It's the hate that has to go, and in most cases does. A Moslem has to be able to walk past orthodox Jews as something normal, and Jews in turn regard Islamic dress as normal."

"Wait a minute!" I protested. "Are you calling my Catholic faith, the faith of my family for generations and millions of others just another cultural meme? Is that what you think it is? A meme?" I was getting my Irish up again.

He was quiet for a minute. I sat there enjoying his discomfort, feeling smug. I wondered if it showed on my face. Then he said, sounding a lot more humble:

"I didn't mean to insult you or your faith. Do you mind me asking, do you regularly attend services at your church?"

"I don't mind you asking," I replied, "but aren't we talking about Ari. How did this get to be about me?" Then I said, without waiting for a reply: "I go to mass about once a month. I dress conservatively and I do all that liturgy and eucharist stuff. I sing and I chant and feel good about it. I don't question it, I believe it...but I draw the line at confession no matter what I just said about confessing my sins. I don't want to tell some old celibate priest what's on my mind."

He laughed out loud at that. I didn't mean to be funny, but I guess I was. I could have been angry, but I let it go.

"To tell the truth," I continued on a roll, "I go with my mom to see my grandma. She's always thrilled to see me; she likes to show me off to her friends. She brings me cookies if she's been baking. My dad goes too sometimes, like, every three months, maybe. And you see the children all dressed up in their Sunday best. And one more thing, and I'm serious, the organization I work for, Catholic Charities, is true to its mission. It assists anybody no matter their background. I believe in it. I feel part of something that is spiritual, something that matters to the poor, the sick and the friendless.

"And yet one more thing. I love the music, not all of it but if you've ever heard Missa de Angelis at Christmas you'd know what I mean. You'd want to be a Catholic too."

Wilson pivoted back to Ari to get away from my rant, I guess: "Ari didn't want to hate anybody or be hated by anybody for his past, his family, his race, especially his religion. He just wanted to leave it all behind and be American, a New Yorker, a Brooklynite in the vigorous urban salad of Williamsburg."

"Do you think I'm the dressing on this 'vigorous urban salad?' A vinaigrette say? for Ari?" I couldn't help asking.

Wilson was master of the wry dry smile and without missing a beat asked me: "Do you think Hadassah, his other girlfriend might claim that honorific?"

This threw me more than it should have. I wasn't sure if either one of us was his girlfriend, but our aspirations were a different matter. I dropped the subject and let Wilson continue:

"It had all seemed to become pointless as Ari mixed and befriended Americans of his generation who really didn't care what his background was, beyond sympathetic curiosity. And even if asked, was easily deflected with 'I was born and grew up in…etc.'"

"That's right," I agreed, "that could have been me asking. I really don't care about his background or the religion he grew up with, just as long as he's Catholic." The last few words I uttered dissolved into a giggle.

But Mr. Wry Smile kept on going: "I know that immigrant tradition holds that Italian immigrants gravitate to Italian neighborhoods, the Irish to theirs, as do the Poles, Jews and so on. But he came alone to liberal family friends that would not try to influence his choices. Youth is his ally and friend, and youth even has its culture, devoid of mature biases."

But his face turned serious again as he continued: "And there he was with all of us eagerly waiting for him to drag up his past, stuck halfway between cultures and communities, for the first time in many months. What the hell? Why bother? But there you were with your burning curiosity!"

"Me!" I yelled, "Don't pick on me, you and Beaty were there, you wanted to hear it too."

"Beaty and I already knew most of the story", he answered calmly, "but to be fair to you, he wanted to, rather he was determined to face his gremlins and exorcise his embarrassment and his self-imposed silence."

"Right," I said, "thanks for remembering that. Anyway, once I saw his beautiful apartment by the river, who cares what his religion was? I wanted in."

Wilson smiled again before returning to his monologue: "You see, simply by being an Palestinian and a Muslim by birth, among youthful Israeli Jews who were serving, or who had served like him in the army, women too, continually raised doubts and questions. Their adversaries are exclusively Arab and Muslim…"

"Yea yea, I get it," I interrupted, "and up until the discovery of his real bio parents was Ari's too." That's what you were going to say isn't it?

"Yes", he answered, "It felt to him like he'd betrayed both sides, both races and both religions."

"Right, he was neither one thing nor the other and could not be truly accepted in either community." I said agreeing with him.

"Right," he said yet again, mimicking me. "Many young Americans would talk quite freely about such things, they switch religions as it suits them, they don't hate their past adversaries in war, except perhaps the British on July 4th." He laughed at his own joke. "Not even them, isn't that true?" he asked me.

"You're not Catholic are you? And you're definitely not Irish" I said, not as a question but as a statement and trying to stop myself laughing with no success at all."

"No, I'm not Jewish either", he answered, "but I get your drift", and I caught another flicker of a suppressed smile on his face as he said it, "but it's a matter of degree for most people, like...," he paused, "think of it in extremes, it's rare that anybody gets shunned for apostasy and it's unheard of to become the target or victim of a fatwa for apostasy," he added.

"I think we've flogged this dead horse for long enough," I said. As I said it, I remembered several Catholics I knew who had "lapsed", walked away that is. Outwardly

110

they shed all interest in taking part in regular Catholic mass but on the rare occasions they attended a wedding or funeral, submitted meekly and naturally to the rituals. If you didn't know them personally you couldn't distinguish them from the committed believers.

All I said was: "OK, OK, I get it. Now can we just move the story along a bit quicker? OK?"

"OK."

Chapter 13 - Fizzles - Maria

"O K, so where did we get to," muttered Wilson as he sipped his Merlot having satiated his appetite. "Oh yes," he said, collecting his thoughts after a few prods and reminders from me.

"The murder?" I asked, "you said there was a murder in Jerusalem

"Right, I did. That got your attention, didn't it? I thought you were going to sleep on me. Bear with me, I want to tell you about the events that poisoned relations between the two communities at that time, keeping in mind Ari was a solid committed member of one of the communities before the solid ground supporting his commitment to it turned to mud."

"OK, I guess," I mumbled. If he hadn't mentioned Ari in that last sentence, I would have shown him the door.

So, Wilson continued: "I think I mentioned there were parallel upbringings of the boys, each steeped in the culture of their respective Palestinian and Jewish families. And it was to both families' pleasure that each widened his contacts in his community and deepened his associations with his ethnic traditions. Each enrolled in a university. Ari, though capable in physics and mathematics, is drawn more to the arts at first, especially literature."

"Ari likes the arts?" I muttered, "If you say so, not that we talked much about that, and anyway, recently he doesn't seem to want to talk about anything."

"Well, there in the arts, he found a rich trove to expand his world view. He moved seamlessly from translations into Hebrew to their mostly English language original forms as his schooling in the language progressed. His participation in the Jewish religion was unthinking and automatic."

"Smart guy, quite a linguist." I couldn't help adding, "I noticed a slight accent, but his English is pretty darn good." I kept up my background muttering trying to slow Wilson down.

"Later he rediscovered elegance in mathematics, especially statistics. The holidays and rituals and meals practiced by his family brought order and warmth to his life, though strict religious observance fell away in time. Wide reading also brought him into contact with ideas that rejected religion altogether but while he may have thought about them, they did not alter his participation in, and acceptance of Judaic traditions.

"So... how do I know all this? Well as I said earlier, I had met this lady, Shona, a fellow journalist, sharp and pretty, who found Ari's biological mother. It was she, Shona who inadvertently set off a whole chain of events. She has a nose for stories and a determination to get them. She has a gentle side though and a mothering instinct which she uses to advantage when interviewing someone for a story.

"You like her, don't you? Do you see her often?

"Not often, and never for long, she's always traveling. For all her gentle side she's very independent and tough. She likes work and never stops"

"Is she good looking?" I asked.

"She is. I think she adjusts her appearance according to her assignment. She doesn't like to intimidate humble people. When in their company she dresses down, doesn't look too flashy, not much makeup. Get her in front of a self-important corporate exec and she's quite different, self-assured, tastefully dressed and unafraid. What were we talking about? Where did I get to? Oh yea, I was talking about the two boys, Ari and Nadeem".

"Each had a girlfriend. In Ari's case it was open and uninhibited, but Nadeem's friendship was secret on account of modesty and discretion requirements in keeping with Islamic traditions in Palestine."   "Now you've got my attention, tell me more about the girlfriends.

He looked straight at me.

"I don't know much about Nadeem, but I do know that he became a committed Palestinian nationalist. His nationalism was reinforced by Islam and a sense of grievance relating to land lost to others, who came mostly from foreign places and did not share his culture, religion or language."

"What do you mean, 'land lost to others,'" I asked.

"How the land was lost was complicated and chronic, some of it legal, some of it not, but that's a discussion for another time."

114

"Some of it not legal? You mean it was stolen?"

"Some of it, yes, stolen, there was no question. There are many examples that some of it that was settled and built upon, was historically part of a village's pasture that went back centuries. Secure legal title in the modern meaning of ownership was not available to the peasant farmers, nor were there, and are there, the financial resources available to mount a legal challenge."

"And the point of telling me all this is?" I asked.

"It's all part of the point, you'll see," he continued. "The grievance was deeply felt and simmered beneath the surface of civil life. An occasional death or injury at the hands of the Israeli defense forces (IDF) blew the top off the entire West Bank cauldron of misery and resentment, expressed in several rebellions called Intifadas. In such cases the IDF was usually acting to prevent or respond to a terror outrage against civilians. Such tit for tat accounting of blame was a bottomless pit. A terrorist for an Israeli was a freedom fighter for a Palestinian.

"Stealing land wouldn't make them very happy, I get it, but why was the whole place a 'cauldron of misery?' Not everybody's land was stolen, somebody must have been happy?" I asked.

"Don't forget, the whole of the West Bank was occupied and largely administered by the IDF that protected an ever-increasing flow of Israeli settlers. And don't forget that these settlers claimed that land was based on their interpretation of ancient religious writings contained in the Talmud. It was not civil law, and not a document valid within any flavor of the Mohammedan religion and not of the kind we know in this country enacted by a Congress."

"The Talmud?"

"Yes, briefly, it's a collection of ancient Jewish laws covering many subjects. It's not an evil book per se, in fact in some respects it's a cultural gem. But honestly that stuff should not be regarded as having legal validity. It would be unthinkable here in the US where religion and civil law are explicitly separated in the constitution. That principle applies in every Western democracy. As you know people here are free to practice any religion they want, but enforceable laws are passed by Congress, and only Congress."

I interrupted, "Yea yea yea, God this is heavy duty!" I held the back of my hand to my forehead and let my jaw go slack in a mock gesture of exhaustion. I hoped to inject a little humor. Wilson smiled thinly again but he wasn't frustrated with my questions or ignorance. On the contrary he seemed to be relaxed, marshaling his thoughts to explain the situation to me in the clearest possible terms.

Then he continued: "The provocations were certainly not all one sided, though. The bomb which injured the boys' mothers is only one of many examples. Many other attacks by Islamists are... I was going to say entirely pointless, but they're not. Their purpose is to spread terror. Many poorly aimed rocket attacks at civilian targets are technically war crimes. Sometimes rockets have been launched from sites that are close to health clinics and food distribution centers to deter a response. And if there is a response there's an immediate propaganda tool available to them accusing Israel of attacking the sick and the hungry. Such cynicism is hard to comprehend."

"Good grief!" I said in disgust.

But it was an Israeli terrorist, Yigal Amir, who assassinated Israeli prime minister Yitzhak Rabin for the purpose of undermining a peace process called the 'Oslo Accords,' which was on the verge of being implemented in 1995. The wish of most people on both sides of the great divide was strongly for peace."

"How do you know that? Everything that gets on our news from over there sounds like they want to kill each other. How many wars have they had in the last 50 years?"

He paused, let out a sigh as if to say he wasn't sure about what he was saying, then continued.

"Orthodox fanatics in Israel campaigned and lobbied hard against the peace process, using terror events as levers to gain a following. The peace process was suddenly leaderless on the Israeli side and in a vacuum of official support."

"Anyway, I was saying... back to the murder in Jerusalem. The Palestinian guy, that's Nadeem, the guy conceived by Jewish parents and brought up Muslim, had a roughly bandaged leg, the result of a bicycle accident that morning. The investigators at the scene had found blood samples from both the victim and perpetrator. Although DNA analysis was not locally available at the time it could be shown that the victim's blood type was different from the rare B-negative blood type that stained the victim's clothes. That rare blood type was identified in a trail of red drops leading away from the incident. Apparently, the victim had struggled with his attacker, at one point deflecting the knife into the attacker's flesh."

"OK...so where does Nadeem come into this? He wasn't the murderer surely?"

"No, of course he wasn't the murderer. But he was snared in a round-up after the IDF had closed several streets in a search for suspects. Confident of his innocence, Nadeem willingly gave a blood sample for their forensic purposes. Unfortunately for him his rare blood type matched that of the drops in the blood trail found on the hard cobbles of the Old City. Although matching rare blood types was by no means proof of his involvement in the crime, his known association with Palestinian nationalist causes cast suspicion sufficient to implicate him."

"Ho boy! So, what did he do?" I asked.

"He vigorously denied any involvement, but thinking he had no chance of a fair trial in Israel he escaped police custody, Lord knows how, that just never happens. He was an engineering graduate and very smart and very popular. It's likely he had help. Then he fled to the country of Jordan across the river of the same name."

"And then?"

"His family on the other hand knew that he was not involved and continued the fight on his behalf. In this, the family had help from lawyers and activists inside Israel. When DNA matching for forensic purposes became available his mother, who lived in East Jerusalem, volunteered a blood sample to match her DNA against that of the presumed attacker. This, of course, was different enough to exonerate her son and the case against him was dropped."

Knowing there was more coming I stayed silent and sipped my wine. Wilson did the same then continued:

"Thus, the boy, oh I should stop calling him a boy, he was far from being a boy anymore; he was a man, mature, accomplished and in all the right ways a man, he, Nadeem returned from exile to his Arab family in Israel."

"And nobody knew yet about his birth to a Jewish mother?" I knew that, but I just had to make sure.

"Right, I'm coming to that. A couple of months later a legal and procedural technicality caused the DNA comparison to be challenged by the prosecution attorney and thrown out. A new trial was demanded. Knowing he had nothing to fear this time around, not needing the sample to come from his mother, Nadeem gave a blood sample himself to match against the crime scene blood evidence and was again exonerated. Nadeem's DNA and that of the perpetrator were clearly from different people."

"To Israeli courts, police and press, the DNA re-unmatching simply confirmed the earlier result. From then on, the police had no more interest in Nadeem as a suspect but reopened the case to search for the real perpetrator. However, my journalist friend who was researching the case in order to write a full feature story about it, did what any conscientious journalist would do. She read both DNA reports, first the mother's then the son's, and compared each to the perpetrator's sample.

119

"She, Shona the journalist, confirmed for herself that DNA matching exonerated Nadeem. She interviewed the lab staff, and even read the lab report from the previous trial. This revealed something unexpected and interesting.

"In addition to exonerating Nadeem, careful reading of the reports showed that Nadeem was not the biological son of this woman who claimed to be his mother. How so? She read the reports three times just to make sure and re-interviewed the lab staff who were adamant that all was good. She made them explain the processes and the safeguards against errors. There were no errors. Moreover, extra care had been taken by the lab staff because this analysis was the second relating to this case. The staff knew that their work would be subject to extra scrutiny after their first test results were thrown out."

"OK", I said, "sounds like Shona got on the scent of a good mystery?"

"That's right, but first Shona also had to ask herself that very question; is it really a good mystery?" continued Wilson. "Will it be interesting enough for a newspaper or periodical to buy it? If she couldn't sell the story the whole project would be a waste of time which she could ill afford. She was now convinced that the lab work was good. The lab technicians seemed professional to a tee and had nothing to gain by corrupting the process."

"So her thoughts moved something like: 'Maybe he's adopted? Maybe there's some easily explained anomaly and a follow-up would be a waste of time? After all, adoption can be at first casual and regarded as temporary if, for example, while a mother is sick and a close neighbor friend cares for her children, the arrangement simply continues. Sometimes an official adoption follows, sometimes not. And yet, and yet..., there was without question an anomaly, and it just might be worth her time to follow up; She had a hunch.'"

"Wait a minute," I interrupted him. "I don't buy it. If he was adopted, then the mother would absolutely know he wasn't her biological child."

"Well...well yes that makes sense, but it works both ways, doesn't it? If she knew, secretly, that she wasn't Nadeem's blood relative, then she'd be sure her DNA would exonerate him. Shona couldn't guess if the mother was that sophisticated. In any case, just sometimes when the families are large and neighbors are close, looking after one another's children in hard times and often exhausted, a poor mother might lose track. Is that too farfetched? Could a poor exhausted mother lose track? Possibly? In the course of her work, she'd seen hordes of children running in and out of small homes in poor communities in third world countries."

"OK, I guess," I mumbled grudgingly. "I've been to Jordan once, but our guide concentrated on tourist destinations. The South Bronx is pretty grim. Do you think it could happen there?"

Wilson was getting to know me. He barely stopped any more for my feeble jokes. He just soldiered on with his monologue: "Having decided then to follow up, the question for Shona was: 'Should she look for Nadeem's mother, and after finding her simply ask her if Nadeem is her birth son or adopted son?' What if she insisted Nadeem's her birth son?

The more Shona thought about it the more that it seemed likely that the mother believed he really was her birth son and would be offended by the question. If she knew he wasn't a blood relative she would not admit it under any circumstances. The mother had volunteered her DNA as a proxy for her son's. She must have been sure that she was not related to the murderer. Or maybe not?"

As Wilson described them, I was getting keyed in to Shona's deliberations and following the story quite well for a change. Wilson continued almost echoing my thoughts: "In any case all that may not be relevant. An educated confident Israeli woman going to some poor Palestinian home and asking such a thing would get nowhere."

And again, he echoed my thoughts: "There had to be another route. If this was not his birth mother, Shona wondered, is there a way to find his biological birth mother? She had an idea. It was a long shot. First, she looked at the police report to find Nadeem's birthday. Armed with this information she went to the archives of the main Israeli newspaper she freelanced for, HaAretz, and retrieved the newspapers for the day before Nadeem's birthday more than twenty-two years ago, and all subsequent editions for the following two weeks."

"OK, ok," I said, feeling a little envious of Shona's profession. This kind of detective work sounded quite interesting.

Wilson continued: "The headline that day was a report about the bus terror incident. Oh well I won't bore you with every detail, but I think you get it. As soon as she saw that two children were born in hospital the day that the bus exploded, she smelled a rat, so to speak, with her acute journalist's sense of smell. By scouring contemporary reports, she found there were two women on the bus, both of whom were severely injured, and both of whom gave birth to healthy boys during emergency surgery to save their lives."

And I finished Wilson's thought: "And Shona went to ask the other mother, the Israeli mother - wait - what could she possibly ask or tell this mother. 'Is your son your son? or somebody else's son?'"

"Well…"

"Oh of course" I interrupted him. I get it. "She could ask either the mother or the son to volunteer a DNA sample. That's right! She already had access to DNA analysis reports of the Palestinian mother and son. But asking that question would not be easy! Wow! Is that what she did

Wilson nodded an affirmative.

"How on earth did Shona persuade them to do that?" I asked in astonishment. "I would have told her to take a long walk on a short pier."

123

Chapter 14 - Kitchen Table with Israeli Mom and Ari - Maria

I had to wait about ten days for Wilson to get back to our conversation. Our earlier chat was broken off abruptly when he looked at his watch, made his apologies and hurried out the door. His journalist work took him to California to cover a four-day tech exhibition, after which he needed to do the rounds in Silicon Valley interviewing startup entrepreneurs. The pause left me time to digest what I'd learned and cool my heels about Ari. I felt like a relationship with him could go either way now and I could take it or leave it.

Good to his word he called me when he got back and came over as he had done on previous occasions. Before he left for California, he was about to tell me how the news broke about Ari's parentage. Wilson's absence had given me time to relax about what I'd learned and was about to learn as we started, as before, with wine and coffee.

He told me: "I'd love you to meet Shona. She could describe the scene for herself when she asked Ari's mom to take a DNA test. Actually, Ari was present too when Shona visited his family home in Tel Aviv. He could tell you."

"How do you mean, present? Present where? How did Shona break it to Ari and Ari's family that Ari may not be their son?" I asked.

Just then my phone buzzed. I looked at Wilson, mouthed "It's Ari" and answered in a neutral flat tone: "Hello," and waited to hear his voice.

"Oh hi", I answered continuing my neutral tone. I felt like I wanted to spit up "Your friend Wilson is here; would you like to speak to him?"

"No thanks Maria, it's you I want to speak to."

'Should I hang up?' I was thinking. "Just a minute," I said. I pushed the mute button on my phone and asked Wilson: "Did you tell Ari you were coming over here?"

Wilson looked a bit sheepish and nodded a yes. I breathed deeply for a few seconds to calm down, unmuted my phone and asked dryly: "What is it Ari?"

"I know you're mad at me, I'm really sorry about leaving you in the street," he continued.

"Do you leave all your girlfriends cold in the street when the mood takes you?" I asked him, trying to sound cool but I was simmering underneath. Expressing my anger felt like a dam had burst inside of me. "What about your beautiful girlfriend I met at the café a while back? Do you stand her up sometimes?" Then I continued with a rant, which is really not like me and I'm not going to repeat it here, but it felt good at the time. I finished off with a less-than-elegant sentence:

"You're supposed to be a smart guy but you're a real flake head sometimes." Here, talk to Wilson."

"I...I...I... but...", I heard him stammer as I handed my phone to Wilson."

It was not hard to guess what Ari was saying to him. This is what I heard; each sentence uttered by Wilson followed by brief silences as Ari talked on the other end of the line:

"Just talking,"

"Yes, just talking…."

"About you, actually…."

"Don't be ridiculous…."

"About how you found out, you know… I'll just spit it out, how you and your family got to know that you were switched at birth when your mom was treated in the emergency room after the explosion on a bus. You know the story better than I do, why don't you tell it?"

Then Ari must have asked Wilson how he found out all about his past because next, Wilson said: "I found out from Shona, she told me, then I saw her article about it reprinted in the English language 'Jerusalem Post', so yes, you're right, this is a second hand account, but I know the bones of it. Why don't you come over and tell us what happened?"

I gave Wilson a very hard stare and said above whatever he was saying to Ari: "This is my place; he has to ask me if he can come over." I didn't want to talk to Ari, but I'd backed myself into a corner by saying he must ask me. Wilson handed back my phone.

"Hi Ari, you'd better come over." I said in the flattest tone I could muster without waiting for him to ask.

"Yea, Yea, I'll come." He said dejectedly. He hadn't been to my place before, but he knew the address. It's not difficult to find so I just said flatly: "OK, see you soon" and hung up.

Oddly, the serious and somber mood that enveloped my little place seemed to clear the moment I hung up. Wilson and I had been sipping red wine the whole time which was beginning to have an effect on me. The whole Ari thing started to feel a bit funny. Like funny ha! ha! I could see Wilson's demeanor was loosening up, he'd taken off his jacket and he looked relieved.

"Think of it Wilson, here's this Jewish guy, living his comfortable Jewish life without the slightest doubt about his patronage, history, tradition, you name it, and all the while he's not Jewish at all. It's all bababalony." The stammer might have been something to do with the wine.

"Not only that, it turns out his real patronage and history is all wrapped up in the enemy camp."

Wilson looked at me quizzically tilting his head to one side which made his restrained smile look crooked and a bit silly."

I felt silly too. I started this silly wine-fueled monologue: "Hey God, I know there's only one God, but obviously there are two, no, three, one for Jews, one for Muslims and one for Catholics like me."

"What about Protestants?" Asked Wilson.

"Protestants can share our God, unless you're Irish, they need two Gods, one that lives in the North of the country and one that lives in the South. But over here, Stateside, even we Irish can manage with one."

"So, what's the point of three Gods?"

"Well don't you see? I answered passionately. "There's a couple of guys that need to switch sides. The God Ref, he's number four, needs to call timeout so they can switch."

At that moment in my mind's eye, two soccer teams of eleven each side, one of Palestinians, one of Israelis, each supported by a bearded God peering through the clouds. The players engaged in animated angry discussions around a soccer field, finger pointing and threatening each other.

The stadium speakers announced, "Time out while two participants switch sides." A guy that looked like a soccer ref with a whistle signaled to stop play, and for the players to get back onto their own half of the field. Then he pointed to one team with the index finger of his left hand and the other with his right, then crossed his arms to signal a switch.

Two players emerged, one from each team, shoved and insulted by their own team members as they elbowed their way into a thirty feet wide no-mans-land between the teams.

Each looked back at his home team holding up the palms of his hands in questioning exasperated gestures as if to ask: "What the Hell is going on?" But the teams jeered and swore some more, some yelling "Get out traitor."

So, each ran across the divide to the other side. But neither were welcomed by their new teams. Both teams closed ranks, shoulder to shoulder, preventing the new members from joining them, jeering and spitting at them when they tried.

My hallucination ended when I heard Wilson say somberly "You're forgetting one thing, one of these guys doesn't appear to be around anymore to switch sides."

"Oh, right," I said, looking down at my feet feeling deflated. "Maybe he tried to switch sides and got rejected."

As a diversion from being reminded of this unpleasant fact, and as I was feeling hungry, I got up to make some food. I had some cooked rice which I took out of the fridge, then I turned on the oven. I fried up some peppers, onions, squash, tomatoes, and herbs into a kind of gumbo, and mixed them up with the rice to make it all stick together. Then I rolled spoonsful of it into vine leaves. All the while Wilson was looking at the photos on my walls, the books on my shelves and my CD collection. Then I popped the stuffed vine leaves in the oven for fifteen minutes.

Just as I was taking the stuffed vine leaves out of the oven there was a buzz from the apartment intercom. While holding the hot food tray I glanced a meaningful glance at Wilson to press the front door open button.

When Ari came in there was no spring in his step, no glint in his eye and no confident posture.

Wilson and I looked at each other, then Wilson spoke first:

"What's going on Ari?"

"I didn't go anywhere with my cousins, just back to my place for now. Anyway, how could I at such short notice? It was all a bit stupid and emotional"

There was silence.

"And I lost my job", he continued.

"What about your apartment?" asked Wilson, "Doesn't that come with your job?"

"Lost that too", he answered.

"Where are you living?" I asked.

"Back with my folks."

"You mean Moishe and Avril, yes, where else, of course" I said feeling dumb again.

"Why did you lose your job?" I asked.

"Didn't go into work", he answered flatly.

I offered my tray of goodies to Ari and said: "Here's a stuffed vine leaf and here's a plate to go with it, don't drop any rice on my rug."

He picked it up, nodded in approval, and at that moment the door buzzer sounded again.

Wilson went to the intercom and we heard my dad's voice: "Hi sweetie, we've got some cookies for you. Your mom's been baking."

I nodded "yes" to Wilson and a minute later my parents, flush from their walk and excited with their modest gift burst into my apartment. I watched my mom's eyes glance at me, then at Wilson, then Ari, then settle back on Wilson. I almost had to laugh. I could see right inside my mom's brain at what she was thinking. Trying not to smirk I introduced first Ari then Wilson to my parents while I was opening her cookie tin and emptying the contents into a bowl. Then I put on some coffee.

"Is this not a good time?" my mom asked. My dad had helped himself to a stuffed vine leaf and was getting out cups for coffee.

"There must always be time for cookies this good," piped up Ari looking a little more cheerful.

"I saw my mom's gaze snap back to Ari as his slightly non-American accent broke the brief silence.

"Ari's a brilliant grad student at NYU", I said. He does things with computers. Computer science is his field.

"And statistics", added Ari helpfully.

"Oh, isn't that something like what you do dear?" she asked me.

She didn't give me a chance to answer as, in unison, my parents' gazes switched to Wilson. I wasn't going to wait for my mother to embarrass me and my guests to say something like "...and what do you do?" so I jumped right in again: "Wilson's a journalist".

"A journalist, oh that's nice." but she held her approving gaze on Wilson who was quite nicely dressed even without his jacket which was draped over the edge of my sofa.

There was no way we could continue our collective dénouement of Ari's past and current predicament with my parents around, so before the guys would be driven away with embarrassment I blurted: "We were having a bit of a conference before you came."

My dad joined in for the first time: "C'mon dear, get your coat, here, let me help you. We need to finish watching our movie before bedtime".

So they left, but it may have been a good thing that they visited when they did. We all seemed to relax after they left. Something as normal as cookies and a cup of coffee sort of got everybody's feet back on the ground.

I looked at Ari and said: "So... Ari, dear Ari, none of what I'm going to ask you is any of my business. In one way, though, you've made it my business. We were friends. You were charming and fun, and now, forgive me, something happened and you're not. You're a fucking pain, so spill it."

Then I shut up and let the silence speak for itself.

Ari looked at me with doleful eyes and I immediately regretted what I said, but Wilson joined in a little more gently:

"Hey Ari, Maria's right it is none of her business." I gave him a worried glance and wondered where he was going with this, but he continued:

"I was about to tell Maria that you may not be a blood relative of the family you were raised with. Shona told me how she found out and I read her article about it. How do you see it? If you won't tell us, as far as I'm concerned, our friendship is unchanged because I just don't care. But you changed for Maria, and you may owe her an explanation."

Ari took a bite of his cookie and a sip of coffee, looked up and mumbled: "OK, why don't you start? If I want to say something I'll butt in, OK?"

So Wilson took a deep breath and started:

"OK now picture the family home in Tel Aviv in which, around a kitchen table replete with coffee cups, a fruit basket and snacks, a bemused mother was being interviewed. It all came out of the clear blue sky. Here at her table was a reporter, Shona, from a well-known newspaper. She and Ari's mother, Ayelet were sitting opposite one another.

"Shona was explaining how she researched the original incident of a bomb exploding on a bus Ayelet was riding, when eight and a half months pregnant, and how after cesareans baby boys were switched.

"Ari's mother understood that Shona was inferring Ari may not be her son but was by no means convinced. After all, Ari resembled her and his father in so many ways. He even seemed to have inherited her sense of humor. Shona told me the conversation with Ari's mother went something like this":

"Yes, cute story," she says. As for my DNA swab? Not a chance. No way. The more I think about it the more I find your question offensive."

And at that moment Ari arrived home from class, excited, hungry, went to the fridge for a snack, mumbled something about a test score, a minor college scandal involving a lecturer student romance and then stopped short, acknowledging a guest at the kitchen table whom he'd heard ask about the DNA. Seeing the angry stare from his mother, assumed it was about his rudeness to the stranger, apologized, politely introduced himself and continued:

"You want a DNA swab from my mom? Why? You think she's not my mom? You've got to be kidding me. Just look at us. We could be twins," he jokes, but the joke fell ominously flat with his mother.

"I made more and better jokes than that," interrupted Ari. I told him some other time would be fine and that Wilson should continue with the main line of the story.

"Well, actually Ari, a DNA swab from you would do just as well" said Shona explaining her presence to him but abandoning any attempt to soften the harshness of the question she'd come to ask, but maintaining a sincere respectful tone.

Ari appeared open to a DNA swab and said something like: "I guess if I did, that would eliminate me for your enquiries… except, I mean you can write in your report that you'd tried the idea and proved I am after all my mother's son?"

All the time Ari was nodding in the affirmative as if to tell Wilson he was getting it right. Wilson interrupted his own second hand telling of Shona's story to look directly at Ari to add "If you knew Ari like I do you'd just picture his sardonic not-quite-a-smirk that characterizes his humor and conveys his disbelief."

In response Ari made a ridiculous contortion of his face that made me giggle but Wilson kept a straight face and continued his second hand telling of the story.

Ari asked his mother: "OK with you mom?" who replied: "Oh I hate the idea. Well what harm can it do? I suppose, maybe... If Ari gives you a swab you won't have any reason to come back here, right?

"Right," says Shona, "unless... well, never mind. The thing is, as you realize, I'm just trying to eliminate all possibilities. If I hadn't asked you and I hadn't been able to find an answer to my question, I would have had to come back just to make sure I'd covered everything. You wouldn't have wanted that."

"So wait, let me get this clear," interrupted Ari at his family's kitchen table in Tel Aviv, "I give you a DNA swab which you can use to establish that some woman that I don't know and have never met is my mother, assuming your suspicions are correct. And this woman here at the table is not? OK I'll give you the swab, then go away. There'll be no need for you to come back."

"So Ari gave the swab, Shona had it tested for a match against the accused Palestinian boy's mother and, yes you know already, she found that Ari and the Palestinian mother were related. Shona also knew, now full of regrets, she'd opened a pandora's box. It would be cruel to tell Ari and his mother of the finding and cruel not to. What to do? The journalist in her wanted the scoop, the sensitive motherly side of her wanted to leave well alone.

"But Ari and his parents, and Hannah, his little sister, did find out. Shona denied it was her who leaked the secret when I asked her how. She told me she was agonizing about what to do and unexpectedly was told by her editor that the family had found out. But the editor denied it too that he'd told anybody but explained that sometimes if they're having a slow news day, investigative tabloid journalists shadow other journalists looking for a scoop.

Wilson broke his monologue: "How did you find out Ari? Shona was going to squash the story."

"Ugh, Ari mumbled, "this really arrogant reporter type guy came to our house asking for the inside scoop and to pay my mom for it. My mom told him go away. I think you may be right. I think he may have followed Shona to our house when she came around to see us that time. He made up a lot of crap about us. But what he said at core was true."

Wilson continued: "Shona told me, there followed domestic anguish that was, or is, rather, so profound it's difficult to describe. Ari opened up about it to me after a few drinks and in a funk about a less than perfect grade for one of his school papers. He's a good student, as you know, very determined to excel in everything he does."

"But getting back to the story," continued Wilson, "the corollary to Ari's disrupted belief in his own patrimony of course was: who were his biological parents? Given the circumstances and timing of his birth it was not hard to strongly infer that it was the other pregnant woman injured in the bus explosion."

"By this time the story had broken in the media and a hundred scoop-hungry scandal sheet snoops and paparazzi hunted down the poor Palestinian woman, son and family before they'd had a chance to catch up with the Israeli news story. Keep in mind that Palestinian media in the West Bank and Jordan, despite their geographical closeness to Israel, live in parallel but separate universes."

"You're telling me this poor woman found out about a private and deeply sad family matter from a scuffling media crowd outside her house?" I interrupted, followed by

136

"God that sucks! God what agony for them!" as I tried to process in my own mind what that must have felt like, then added "wait, just give me a quick rundown of what happened in the West Bank?"

Wilson patiently explained in more detail than I really needed that it is a large area mostly populated by Palestinian Arab people within the old boundaries of Palestine, on the West Bank of the Jordan river. It was conquered by Israel in 1967 and was originally held as a bargaining chip in a hoped-for peace treaty in peace negotiations. The negotiations happened a-plenty but there was no treaty - well, except with Egypt, and er, maybe Jordan I think he said, or something like it and other arcane political stuff but I got the gist of it. Everyone in all the countries involved ended up very angry and distrustful of one another. At least the worst of the fighting was over, until 1973 that was, when there was yet another war, and then more terror, year in, year out, but all that's another story.

I stared at the floor, for how long I couldn't say. Then I looked at Ari who mumbled:

"Yea, that's right, that's how it was. She got the details; she wrote everything down." And then he put his head in his hands and wept softly as tears dripped between his fingers.

"She's my mom." He was sobbing openly now. "She'll always be my mom no matter who my natural mother is. I don't mean anything bad about my biological mom, but my real mom is the one back in Tel Aviv."

I couldn't look at Ari or Wilson in the face. Then I heard the door close gently. I looked up and around in a daze and saw that both had left. So, I stared some more at the patterns in my rug and let them drift in and out of focus trying to fit Ari into the story. I imagined a young man and his mom and Shona at a kitchen table that looked like the one at my mom and dad's place. The silent intense atmosphere carried with it paradoxical angst and defiance but all the while having some semblance of gentle mutual respect as they tried to adjust to some uncomfortable facts. And how all this contrasted with the crass and cruel circus of its counterpart which happened a week later and just a few miles East of it!

Next morning, walking to work I was caught in a rainstorm driven by a wind so strong I had to hold onto my umbrella with both hands and I was drenched from head to foot. When I got to work, I hid in my office and stripped off almost naked to dry my clothes over the radiator, which thankfully, sort of worked, almost. I'd walked to work in sneakers which, of course, were soaked.

So I slipped on my demure heels which I kept at work and carried my sneakers over to the cafeteria. After checking them for metal and removing the laces, popped them inside the microwave, slammed the door and set the time on full for five minutes. They steamed and hissed and dried and stank a bit too. Feeling idiotically pleased with myself I tried to slip them on after they'd cooled but could not. They had shrunk! So next I had to try to stretch them. Fortunately, my workplace has a toolset. Gripping the back of each shoe with pliers I managed to get my feet into them without socks.

'Should'a taken the subway,' I was thinking when I looked up to see Marty with that smug superior expression he wears.

Chapter 15 - Marty the Healer and Nadeem's Disappearance - Maria

Hi Marty", I croaked while bent over, pulling on my shrunken shoe, "How's your Japanese girlfriend, what's her name...er At..At.."

"Atsuko", Marty interrupted. "And yes, we are seeing each other," he answered after turning a bit red, which I thought was sort of cute. "What are you doing down there with the pliers?" He asked.

"Never mind," I answered. I think I must have looked flush from bending over, tugging on my shoe.

I stood up, looked straight at him and said: "I think Atsuko's a lovely person and I'm happy for you."

"It's kind of you to say," he answered, "I don't think my parents are super happy about it, but I think she's..., let's just say I'm quite fond of her."

"What's their problem? Is it a Catholic/non-Catholic thing?

"I guess..., they don't come out and say it, but I think it is. You know what I mean?"

"Hmmm, I think so, do you want to get a cup of coffee?" I asked him. I was ready for one and we were already in the cafeteria.

So we sat, and he told me about how his parents just couldn't get their heads around someone so different from their expectations of what Marty's girlfriend might be like, 'but so nice too,' his puzzled mother added. "Actually, I really don't care what they think. They're not openly hostile and I think they'll come around. Either way I want to keep on seeing her and what happens, happens." After a paused he asked:

"So what's going on with you?"

I told him about Ari and what I knew of his problems, and he asked. "Had you met him before we went out to Ground Zero a few weeks ago."

"Yes" I said.

"You were preoccupied thinking about him, weren't you?" Continued Marty. "I knew there was something going on with you. There must have been a lot to think about with that guy."

"Yes, there was." I answered.

He continued: "But all that stuff about his 'cousins' coming to get him hadn't happened yet, nor had his...I want to say brother...but not his real brother...?" and stopped mid-sentence.

"Disappeared" I interrupted.

"Yes disappeared, that's what I meant to ask," continued Marty. "I don't mean to sound disrespectful, but it was not quite clear to me the way you were telling the

141

story. Forgive me but...do you know exactly how he disappeared?"

"Actually, they didn't say. They, his cousins, just said he's gone, or to be precise "he disappeared" that's exactly what they said. They didn't say from where he disappeared or how, and it seemed insensitive to ask. I worried it may have been suicide which is regarded as shameful in their community." then I added without thinking about it: "unless of course the protagonist has a bomb strapped around their middle."

"I don't think that's fair," Marty answered, "you can't judge a community or a nation by its extremes. Heaven knows, we've got our own homegrown bombers and weirdos. Remember Oklahoma City? Anyway, you said Ari, spent some time with his cousins after he left you that evening. Maybe they told him then?"

"You're right. I'll ask Ari how Nadeem disappeared. If he doesn't know he should ask his cousins assuming they're still around." I'd deliberately quit calling Nadeem and Ari brothers. They weren't, and it didn't make sense to me.

I mentioned a café by name and told Marty I was going to invite Ari to meet me there on Saturday morning. Perhaps, if he wasn't busy, he too could "meet us there, for brunch, maybe? Please?"

When they left my apartment a few nights ago Ari and Wilson had left me in a funk of gloom. I wanted to see Ari again. I wanted to be friends with him even if I could never be anything more than that. And if Ari's girlfriend, Hadassah, who I knew liked that café showed up too, with both Ari and Marty there, it would just look like a casual chat with a couple of guys, and who knows? maybe I could normalize my relationship with her and stop appearing to be a rival.

There was something else too, at the back of my mind. Marty had an advanced degree in psychology and a calm sympathetic personality. It was obvious Ari was deeply troubled and perhaps Marty and Ari could talk? Perhaps Marty could help?

So when I asked if he would meet me, and hopefully Ari too, he nodded slightly and smiled slightly and said: "OK, I'll think about it. I've got to get back to work, nice seeing you again."

There was a cold wind blowing off the East River that early that autumn Saturday morning. The café I chose was a warm refuge from it and had booths which made conversation possible even in Williamsburg's boisterous heart. I arrived early, ordered a coffee, took out my phone and dived into social media trying not to think about how many things could go wrong with my scheme. Ari and Marty had never met, and both came early. I didn't see Ari until he came right up to me and said "boo" in my left ear and smiled a smile more like his old self.

I turned to him, looked him in the eye and said: "You stinker, the last two times I saw you, you left without saying goodbye." His face fell. "But I forgive you, I added, quickly, and kissed him on the cheek to show that I meant it. That seemed to restore his face to something like normal.

He made some lame excuses about leaving me on both occasions, but I wasn't really listening, just nodding to make it look like I was. Then I told him that someone I work with may be coming too. "At least then, with three of us chatting we'll look less like a couple if your girlfriend, Hadassah, that's her name, isn't it? shows up." I told him.

He nodded without looking at me, took out his phone into which his consciousness disappeared. Was he just being rude? I felt embarrassed for him. I was relieved to see Marty walk through the door at that moment. I caught his eye. He waved and started weaving his way towards us with Atsuko, his new Japanese girlfriend right behind.

'Oh, depression!' I thought, glancing at Ari. 'I'm no doctor but I bet he has something like clinical depression.' I had the sense for once, though, not to mention it.

It was quite pleasant in the café. Ari seemed to wake up when the food came, which, incidentally, was good. He and I talked to Atsuko about her home in Japan, and how she likes it here in the US. She in turn asked Ari about Israel and Marty joined in with all sorts of questions about sports and tourism and the price of apartments in Japan. Ari seemed to shake off his glum mood, talking a little about NYU, his classes and what it was like moving back in with Moishe and Avril again.

When we'd finished eating Ari offered to walk me home and, of course, I agreed. But even then, it didn't seem opportune to ask him anything, not least because of the howling cold wind.

"Hey, would you like to come and meet my replacement American parents Moishe and Avril?" he asked.

"They're not often home on a Saturday and they're very sociable. They like meeting the younger generation."

It seemed like he had sensed I was going for a heart-to-heart talk, and he'd found a way to avoid it. It was possible too that he wanted to avoid being alone with me in my apartment, for what reason exactly, I'll leave you to speculate. After a pause I told him that I'd very much like to meet his "replacement American parents."

I found Moishe and Avril's 6th floor warehouse apartment and artist studio to be breathtaking. It was so bright and casual and relaxed and practical. It helped too that the furniture, kitchen appliances were all high end and expensive looking, and the furniture comfortable. Just as Ari had said the couple were sociable. And they were kindly towards me, managing to ask questions in such a way that they found me interesting and likable, but not like they were prying. Moishe gave me a tour of his paintings which I loved. I asked questions about their meanings and what his inspirations were, and he was quite open about it. Avril teased him about paintings of some of his female muses, noting that none of them was of her, asking if that could be on account of her age? They both sounded English to me. I said so and turned out to be right even though their accents were markedly different, Moishe's, as Ari explained being from London, and Avril's from Yorkshire.

Quite out of the blue Moishe asked me if I'd seen Ari's lovely apartment in the high-rise by the East River. I hesitated, looked briefly at Ari then answered: "Yes it was beautiful".

"Silly bugger" said Moishe, "moped around feeling sorry for himself, didn't go to work, lost his job and his apartment. You can't blame the company."

"You never had to go through what he went through," joined in Avril. "She looked at Ari and added "Don't listen to him dear, you're welcome here, this is your home and don't you forget it."

Then Avril looked at me and asked: "You heard what happened, about Ari, I mean, and his recent family difficulties didn't you?"

"I'd heard that Ari's brother is called Nadeem, that he was not really Ari's brother and that he disappeared, and that Ari grew up in a family with parents that turned out to be not his own biological parents because as a newborn baby, he was accidentally switched with another." I answered without taking a breath. Then I added: "Ari's mother gave birth to a son who grew up with a Palestinian family, that's who Nadeem is, and that's why he's often referred to as Ari's brother."

"You heard he disappeared, but do you know now how he disappeared?" asked Avril, looking confused.

"Nobody told me how, all I knew was that he disappeared."

"The official version is that he disappeared without a trace in Cyprus, but we don't believe that" said Avril". "Ari, why didn't you tell Maria that?"

"Cyprus?" I asked. "No trace of him? Why Cyprus? What do you mean 'official version?' Do you have another version?" I gasped.

At that point Moishe got into the conversation rather clumsily: "Ari, why don't you tell Maria what the hell is going on? You need to slay the ghost." And with a glance at Ari's hangdog look added: "For crying out loud man! It's not your fault. Get over it and move on."

"It's my fault, it's all my fault, OK!" Ari yelled in anguish, more to the ceiling than at any one of us. "I'm ashamed. That's why I didn't want to say. If I hadn't been so stupid he would still be with us." Now in silence, he sat on the couch, his head drooping towards the floor and holding himself by wrapping his arms around his chest, doubled forward as though he had a pain in his stomach."

Avril went to put her arm around his shoulder and said affectionately in his ear: "C'mon dear, you're among friends, you did nothing wrong, in fact you did everything right. Do you mind if I tell Maria what happened? I can see you're not in the mood to do it right now. You can butt in if I get anything wrong."

He nodded to say that was OK but continued to look deeply distressed and upset.

I looked at Avril in the brief silence that followed. It seemed she was thinking of what to say and how to say it. Moishe had handed me an atlas open on a page showing the Eastern Mediterranean, then Avril started talking again.

"Ari's Israeli mother, Ayelet, told me on the phone that some people back in Israel have been deeply disturbed by all of this. By that I mean Ari having to leave Israel and his counterpart in East Jerusalem having to leave too, then disappearing. I can't, and I won't, attach any blame to any of

147

them. They suffered terribly. There's a strong suspicion in the family that Nadeem may have been murdered and if his body is discovered, made to look like he took his own life. The suspected reason being to deflect blame, of course, to obviate a hunt for the perpetrators, but also to bring shame to his, and his family's reputation."

"But why would somebody murder him? Was it a robbery gone wrong? Was it a revenge attack? There has to be a reason," I asked, managing with difficulty to stay calm when speaking.

"OK, correct me if I'm wrong Ari." continued Avril, "after Ari discovered he had been switched as a baby it was natural that he went looking for the guy of exactly his own age that he was switched with. It was not hard. The tabloids had made a meal of it and putting two and two together from newspaper reports, he found out who he was switched with and then found his email address."

Avril continued to explain what she had learned from his Israeli mother. She said she had gathered that Ari's and Nadeem's email conversations were rather good for them. She was glad the two of them were talking, hoping they would get together. What's more, though her love for Ari was undiminished, she ached to see and meet and talk to the boy who was her very own natural firstborn. She knew that Nadeem's mother would feel the same about Ari. And for that matter their fathers would feel that too.

At first the two boys contacting each other went quite well. She looked at Ari who nodded in agreement when she said it. "They were both math and engineering nerds. It was a great help that they both knew English and had English language keyboards in addition to their native language keyboards, one Arabic the other Hebrew. Naturally English was the most convenient way for them to communicate.

Then Ari mumbled something.

"What?" I said.

"Sports!" he yelled. "That's what got us going, that's what was great about talking to Nadeem. He wasn't into my music at all, but we clicked when it came to sports."

"OK," I said cautiously, not quite understanding this mostly guy thing about sports.

With enthusiasm for the first time in a while Ari said: "I like Manchester United, and Liverpool and he liked Chelsea and Arsenal."

"Nadeem had very good taste," said Moishe, the former Londoner.

Avril explained that Chelsea and Arsenal are both London soccer teams, the other two being based in Northern England.

"Then their emails got political and edgy", said Avril.

"Politics not my strong point," I said with distaste.

"Edgy is the word that springs to mind. It's nothing like politics here. The best way to get some understanding of it, is maybe to see some of the emails they exchanged," Avril said looking at Ari.

Ari got up and walked over to the computer. While he was fiddling with it, Avril went to the wine cabinet and took out a bottle of Riesling, extracted the cork and put some glasses on the table along with some cookies.

"Help yourself," she said above the humming and clicking of the computer printing.

A few minutes later Ari picked up about fifteen sheets of printed emails and put them on the table. At the top of the pile was one from Nadeem to Ari. It started off all about why London soccer teams would always be better than anything provincial teams could muster, because, well it doesn't matter, but at the end he went on to say:

Well, my dear brother Ari, enough of sports. By default, now that you know that you're really an Arab, and because of that should be a Muslim and hopefully will become one someday. It is time for you to take pride in admitting that:

1. Israel's treatment of its neighbors is beyond contempt.

2. By virtue of their righteous cause the Arab peoples will remain united in their determination to return all the land in Palestine from the Mediterranean to the River Jordan to its rightful owners.

3. Those of us who have been displaced and are living in squalid camps in Lebanon, Syria, Jordan, and the West Bank of the Jordan will return to reclaim their land and homes and, in the process, drive out those who now illegally possess them...etc.

To which Ari replied:

...It behooves me to answer your email thusly, that inasmuch as I am an Arab and by your lights a Muslim, you therefore, must be a Jew by race and by religion. And in respect of your other assertions:

1. Constant assaults and rocket and terror attacks on the peaceful people of Israel invite nothing but contempt.

2. I grant that some land on the West Bank was acquired illegally, and many Israelis condemn that. Most of the land within the 1967 boundaries of Israel proper, was acquired legally by purchase, or taken over when abandoned. It must be acknowledged that most people who now settle that land were themselves displaced by coercion, harassment and persecution from Arab states: Iraq, Syria, Lebanon, Egypt, Libya, Algeria in even greater numbers.

3. The Arab and Muslim peoples that inhabit your neighboring countries have done little, in spite of their fabulous wealth, to help displaced Palestinian Arabs. And far from being brother Arabs, with few exceptions, deny them citizenship in those countries and limit their employment to menial tasks.

No doubt we could go on scoring points off each other. I left out a whole lot of grievances, as, I note, did you on your side. Assuredly the argument would go on forever. But just as surely, you and I of all people should be aware that nobody can help the circumstances in which they are born.

The emails continued in a similar vein, each finding something to condemn in the other's camp without ever being personal.

Avril put down the wad of emails she was holding and invited us to read through them, which we did. There was a lot of small talk and sports talk which was a fun diversion, but in summary the gist of it was:

In Israel, social media was full of diverse opinions about relations with their Palestinian neighbors. In West Bank Palestine, hostility towards Israel and its people and government was almost universal.

Though he was reluctant to concede a point to Ari in their email exchanges, in some of his social media postings Nadeem began to question the use of some of the violent provocations, bombs, missile attacks, and other outrages. This attracted hostility and death threats which at first, he was able to ignore. Then came an innocent post which talked about the circumstances of his own birth.

It was not about just another outrage. This time, reading between the lines, Islamist fanatics picked up that he was by birth a Jew now living among them, and it seemed, promoting Israeli propaganda in his Facebook posts. He became, to some militants, a target, even an easy target. Nadeem's family and most of his friends backed him and supported him by all means possible, but death threats became too frequent and credible to ignore."

After going into hiding in friends' homes for a while fled to the nearby peaceful Greek section of Cyprus. Then he disappeared.

"It's my fault you see, you see, Ari yelled. If I'd stuck to sports none of this would have happened."

There was a silence for a few seconds, and I felt I understood at last what was upsetting Ari. I felt angry about it, angry that someone should be targeted for expressing an opinion about an event he was caught up in but did not cause. On the other hand, I was a little skeptical about the story. There could be no doubt that he had disappeared, and possibly at the hands of Islamic terrorists. But just for posting on social media? I couldn't help thinking there may have been more to the story that nobody had yet uncovered. Facebook was unable or unwilling to police postings which promoted violent reprisals for perceived un-Islamic sentiments.

Knowing how disorientated Ari had been over the last several weeks, perhaps Nadeem had been driven to take his own life? No. That didn't make sense. There had to be something more.

Ari's arrival in the United States had been cushioned in every possible way. He had landed at the home of a sympathetic, loving and let's not forget, very financially secure couple. He knew the language well, had a place at a first-class university and found supportive friends.

In stark contrast, Nadeem may not have known anybody in Cyprus. He did not know a word of Greek, he had no immediate way to earn a living or place to continue his studies, and he had no friends as far as I knew.

I stared a hard stare at Ari and told him: "One thing's for damn sure Ari, it's absolutely not your fault. And we have to figure out what to do about it. I think a good place to start would be to find exactly how Nadeem disappeared. We may get some clues if there's any kind of police report in Cyprus about his disappearance."

To this Moishe added: "I think you're right Maria, there's been too much guess work going on." Another silence in the room suggested there was agreement with what Moishe and I were thinking. Then Moishe continued "At least language difficulties for Nadeem may not have been as bad as you think. The Brits owned the island for a long time and still own small bits of it."

I supposed Moishe, being an ex-Brit would know that, and it came as a slight relief to me. But just what to do about the whole mess I had no idea. Judging by their blank stares nor had the other three people.

Then Moishe piped up again. "Let's sleep on it," he said. "I have a few ideas about what we can do to start, at least. If you guys want to come around tomorrow, Sunday, we can jaw jaw about it. It may lead to nothing, but I don't want to let this go without even trying. Anyway, I'll make some lunch for us all and I'll have the pleasure of seeing your faces again."

"I'll come." I said. It was an easy decision for me. I would get to see Ari again and it would be a nice place to spend a good part of Sunday. "But is there a reason we can't jaw jaw about it now?" I asked.

"Well, actually, I intend to start now," answered Moishe but it means me making some phone calls to old friends who may not be immediately available, and I need to do some searching online. Also, it would be helpful if someone could come up with an idea about how to find out approximately where he disappeared. His mother may know that or did someone say something about his 'cousins' being here in the city?"

"Oh yea, maybe that was me," I said, but I wasn't sure. "There were these three guys, called themselves Ari's cousins, who persuaded Ari to go with them a few weeks ago. Evidently you didn't go very far because you're still around. I guess you just went to your apartment by the East River, right? Ari?"

"Yes, that's right, we went back to my place and had a long fraught conversation about what to do which turned into an argument but got nowhere," he answered.

I wasn't really satisfied with this answer, I was confused about what they wanted from Ari, so I asked: "What did they really want you to do?"

Ari struggled to explain: "It doesn't really make any sense what they wanted, but the fact is they were very upset, and I sympathized with them to a point. Back on the West Bank it's really a different world. Family ties are very strong there. They were so upset about Nadeem's disappearance, some of them believed naively that if they brought Nadeem's mother's real birth son to her, it might somehow calm her grief.

"How so?" I asked.

"They're not sophisticated people," he continued. In their upended logic, if three cousins come to get Ari to take Nadeem's place it would satisfy some warped idea of justice. To them, if Ari came back to join what they regarded as his family, a man born of an Arab Muslim woman would be returned to his rightful place."

I couldn't quite get my head around all this. I looked at the floor when I said: "It still seems far-fetched to me."

Ari kept on struggling to explain: "I know, I know it does, but there's more. It seems the family was under some pressure from extremists. There had been suggestions that somehow the Jews had stolen a fine healthy Muslim baby,

155

then converted him to Judaism. Incidentally only one of them had some family connection. The one called Anwar. The other two were just plain weird."

"Convert a baby?" I said almost to myself. "How could anybody convert a baby? What a notion! What a load of crap!" I wasn't going to let him get away with that one, but he came back at me with more

"C'mon, every religion has their head cases, I know Judaism does and I'm pretty sure Christianity does too. Stir up unquestioning religious observance in the same pot as nationalism and an overarching sense of victimhood - that's when deprived youths become angry fanatics."

"I guess, maybe?" I said doubtfully.

But Ari hardly stopped to take a breath: "And if that hasn't stretched credibility far enough, my visitors said that the Jews, having stolen a pure Arab baby gave one back by planting a Jewish spy in their midst. I know it's nonsense, but these extremists were getting at the family because they didn't like what Nadeem was posting on social media. They have a warped sense of reality. This is the depressing stuff I got from these guys squatting in my apartment, two of them at least. It seemed like they'd been sent on a mission."

"A baby adopts the religion that surrounds him," I mumbled with babies still on my mind.

Avril rejoined the conversation at that point by asking Ari "Why didn't you tell us all this before?" She asked it more in sympathy and frustration.

"It's difficult to explain," he said. One minute I just want to get back to my life here, back to my studies and maybe even back to work. The next minute I'm in the most dreadful depressed state thinking of the young guy I was just getting to know and like on email and texting, then thinking of the grief that my birth mother must be feeling. I just feel like the whole thing is my fault."

"It's not your fault!" three of us said emphatically almost in unison.

Ari looked a bit startled at that rejoinder and then continued: "So I said to my 'cousins' something like: 'What could I possibly achieve If I came with you back to Palestine? My birth mother doesn't know me, my Israeli family would be terrified for my safety. I'd be targeted the moment I said anything favorable about Israel or negative about Palestine. I feel terrible about it all, but my life is here now.' After I said that their hostility was palpable. I felt wretched and sick, I couldn't move, and I didn't move. I went to bed; I didn't go to class, and I stayed in bed until my work called."

"And then?" I asked.

"And then I hung up and went back to bed."

"And then? I asked again.

"And then work called again and again and again. Eventually Mr. Roth pointed out, the bottom line was that if I didn't come to work, I'd have to move out of the apartment. So, I moved out and here I am.

"What about your so-called cousins? Did they show up again? I asked."

"Well I thought you knew. As I said, they'd shacked up at my place. They didn't give me much choice about it. About two and a half weeks ago the three guys left me one morning when I was still in bed. They went to walk around Manhattan, they said, and that they'd come back later."

"One of them had my spare key so I called a locksmith immediately after they were gone. Then I packed my stuff. When the locksmith had finished, I locked the door behind me. The three guys returned later, and found they were locked out. Anwar called me to ask me to let them in. I told him to 'piss off' and take his weird cousins with him. They don't know where I went; I never mentioned this address. Last time they found me they followed me home from class."

Feeling my humor bubbling through the stress I said with absurd understatement: "You didn't like them very much did you?" Then added after I'd thought about it: "And if they stick around they could do the same again and find you here by following you from class."

"Guess so," Ari replied with a hint of a smile and forced nonchalance, then continued: "But I couldn't take any more of their crap, no matter how much sympathy and guilt I felt. Actually, I still do feel sympathy and especially guilt. By the way, Anwar was OK, the other two, you don't want to know. They were just nuts."

At least he didn't say 'it's all my fault' yet again. "Then," he continued, "I put the new key in the mail and sent it to my former employer with a note to explain. I thanked them heartily for their generosity and told them I was working on my personal problems. And thank you Moishe and Avril, what would I have done without you?

"Wait a minute," I said, "did your cousins ever tell you where, exactly, Nadeem disappeared? We know it was Cyprus, but could they have been more precise?"

"Maybe I could find out" said Ari, "I'm sure all three of them have left this country now, all they possessed were tickets home. They kept sponging money off me and claimed they had none of their own. One of them, Anwar, had a cell phone which worked here. He called me a few days ago to say he was in Palestine and the other two guys had gone to Cyprus to look for Nadeem. Wait a minute, let me see if he'll answer that number."

After a brief conversation with Anwar, Ari looked up and said: "Paphos, - the last time he was seen was in a town called Paphos. Big-beard and Little-beard had gone to look for him there."

"What in God's name could we do about a disappearance that took place a few weeks ago in Paphos, Cyprus?" I blurted, but I'm sure I was not the only one thinking it. I looked round at faces that looked back at me with confused and questioning stares, Avril was the exception.

"Hey guy's", said Avril, "I have an unusual case tomorrow that I need to research, a surgical case that is. And I need Moishe to do some shopping and to fix the kitchen drain and make some phone calls he was hinting about earlier. So…, Maria, it has been such a pleasure to meet you. Ari dear, be a gentleman and see Maria home. And yes Maria, I hope you will come back tomorrow so we can pick up this discussion where we left it."

159

Chapter 16 - An Immediate Solution Does not Come to Mind - Maria

There was a brief look of alarm on Ari's face when Avril casually asked him to see me home. But he said nothing and crossed the room willingly to take my favorite slim black raincoat off the hook near the door. I followed him smartly enough and slipped into it as he held it for me with silent exaggerated consideration. I smiled to myself and grabbed my scarf from the same hook to save him from the challenge of helping me wrap it round my neck. Then he put on his own expensive looking down-stuffed jacket which he must have bought before he lost his job, and out we went into the blustery Autumn day. There were few people around McCarren Park as we walked through it. Leaves were blowing around, and those few left on the trees tried to hide their bold fall colors in their curled wrinkled forms.

The cold made me snuggle up to Ari as we skirted around the puddles that had formed from the previous night's rain. I took his arm while trying to banish from my mind the thought that Hadassah might see us and worse, that we would be pursued by "cousins" appearing out of nowhere to snatch him away into some inscrutable void. He accepted my snuggle and even snuggled back a little. When approaching my front door, I said to him: "You'd better come in Ari, I'll make you a coffee. And…" I said with a hint of deliberation in my voice, "I have some questions for you. Oh, don't worry," I added hastily, "they're real easy questions", and I gave him one extra snuggle before taking out my key to open my front door. I saw my neighbor, and said a quick hi to her, not wanting to get into introductions. She did a discreet double take, if there is such a thing, when she saw me on the arm of a handsome guy she hadn't seen before.

When inside, I pointed to where he should leave his coat and shoes and I went to make some coffee in the kitchen at the far end of my all-in-one kitchen-dining-living room. Just as Wilson had been drawn to photos on my walls a few days earlier, Ari was now perusing photos of my parents, my brother, his wife, children, and my baby cousins. And just as Wilson had, he asked about them, what they did, where they lived etc.

My favorite photos of vacations, college, friends, people I work with, and some prints of my favorite Impressionist paintings scattered around, all in a way I like to think of as tasteful, but probably isn't. So I told him general things about my life. After all, I knew quite a lot about his life, and he was curious about mine. He didn't know anything about Catholics although he knew a little about the Eastern Orthodox Christian churches in Jerusalem. I really

161

didn't want to get into all that, though, because, frankly I didn't really care about it, especially at that moment.

In fact, I showed him what I cared about a whole lot more by gently planting a full unabashed kiss directly on his lips in a way that left him in no doubt what opportunities lay ahead for him in the immediate future. In returning the kiss he made it equally clear to me he was ready to seize the moment. It also removed any lingering doubts I had about his sexual orientation.

I don't want to get too detailed in my descriptions of what followed because I can't. Didn't I tell you? I'm a demur Catholic girl. But I will tell you this. I was barely conscious of, but responding to, a longing in my body to be close. Close to his, which mysteriously insinuated its presence by a trace of coffee on his breath, of a discrete anti-perspirant and of a newly minted hint of body odor. I sensed that on both our parts there had been some tension when we were close which had the effect of drawing us closer, resolving at first into innocent cuddles. Touching, just touching was stimulating, and with scarcely mindful intent became a more intimate caressing, followed by consummate love making that was deeply satisfying for me, and I hoped equally so for him. He was slightly awkward which suggested to me that he was a virgin, but he was a fast learner. In any case I was willing and ready to help between the sheets which he accepted with grace.

It was early evening before I threw a robe around my shoulders and crept into the shower while he snoozed.

162

Following my shower I went to the kitchen to prepare some rice and beans for us. I could hear Ari moving around and then I heard the hiss of his shower. He emerged a few minutes later with wet hair and an appetite, as had I, so we ate our fill of rice and beans with some hot sauce and steamed asparagus, and washed it down with a glass of Merlot. While finishing up with yet another cup of freshly brewed coffee Ari's phone rang, which irrationally filled me with dread that Ari's dark mood might return at any time if faced with any dark news.

I need not have worried this time. He looked relaxed about the call just saying OK, OK and then hung up and looked at me.

"Just Avril," he said, "she wants me to call in at the grocery store on the way home to pick up some stuff. She said she'd asked Moishe to get the groceries, but he got a phone call followed by a visit from a client and couldn't."

I needed to go to the grocery store myself so the two of us left the apartment together, saying our goodbyes half an hour later at the store.

Late next morning I got a call from Ari. "You coming for lunch?" he asked. "Avril said she thought you were coming over." It was not what he said but the way he said it that caught my attention. He sounded like he'd got his mojo back. Does anybody say that anymore? But anyway, that's what he sounded like, not the confused and conflicted Ari but the bold bright guy I'd caught glimpses of in previous encounters. If I have such a thing called mojo, I think a little of it crept back into me too.

163

So of course I went for lunch. The four of us, by our conversation the previous day, had made implicit that we intended to do something about Nadeem's death. When I raised the subject, Avril intoned a bland but altogether memorable reply:

"An immediate solution about what to do does not come to mind.

There was really no arguing with that, and after fifteen seconds of silence she added: "However, I have an idea that might help."

"Here's what happened with us so far," she continued. "Moishe made a phone call to a number he found on a British website. The number was a help line of the local Paphos police for British people trying to find the gravesites of family members who had died in Cyprus. Unfortunately, Moishe forgot to find out the date Nadeem disappeared, or even his last name, or surname, as it's called in British speak. He didn't ask Ari what Nadeem's surname was and now, being Sunday, that phone is not staffed, and if it had been, it is 9:00 PM in Paphos, so this piece of the puzzle will have to wait until tomorrow."

"I'm sorry," said Moishe," looking a bit sheepish. "Look, I had a call from an important client who I think is going to buy several of my paintings for his gallery. I was distracted."

Ari logged on to his email while Avril was speaking. "His last name is Mohammed, that's Nadeem's last name," he said to Moishe.

"Good, maybe we'll have better luck tomorrow with a phone call," Avril answered, making sure Moishe could hear her. "Is there any way you can figure out what date he disappeared Ari?"

"Not really," said Ari, "but we have a pretty narrow range of dates, like from the last email I received from him until the day I learned of his disappearance from my 'cousins'."

"And then," I asked. "How much closer will we be to finding the last place he was seen? and if he died, how? and if murdered, who was the murderer?

"I don't know, we can ask around," said Avril vaguely.

Avril is not a vague kind of person, and this answer had me asking the obvious: "Who on earth in Brooklyn are you going to ask, even if you wait until tomorrow when more things are open?"

"Actually," she said slowly, "I was thinking of going to Paphos to ask around."

Nobody said anything for a few seconds, then out of the blue something occurred to me. "Ari," I said, "if I remember rightly, Wilson told me that Nadeem had a girlfriend. Did Nadeem ever tell you about her?"

"Yea, yes, just in our emails, that's the only way he could have, but yes." he answered.

Do you think you could dig out some of the emails he sent you in which he mentions her and print them? Maybe we can get a few clues about what happened.

So for a while Ari was tapping on the computer keyboard and the printer buzzed occasionally. Moishe, who hadn't said anything up until that point, excused himself to work on a painting. I guessed it would be one his client was interested in buying. And then I got to talking to Avril out of the hearing of both of them. She asked me how long had it been since I'd had a vacation and am I due for another? I guessed what she was going to ask me next, but I beat her to it.

"You want to know if I want to take a vacation in Paphos, right?" I asked.

"Right", she answered, "and by the way, whatever happened to you two yesterday, Ari was gone for hours?" and when she asked it, I saw a twinkle in her eye and a quiver in her lip as if trying not to smile.

"You set me up," I shrieked then quieted my voice as the two guys' heads turned towards us. "You knew what would happen, didn't you," I asked.

"And did it?" She asked.

I looked at her and smiled. I didn't need to say anything. This woman could read me like a book. Just as she knew I'd wanted Ari she knew now, in a manner of speaking, I'd got Ari, and very likely she had Ari figured out just as well.

Avril, I was thinking, knows about people, and was going, in her own mysterious way, to investigate Nadeem's death and to involve me in the investigation. What had seemed like an impossible task still seemed like an impossible task, but at least mixing it in with a vacation in Cyprus, a place that I'd never been to, made failure seem almost as good as success in the venture. Not only that, but I liked Avril. But there was something else on my mind and I had to ask her: "Supposing we find out what happened to

Nadeem, what can we possibly do about it? Do we just tell the police and leave, hoping they'll do something?"

"That's a good question." she answered. "There's a lot we can at least try to do. From a simple human perspective there could be some kind of closure for Ari, his family and for Nadeem's family. If we can find absolutely no trace of him, it may be that he doesn't want to be found. Although I doubt that. I have a friend who's a journalist in Israel, Ari knows her. She's resourceful and I know she'll help. Anyway, if we start stirring up a hornets' nest of spies and fanatics her experience may come in useful."

Then I remembered that Avril used to be a photojournalist before she trained to be a doctor. She had a faraway look in her eye for a few seconds, then she looked at me in earnest and said: "I'm going to rent a place for the four of us for a couple of weeks. If I can swing some vacation time, I'm overdue for some, and if Moishe keeps his clients off his back for that time, and if you can swing some vacation time, and if Ari can take his class assignments with him, maybe we can take a vacation. Lots of ifs there. Gotta start somewhere, though. Moishe might be a problem, but if he can take his easel and paints and brushes, he might be persuaded."

"Lots of ifs," I repeated, "but I'm on board." It was true what I said about being due for a vacation. It was almost two years since I was in Jordan and since then I'd barely been out of the city.

Meanwhile groans and grunts between curses were coming from Moishe's direction at the other side of the room as he brandished a half inch brush bearing a blob of orange towards a dark unsuspecting sky. "You need a vacation," yelled Avril as she winked at me, "You need to see a real sky, then you'd have less trouble painting one."

"What do you have in mind?" He yelled back.

"A vacation in Cyprus." yelled Avril.

He stopped, brush dangling, orange blob dripping to the floor, and looked at us. "That's his thinking face," said Avril, "he'll need to grunt and curse a bit more before he agrees to it, but I think he'll come around. In the meantime, I, I mean we, need to work on the dates we can get off work, and what vacation or rental homes are available during those times."

Ari took some papers off the printer; I don't think he'd heard anything we'd been talking about but he seemed excited. He scanned a page with his eyes then said: "Here's something, Nadeem had been writing about low water levels in the Dead Sea, real nerdy stuff, then he switched to this, I'll read it to you:

"There's something that weighs heavily upon my heart, my brother. Is that how you would say it in English? I think so. Even if not, I think you know what I mean by heavy heart. I write about many things, but I have a private disposition and talking about this I find especially difficult.

Several months ago, my parents arranged with another family for me to meet one of their daughters. She is called Hiba; it means gift in Arabic. They could have not made a better choice for me. She was truly a gift. She was sweet from the first moment I met her, and I tried to be sweet in return, I was quite taken with her. We urged our parents to arrange several more meetings which they did. After exchanging email addresses with her we started to arrange our own meetings without their help. As I got to know her better, I found she was more than just sweet. She had broad interests and could talk about them, and she loved books, English novels mostly, that's how she knew English well. She occasionally expressed an interest in politics. This is unusual for a woman in my country. I should rephrase that; I believe many women are interested in politics but not many talk about it.

One day my father came to talk to me and told me to cut off all communication with Hiba. He did not explain why, although I asked him to, several times. I asked him if Hiba's father had demanded that, and he could not find an answer, or at least did not give me an answer, he just looked at the floor and said: 'Don't ask me', then he walked away without another word. He reminded me to stay away from her several times after that on the occasions that he and I were alone together.

In my life I have rarely disobeyed my father, and if I did it was mostly when I was a child, when I would take a sweet cake from a cooling rack, for example, or play football in the street when car traffic made it dangerous, you know, that sort of thing. But he had never before ordered me to not do something like this with such solemnity, such firmness.

He is not familiar with computers, he did not know my email password and if he did, he would not have known how to use it, so, of course I continued to contact Hiba. I told her by email what my father had said. When I told her that she made no comment but continued to contact me and meet me.

169

At first she acted no differently than before, she continued to be affectionate and attentive to everything I said. We would meet in a restaurant or some other public space, and we were never alone together. In our culture it is not acceptable to touch unless you are related or married.

In one of our meetings, she seemed distracted and plainly didn't listen to me when I talked. She would look away into the distance, then she'd ask me to repeat what I'd just said. It was not like her at all, and then without warning she said, with uncalled for passion, "Don't listen to your father, he doesn't know what he's talking about."

'Obviously,' I told her, 'I haven't listened to my father or why would we be talking now? You're not making sense.'

'"Oh, oh, of course,"' she answered and then: '"I have to be somewhere,"' and disappeared into a narrow street full of merchants with stalls and barrows."

"Are there more mentions of Hiba?" Asked Avril.

"Not in this email," answered Ari, "but there's some more about her a couple of days later. Just one sentence in his email. Like it came out of nowhere he just said": 'Hiba asked me in a one-line email: "I'm told you're born Jewish. Is that true?"'

"That's it?" Asked Avril, "did he answer her?"

"Nadeem never answered that question to my knowledge," replied Ari, "but there's more here, much more," he said after sifting through several pages. "This is the last one I ever got from him. Hiba's mentioned, as is his father, and it's quite long. Here it is, just the most relevant bits." And again, he read to us:

170

"My father asked me again today if I'd seen 'that woman' again. He'd never called her that before, he would always mention her by name. Then he said to me in the gravest possible tone: 'You must not see her again, ever. Do you use your computer to write to her? I hear computers can do that sort of thing.'

I was really upset. I love my father and couldn't lie to him and I admitted that I had, and even cried a little for the first time since I was a child.

"But why father?" I asked, "And why has she been so cold with me recently?" The strangest thing of all is that she was distant with me, like short tempered. She said I shouldn't listen to you, and we should keep up our email correspondence.

My father looked thoughtful for a few seconds, then he gripped my shoulders tightly and pulled me close. I am a little taller than he, and felt uncomfortable looking down at him. He said to me in his clearest standard Arabic without using local Levantine dialect words.

"You are in danger my son; you have been targeted by fanatics. I believe Hiba, poor girl, has been targeted too, but unlike you, her life is not in danger just so long as she does what is asked of her."

"What do you think is asked of her?" I asked my father.

"I think her task will be to persuade you to meet her at a place of their choosing," he answered.

"To what purpose?" I asked not really believing what my father was saying.

"I think they're planning to kidnap you," said my father

"Whatever for?" I asked him, I also used formal Arabic as he had. "I'm a good Muslim, I pray at prescribed times, I have never criticized the faith. I have never talked about other religions or even had any interest in them. I even work for our causes and express disgust at Israeli settlers' annexations in Palestine near Hebron, and Nablus and Ramallah and Jerusalem and Bethlehem and everywhere they trespass. They couldn't possibly want to harm me. And what use to them would I be if they kidnapped me?"

"I know all that my son," he said, "I'm so proud of you. But you know I have many friends whom I've known since childhood, and they would not lie to me. Some of them have family members who are simply fanatics. Often, these fanatics have suffered in some way, and now are bitter and lash out with irrational anger at anything remotely Jewish. And you, my dear son, are the natural son of a Jewish mother. A good and old friend told me that on account of this, you are a target."

I was exasperated: "Nobody chooses their mother!" I yelled at him. "And in any case, you haven't told me what possible use I could be to them if they kidnapped me?"

"To exchange you for one of our violent extremists in an Israeli prison," he answered simply.

"That makes no sense!" I yelled again. I'm a nobody. "Israel couldn't possibly attach any value to me for such an exchange."

"You have more value than you think." My father said.

"How so?" I asked.

"Well, it's like this." My father paused to collect his thoughts then continued: "The Israeli government would get pressure from two sides of the political spectrum. To people with divergent religious convictions, you are by birth Jewish, and therefore always Jewish. To them you are worth much more than a Muslim counterpart. To more liberal Jews, not so bound by orthodoxy, your unique conundrum would attract a lot of sympathy. Your natural Jewish mother is still alive and must be aching to see you. That alone would be a popular story in Israeli newspapers."

I looked at him and he at me, as yet again he seemed to be collecting his thoughts. Then he continued:

"What mutually outrages our two communities more than anything, are the deaths we inflict on each other. And as we do, each side calls the attention of its people to the violence inflicted by the other, to justify a violent response."

"Do not forget' he continued, "your misplacement in our family is the outcome of a violent attack by our side, on innocents. Among these innocents were your own mother here in the Palestinian area of Jerusalem and your birth mother in Tel Aviv. The Israelis will make the most of that for propaganda, for a second time. They will pay dearly to get you back among them."

I felt sick when he said: "your misplacement in our family." For a moment I felt like I didn't belong anywhere. Like I was a 'misplacement' everywhere. But when I looked

173

again at my father, at the love in his eyes, and I saw there the desperate concern he felt for my safety I knew that nobody could have had a better 'misplacement' than I'd had.

And when I stopped to think some more, I was amazed at what my father had said. He is a tailor by trade, a simple working man, he seemed to understand the dynamics of Israeli politics as well as our own. He'd made his case well and I realized, slowly, that he was right. Then for the second time that day I cried.

'If I simply volunteered to be exchanged for one of our fanatics they wouldn't have to kidnap me, would they?" I sobbed naively.

"They'll shoot you before they'd let you do that. Pack your suitcase, now. Say goodbye to your mother and avoid your sister. I'll deal with them later. I know you love them, but you cannot expect them to understand. I know a safe place for you to go for a short while and I'll work on a longer-term solution. Things are going to be difficult for you at first."

"Is that it, is that the end of the email? Avril asked.

"Not quite, there are a few things here about what he packed, and he was told to stay indoors waiting for nightfall. At the very end he says":

My father left me alone while I packed my suitcase in silence and sadness. He returned an hour later with a cell phone he'd bought for me. He has a simple Nokia cell phone and didn't know about texting. The store where he bought my phone explained texting and he chose one with English

174

rather than Arabic characters. I thought he'd made a mistake but said nothing because he only made voice calls anyway.

So my dear brother, I know in some ways your predicament is similar to mine. I hope you find a more agreeable way to resolve it than is my lot. Goodbye for now. It may be several weeks or even months before I contact you again. I look forward to that time.

"Wait," I said, "he got a phone that he could text you with, did he tell you his phone number?"

"I was lucky," Ari replied, "I read his email the moment he sent it. I asked him for his phone number and he sent it to me right away. His father was smarter than Nadeem realized at the time"

"So you texted each other following that?" I asked.

"Yes, but...," he stopped speaking, looking embarrassed and confused, while we watched and listened, feeling embarrassed and confused too. Then he continued: "To tell the truth, I got sick of it all. I felt there was just nothing I could do about it. But he kept texting me, and texting me, and the texts became ever more desperate and weird. Then the texts stopped and his 'cousins' or to be strictly correct my cousins and Big and Little Beards showed up."

Thinking back to when he left me cold that evening when we were walking together and feeling irritated still, I asked: "What exactly happened with you, Anwar and the Beards?"

"Well, you know," he said, collecting his thoughts, "they came back to my place. They'd been staying in a hotel and were fast running out of cash. They had no clear idea of what they wanted to do or what I could do for them, beyond going with them. The arguments they used made no impression on me except to make me more miserable. Anwar told me that Nadeem had called him to tell him he was in Cyprus but little else. He didn't text him. And then they lost contact, I guess that's when Nadeem disappeared. So, they wanted more information from me about what went on between us in our emails and texts. Anyway, they insisted they should stay with me until their flight home in three days' time."

What Ari had just told us generated more questions than answers. I knew that for several weeks his moods had been up and down. I'm no psychologist but I'm pretty sure he'd had bouts of clinical depression. I started to think we'd been too curious and too insistent on knowing everything that happened when he would have preferred to let the whole thing go and immerse himself in computer code and statistics. Moishe and Avril were both silent. I knew they understood how difficult it had been for him. This is a young man with a conscience, I thought. The greater was his success, the greater the contrast between him and his opposite number that had fled for his life.

"I'll print the texts," Ari said suddenly, taking out his phone.

Ari read the first text: "'I'm still in East Jerusalem,'" and continued: "he means he's in mostly Palestinian East

Jerusalem, that's the part of Jerusalem annexed by Israel after the '67 war."

Then he read the next text: "filled in lots of forms, I'm waiting for my passport." and then "still waiting." Then the conversation ran as follows"

Ari: 'What is it like where you are?'

Nadeem: 'I can't go out; I'm told that would be dangerous for me. There's an old man and a young woman here. They're father and daughter and they're nice to me. The daughter is pretty but distant and formal."

Ari: 'Where in East Jerusalem are you?'

Nadeem: 'I don't know. I came here at about 2am lying on the back seat of a taxi with very dark shaded windows to what looked like, when I got out, a pleasant section of town that I haven't seen before.

Ari: 'Then how do you know you're in East Jerusalem?'

Nadeem: 'The man here told me. And there were no checkpoints on the way here. If we were in the West Bank I would have known. The taxi meter wasn't going and the "For Hire" light was out. The driver told me to sit in the back and keep my head down so I couldn't see which way the car was going. The man at the house said I should stay here until my passport comes, then I would be able to move more freely."

Ari: 'Move where too?'

Nadeem: 'They hinted, to the West Bank, then Jordan, after that I don't know. I'm sure I wouldn't be any safer in Jordan. This house where I'm staying is really nice. It's a traditional Palestinian house. It has a tall outer wall enclosing the whole U-shaped house, and a courtyard garden which has some palms for shade over a table and chairs where I eat and read as the weather allows. There are some flowers and a small pond with a fountain.'

The next text was Nadeem again: 'I called my dad, he sounded like he was crying while he was talking, so did my mom when I talked to her.'

Ari: 'I know how hard that is. Courage, courage my dear friend and brother.'

Then Ari added: "I'd never met Nadeem but when he said stuff like that I really choked up. I knew what he was going through. He felt like he was a traitor and yet there was nothing he could do, nor could ever have done about it. He seemed comfortable and fairly well settled at this house.

"The next dozen or so texts are just about what he's reading, which tv programs he's watching, liking, that sort of thing. He spoke to his mom and dad and little sister. He said that his dad thought his home was being watched. He told him there were a couple of guys standing in the shade every day and the shadows every night doing nothing, trying to look inconspicuous which meant, to him, kidnappers were trying to keep tabs on him and thought he was hiding at home."

"He told me there were shelves full of books in the house, half of them in English and he guessed the man who lived there was an academic of some kind and his daughter a student."

Then Ari started to read some more texts:

Nadeem: At seven this evening my host told me his daughter had called at my house to pick up a package sent from the Israeli passport office. It turned out to be my Israeli passport. Of course, I knew it would be an Israeli passport when I was applying for it, but it feels very strange. In all respects in my life, I am Palestinian, and yet since I live inside the borders of what is now Israel, to the Israeli government I'm Israeli.

Ari: It's just some paper. It's not you. Don't think about it that way. It's just a piece of paper that will get you into other countries.

Nadeem: OK but it's still weird. At least I can buy my airline ticket to Cyprus now.

Ari: Cyprus? Why Cyprus?

Nadeem: It's relatively affordable and close and peaceful, and there are some people there that can help me at first. It's complicated, but other Palestinians who live in the West Bank, the people who will help me, they have Palestinian passports and travel is much more restricted for them. They need visas to go just about anywhere except Jordan. They even have to get a visa to go to Cyprus, but at least they can go there, and visas can be obtained to travel to Cyprus at their consul's office in Ramallah. I know I'm rambling. It's just so boring here waiting, waiting, and waiting some more, and not going out.

Ari: Wow! At least with the Israeli passport you may be able to get farther away sometime. That's if you want to, of course?

Nadeem: That's right, and here's the other really big thing about Cyprus. A lot of people speak English there.

That's the only European language I know. Later, who knows I may be able to get to the UK or US?

At that moment Ari's phone rang. I heard him say: "Oh hi, er, OK...where?...When?..., OK, see you there then.

"He looked at me and seemed somewhat embarrassed. "Who was that?" I asked him.

"Hadassah," he answered.

"The same Hadassah I saw you with a few weeks ago?"

"The very same. I need to tell her what's going on. I arranged to meet her."

"You could have told her on the phone." I said, listening to myself sound sulky.

"I need to tell her to her face."

"You think she'll listen?"

"What choice does she have?"

We looked at one another, steadily, wordlessly. This is a guy who left me cold in the middle of a street. And that was just "to go with his 'cousins,'" I was thinking. This is a test for him. I'll let him tell me about their meeting. I was not invited. That's OK, I wouldn't have gone anyway.

Chapter 17 - Hadassah and Me - Ari

Hello, it's me, Ari, again. As Maria explained in the previous chapter, I had arranged with Hadassah to meet her the following day in a cafe in Manhattan after my class at NYU. We arrived at the same time and were shown a table together. Hadassah removed her paisley headscarf, slipped out of her long black raincoat, and nonchalantly handed them to a young male server, saying "Would you mind please?" He took them to a space by the door to hang with other coats but made no such offer to me, asking on his return if we'd like to order drinks.

She was so beautiful, so carefully dressed. Her makeup so precise but understated, her body so slim and lithe and movements so graceful, cat-like, and her perfume so subtle when she brushed against me as we made our way to a table. A waitress attended us quite quickly. We ordered our food then looked at one another across the table. I was unable to speak as I took in her smooth olive skin, jet black shoulder length straight hair and her eyes with their dark brown pupils sat in pure white ellipses.

And what could she be thinking as she looked at me? I felt uncomfortable as I remembered how I must look to her. I'd just come from class, my hair uncombed, wrinkled shirt, crumpled jacket draped over the back of my chair, ink marks on my fingers.

She spoke first, and I watched stupefied by her perfect white teeth and perfect diction as she delivered via a refined accent: "So Ari, the girl I saw you with, she is your girlfriend, isn't she? I guessed right when I saw you with her didn't I?"

I nodded mutely.

"I had hoped it would be otherwise, but I wish you luck. Perhaps I could meet her someday?"

I didn't know what to say about this, but I saw a tear form in her eye and roll down her cheek which she wiped away quickly with her napkin. Then she continued:

"Maybe it's for the best. My mother learned your story from Avril. When she found out that you were born to a Palestinian mother, she became subtly hostile to the possibility of us associating with one another. It's true she was charming when you came to our house for dinner. At that time, she thought you were simply a bright Israeli kid, come to New York for your education. Her attitude changed when, after quizzing Avril about you at work was told the circumstances of your birth and the underlying reason you came to the U.S."

"How do you feel about the 'circumstances' of my birth?" I asked her, feeling in part regret and in part flattered that as she spoke another tear rolled onto her cheek. It dawned on me that perhaps I'd unconsciously put her on a pedestal, that her outward perfection made her inner person, her natural warmth and pure patrimony out of reach to mongrel me.

"My first reaction was astonishment," she replied through a watery smile. "I guess we're more tribal than we like to admit."

"Some more than others." I answered, feeling sad but probably looking angry.

"Do you know, my mother and I had the most ungodly argument about you?"

"How could I know?"

She ignored my sulky answer and continued: "She said I should concentrate on my education, forget about notions like 'gap year' and 'traveling' to Europe and even to Israel. The family tradition is medicine, to which we Sephardic Jews are well suited. It accommodates our intellectual talents, provides a good living and the means to associate with others of similar backgrounds."

"That's weird. Did you ask her what Palestinian Arabs, raised as Israeli Jews are well suited to?"

"I took your side," she answered, getting a little aggravated with me. "I told her that nobody can control how or where or to whom they are born. I quoted Martin Luther King and told her that a person's real worth is the 'content of their character.' Telling her that made her think we were seeing each other regularly. Just to rile her up some more I called you at that moment."

I smiled, thinking it was more like something Maria would do, but the smile faded as I wondered how to wind up this conversation in a different way. The thing about Maria was that she accepted me exactly as I am from the moment we met and never changed that acceptance the more she learned about me. What's more, she had told me about her Catholic background and limited associations with others outside the Catholic community but that had made no difference to her. I owed her the same compliment, namely that her totally different and unfamiliar background should make no difference to me.

While I was thinking about this someone put his hand on my shoulder and said: "Hi Ari, are you going to introduce me?"

It was Wilson. I'd chosen a venue to meet with Hadassah remote from Williamsburg so that she and I could lay the ghost of our relationship to rest without interruption, but here was Wilson, out of the blue whom I hadn't told about our meeting. "Oh yes, of course, this is Hadassah, a friend of mine. What brings you here?"

Wilson looked at her appreciatively. She held his gaze and looked back at him. I watched his eyes go to her, then back to me and his face turned into one big question mark which he could not and did not put into words, as if needing help.

"We were just splitting up," said Hadassah helpfully in a bland tone, but Wilson did not appear much helped, retaining his confused expression.

"Would you care to join us?" I asked him, not knowing what else I could possibly say and relieved at the opportunity to change the subject of the conversation I was starting with Hadassah.

"Oh, thanks, is that OK with you Hadassah?"

"Yes, please join us, how do you know Ari?"

"Well, er… I know him through a mutual friend of his mother, it's complicated," answered Wilson.

But this didn't satisfy Hadassah who indicated she knew a lot about my background by asking: "Which mother would you be talking about, his Palestinian mother or his Israeli one?"

This is me she was talking about as if I wasn't there and as if it could be a private joke between them. Wilson looked uncomfortable; he could see that I was embarrassed and paused before replying: "A journalist friend of mine met his mother, that is, the mother who raised him in Israel."

Hadassah looked at him and said, continuing as if I weren't there: "The conventionality of his appearance belies the complexity of his past, through no fault of his own, I hasten to add. I was just saying to him that the 'content of his character' is what anyone should be judged bye."

Wilson got up the leave, saying, as he pushed his chair back under the table: "I think this is something you should be discussing between yourselves." The young server hurriedly returned and asked Wilson if he'd like to order something. Before he could say no Hadassah and I said in unison without thinking:

"Please don't go." He looked at our imploring faces then turned to the waitress to ask her what today's specials were, ordered, sat down again, and asked: "How can I help?"

Of course he couldn't help. Neither us said anything as the three of us sat in silence for about fifteen seconds. Then Wilson said: "I made a mistake, this has nothing to do with me, I'll cancel my food."

"What do you do, Wilson?" Hadassah asked abruptly. Wilson looked unsure about how to answer, hesitating at first, he then started to explain his journalist assignments, inevitably getting to a description of his friendship with Shona, the Israeli journalist who first discovered my complicated birth situation. I sat in silence thinking of my mom's hostile stare across our kitchen table at Shona, as the implications became clear of what was being revealed to her. I also felt a profound nostalgia for what used to be my home and my family and even my country. I looked at the two of them as they continued to talk. It was surreal how I kept hearing my name as if I wasn't there. Also, it was not lost on me that Hadassah had taken my side, my part if you like, in the arguments that she'd had with her mother that she'd told me about.

In her mind I could and should just sort of step up and do the necessary conversions and oaths and prayers that would make me into something else. But how would I know what's in her mind? How arrogant of me? But she had, after all, I remembered, asked me to "convert", the prospect of which sounded ridiculous to me. So maybe I was right about what was going on in her mind? What she appeared not to recognize even in herself, was the pride that some people have in their heritage, that perhaps I too had had before the ugly truth came to light that I was of a different race altogether.

Then I thought about Maria and was enveloped by calm. Again, I smiled to myself as I remembered that unlike

Hadassah, I had met her parents only very briefly when they came to Maria's apartment with some cookies a few weeks ago. I was not so naive to think they would accept me as I am. It seemed quite likely that they would disapprove of me, but that could wait. Maria knew everything about me and was just fine with it. Or maybe, just maybe, it's a matter of love conquers all, and nothing else really matters. Perhaps?

"I hope you'll excuse me, I have to be somewhere," I said as I stood up and lifted my jacket from my chair back. Wilson stood up too, offered his hand for me to shake, which I took and shook warmly. I looked at Hadassah, and she at me. She blew me a kiss as another tear dripped onto her cheek with an expression that showed a softness and tranquility that I hadn't seen before. I fished in my pocket for a twenty-dollar bill which I left on the table and headed for the door. Wilson and Hadassah were still talking as I stole a glance at them before exiting into the bustling sidewalk on University Place, and without thinking, walked North towards Union Square where I could catch the subway back to Williamsburg.

For a few city blocks I lost myself in thoughts weaving my way through a slice of busy varied humanity. I knew I would regain a sense of purpose and prosper in this place. There was no doubt that my upbringing inside a close and loving family with an outgoing and liberal perspective had equipped me well to thrive. I was a biological imposter in the eyes of some religionists, as was my unfortunate opposite number across the great cultural and religious divide. It was comforting to know that Maria was unconcerned about my religion.

For Hadassah, on the other hand, I had to be placed in an identifiable, predictable slot before our relationship could progress. I had no identifiable slot, and that, as far as I was concerned was the way it was going to stay and was quite prepared to own it. I have not expressed this before, but now that I think about it, I know that a rejection of either religion had crept into my subconscious over the previous few months.

As far as I knew I was in a minority of one and perhaps two if poor Nadeem is still alive. One of us an Arab Jew and the other a Jewish Arab. Who is which? I don't know. Perhaps we'd both be both at the same time. Then I thought of Avril and Moishe. They were both English originally, it's true, but other than that they had completely different backgrounds and they didn't care about it. They just got on with the lives they wanted to live and accepted others, like me for instance, or like their friends, the totally different Cardozo/Mendez family just as they are. It seemed not to occur to them to do otherwise.

If Hadassah felt alone without me, it would not last, I was sure. She was too beautiful for that. Then I thought of her talking to Wilson as I left the cafe and smiled to myself as I muttered: 'I wonder where that's going?' I might not have been so relaxed about their meeting had it not been for Maria.

I must have had a thoughtful faraway look when I got home. I flopped, sliding low so my shoulders barely rose above the back of the couch. Avril and Moishe were conversing about thirty feet distant from one another as

Moishe painted at one end of the space and Avril cooked in the other. On account of their raised voices, they didn't hear me close the door as I came in and sat down still wearing a frown.

"We can celebrate that at the same time we celebrate your birthday," Avril yelled, "Oh hello dear," she said when she finally noticed me, "I didn't hear you come in. You look very serious, is everything alright?"

"As long as you don't invite any of my clients," Moishe yelled back from behind a painting he was working on.

"Agreed!" she yelled back, "I don't want them anywhere near."

My serious look must have changed to a questioning look because she turned towards me and said: "We're going to celebrate Moishe's birthday and his very successful exhibition which was followed by many sales. We're going to have a dinner party."

"Here?" I asked incredulously.

"Of course, here," she answered. "Where else? And you're invited, of course, as are your friends, especially Maria." She paused and then added, you look puzzled."

"I guess I am, a little bit," I admitted. "I'm familiar with dinner parties on high holidays and less formal family ones on Friday evening seders, but for a birthday?"

"And Moishe's rising art career," she added. "Anyway, c'mon Ari you even hosted a dinner party yourself when you had your posh apartment by the river. Maria told me about it."

"Who will cook?" I asked.

"That's not decided yet. We may hire a chef, but if we have enough volunteers among the attendees, we may self-cater. I'll buy all the food. But it will be a sit-down meal around our large table. Nobody will be sulking in a corner getting drunk."

By then Moishe was standing behind me in his paint splattered smock and stained hands. "Yes, my boy," he said, raising his voice as he placed his hands on my shoulders from behind the couch, took a lung full of air and announced as if to a crowd of doubters "that's right. An unabashed secular dinner party, anything goes as far as conversation is concerned."

"Moshe! For Heaven's sake look at his shirt, you got paint all over it. And remember, dear," she paused to draw in breath to equal Moishe's tone and volume, "conversation is one thing, ranting is quite another."

"I will gently remove my hands from Ari's shoulder's and restore it to a wearable condition. But not for Heaven's sake, but for Ari's, and yours dear, of course," mumbled the humbled Moishe."

"Is it mandatory to attend?" I asked Avril, knowing that nothing like this could possibly be mandatory but unsure why she would want me drawn into a circle of her friends from her generation. Was she just being kind to make me feel wanted?

"I intend to invite the Cardozo/Mendez family, including their pretty daughter Hadassah. We've been doing it for several years now. You must have noticed we're firm friends with them. Return dinner parties on the occasion of

Moishe's birthday have been delightful thankyous for their Rosh Hashanah seders," she replied. "I urge you to invite some of your friends, especially Maria, I know that may cause tensions if they both agree to come. But you should invite others too

"Aren't we going to Cyprus soon?" I asked.

"I'm working on it, I'll let you know when I get things straightened out. We have time to celebrate Moishe, his birthday, and his art success.

The conversation continued like this for several more minutes until I was finally convinced that Avril really wanted my friends and me to be there. I asked Maria first, she hesitated when I told her that Hadassah would be there too, but I also told her I'd drawn a line under my relationship with her, the neo-romantic part of it at least. She asked if she could invite her work friend Marty who may also want to bring his Japanese girlfriend, Atsuko. 'What about Wilson?' you may ask, 'should he come?' I told him Hadassah was invited even though I was not sure yet whether she'd come but I guessed she would.

There were others that Avril and I invited, but only those mentioned agreed to come. Wilson's architect friend Beaty didn't have a date and consequently declined. It turned out there would be ten attendees altogether, not too many for Avril's extended table, and if some agreed to help, hiring a chef would not be necessary. When asked, Maria was eager to help, provided she was given clear directions. I volunteered too, and that was enough for Avril to go shopping for food which we would prepare ourselves.

Avril declined my offer to go to the store with her but accepted help bringing in her purchases from the taxi. Except for generous and expensive looking wines, the food I helped her unload was surprisingly pedestrian, like leeks, potatoes, ground beef, various herbs, apples, cinnamon, nuts, and salad ingredients, all in generous quantities. I asked her what she would cook.

"Shepherd's Pie," she answered. I had no idea what that was and told her. "You'll find out. It's simple and delicious and I'll hold you to your promise of help in its preparation.

"Moishe dearest," she yelled, "give that canvas a break, take your nose out of it, you're agonizing. Do me a favor and get me some oregano, for some reason it's not in my shopping here." Moishe looked relieved and complied willingly with her request. He parked his brush, donned his pea jacket and flat cap in mere seconds saying with ridiculous fervor: "Duty and honor summon me to the grocery store." And slammed the door behind him as he left."

Avril picked up a bunch of fresh oregano from the ingredients she'd already set out and hid it a few inches down in the trash can. Then she turned her attention back to me and said:

"No, I'm not crazy, I didn't want Moishe to hear this, I had to get him out of here for a few minutes. The party may be a disaster, but I think it may be magical. I'm doing it mostly for him. I'm doing it for me too, and I flatter myself that I'm doing it for you young people too," she said with an enigmatic gaze into the middle distance. "The more I think of it, the more I know I'm doing it for Moishe. You see..." she paused to think, "his newfound success and celebrity in the art world delights him and frustrates him at the same time. He mixes with rich collectors, galleries, museum curators, all of whom evaluate his work based on its originality, technique, its visual shock and its craftsmanship. But he's also trying to say something."

"OK," I answered, "but I guess I'm not quite connecting the dots. Do you mean they like his stuff, but they don't really get it?"

"Yes, that's about it," she answered, still looking thoughtful. "That is something you could ask him about, I guess: What is he trying to say through his painting?"

"OK, but how does a dinner party featuring shepherd's pie, and with none of Moishe's clients at the table, help Moishe's clients get his art?" I asked.

"You're right, it doesn't," she answered slowly, "but it helps Moishe."

That was good enough for me. I still didn't really understand how we were going to help Moishe or even why he needed help, but I'd grown to love Avril and Moishe almost like my own parents and instinctively wanted to help.

"Here's the thing," she continued, "It's in Moishe's makeup, in his personality, that he's intensely engaged in what's going on around him. He's trying, through his art, to show others what he feels and sees and thinks. If you spend all your waking hours producing and promoting and selling, there's no renewal. Nothing to stimulate fresh thoughts and outlooks. You guys are smart and fresh. OK you're pretty dumb and green too, but still smart. You ask him questions that make him think. You show him respect as an individual, but you don't revere his celebrity. You're just natural around him. He likes you and Maria and those other friends of yours that show up here from time to time."

"Isn't travel a stimulus for him?" I asked, while trying to reconcile being 'pretty dumb and green' as being part of a compliment. Everybody else says I'm smart but Avril cheerfully calls me dumb, and it doesn't bother me. Oh well?

"Yes," she answered, "but let's not forget that our upcoming trip has a somber purpose and I want him to help me and stay focused on that. If we can find out what happened to Nadeem perhaps there could be some kind of satisfaction for you and your families, Palestinian and Israeli. I had in mind if conditions were right, to invite Nadeem's family to Cyprus. You may get a chance to meet your birth mother for the first time and even your Israeli family there. I just don't know yet, but I'm working on it. It's true, artists need to travel but on this occasion that is a secondary purpose."

Chapter 18 - Moishe's Birthday Party - Ari

Hello again, still me, Ari talking. It's Sunday, Avril got all the food out ready to prepare for the party, not that much really when I look at it. It seems to be blowing up a storm over the East River and the Mayor was advising an evacuation of the Rockaway Peninsula; all of it! New York City can be as hot as Tel Aviv but a cool wind in October brings a chill like I've never felt in Israel. And just as I stood in a kind of reverie looking through the window at the swaying tree tops, shedding their leaves and in some cases their branches, Maria burst in through the door carrying a backpack, wearing a long dripping raincoat and a peculiar hat with a chin strap called a sou'wester. "Keeps your hair in place and dry," she said looking at me as I went over to greet her and help with her backpack.

Avril came to her too, hung her coat and hat for her, took her backpack from me and led her to her room where the two of them disappeared for what seemed like half an hour. During that time Marty turned up with Atsuko,

Wilson, by himself, followed by the Cardozo/Mendez family. A generous wall space with hooks by the door afforded room enough to hang all their outdoor garments. Moishe was there to welcome the arrivals and motioned to me to help hang up coats. This included Hadassah and her mother, Dr. Gillian Mendez, Avril's friend. All but Maria had come in cabs to the apartment house door and had been only slightly disheveled by the weather.

Marty and Atsuko gravitated towards Moishe's jaw-dropping bounteous and busy studio. Wilson joined them as did Moishe and all three of the Cardozo/Mendez family. Moishe was, holding forth with good and easy humor explaining some of the tricks of his trade to an admiring audience. I'd grown used to the ever-present aroma of linseed oil and turpentine and tended not to notice it so much those days. But it was instantly interesting to a newcomer. Seeing their absorption in paintings large and small, and in all stages of completion brought back memories of my own first surprised encounter with it. Wilson was showing a lively interest, asking questions about everything he looked at, as Hadassah hung on his every word. Marty and Atsuko maintained a polite silence.

Wilson asked Moishe: "How can you tell if a painting will sell?"

"I can't tell what people may like, or to be blunt what they'll buy. I do know that when I try to pander to what I believe is popular it doesn't work for me. I admit, I've tried to do that. I have in the past conceived and completed a painting with no other purpose than to sell it for the highest possible sum in the least possible time. Galleries and sophisticated buyers see right through me and ignore it when I do. Paintings generated by emotion work best for me. I would not be so bold as to compare myself to a great artist, but I think emotion is what makes the best art and the best artists masterly."

"How so? I think I understand you in the abstract, but could you give me, or show an example?" Wilson asked as Hadassah took his arm in such a way that I would call affectionate. It flashed through my thoughts that he was somewhat older than she, maybe six or eight years. In any case, none of my business, I thought. Reflexively I turned my head around to see Hadassah's mother staring intently at them. I knew Wilson was not Jewish; was she doing this for her mother to see? Why, I wondered, was religion such an issue when she was my - sort of - girlfriend? Well, never mind. Maria's much more my type, I thought, as my eyes wandered back to Hadassah. I could well imagine an artist getting emotional about her. She was just so beautiful and so exquisitely turned out. Understated but exquisite; how could that be? It's like a contradiction, almost nothing there, but to make a statement like that, like fashion or jazz, you either get it or you don't. I know she was a spirited talker when the mood took her, but today she was quietly hanging on to Wilson's arm. They were a couple.

She wore a white gold necklace from which hung a pear emerald pendant coordinated with a similar gem mounted in white gold on her right middle finger. Her dress was simple and black with discrete matching cloth belt and cloth covered buckle which suited her well, in my inexpert opinion. It perfectly comfortably fitted her slim form, which, further in my inexpert opinion, she was quite aware of. Her shoes were black too, of course, moderately high heeled, managing to be elegant but comfortable at the same time. I guess Wilson looked pretty good too, a cool looking guy, unassuming and sophisticated, sports jacket, slacks, a little taller than Hadassah in her heels.

Meanwhile Moishe was holding forth replying to Wilson, "Well firstly, pouring emotion of any kind into your work doesn't guarantee a worthy or salable painting..." but as he drew breath to launch into a rant, he was interrupted by a question from Dr. John Cardozo who had hurried over to the group to join in the conversation: "What do you think of this gallery owner guy Salander?" he asked.

At that very moment I felt Maria taking my arm and gently leading me to a pile of carrots on the countertop. She and Avril were preparing the main course Shepherd's Pie, out of earshot of Moishe. Maria looked meaningfully at the carrots as she placed a peeler in my hand, and I had to admit I wasn't greatly interested in a gallery owner guy called Salander. Nevertheless, I heard myself asking Avril: "Who's Salander?

She replied: "For once, dear inquisitive Ari, let it go and peel the carrots."

I looked over the counter, first again at the carrots then at the spread of more carrots, but these were already cooked, fresh sweet peas, onions, garlic and various herbs, oregano, rosemary and thyme, Worcestershire sauce and other ingredients that made little sense to my Middle Eastern sense of cuisine.

"The carrots are cooked already, what are these for?"

"We're going to have a meal that's good for a cold autumn day in Yorkshire, and Brooklyn too." I peeled the fresh young carrots, sliced them into thin sticks and popped them into several glasses with ice water and a sprig of parsley in each, then put them into the fridge all per Avril's directions. No sooner was it done than a bowl of hot cooked potatoes was pushed in front of me, with implements to mash them, together with butter, salt, and a carefully measured quantity of milk in a jug. I took the hint and got to work, glancing up from time to time to look at Maria, attractive, even as she was, dressed in Avril's white medical coat. Her hair was tied back while she vigorously stirred a quantity of ground beef in a fryer on the stove, embellished with all kinds of aromatic herbal additions. Avril was busy preparing two great bowls of salad, one for each end of the table.

"Hurry up with the spuds." Avril said.

I obliged, then Avril and Maria sprang into action like a well-oiled machine. Avril checked the oven temperature, nodded at Maria. In response Avril poured the ground beef goulash into a large glass baking dish. Then she picked up my potatoes and spooned them atop the ground beef into a flattened layer which she textured by painting it with a fork, back and forth. Maria added a layer of grated parmesan cheese. Lastly Maria opened the oven for Avril to shove in the loaded baking dish and closed the oven. The two stepped back and high-fived each other in front of an admiring audience that had migrated discretely from Moshe's art monologue toward the cooking aromas.

Not to be outdone Moishe drew the attention of his guests to the drinks table, pointing out aperitifs, sherries and miscellaneous bottles or red and white wine. He was not much of a drinker beyond red dinner wine with practically anything. A sweep of his arm over an array of bottles was all the help he could give in the way of recommendations. Dr. Gillian Mendez came to his rescue, mixing and serving cocktails, calling upon a skill learned during her student days. She offered her first creation to Wilson whose arm was still gently clutched by her daughter, Hadassah.

It was a relaxed affair, conversation hummed naturally and constantly in all directions quite different from the formal chronology of the seder a few weeks earlier at the Cardozo/Mendez home. Maria put the salad and wine on the table and pointed out the place names. It was the one organized formal touch of the entire evening. Then she disappeared into Avril's room for a few minutes. The guests complied unquestioningly with the assigned seating. Dr. Cardozo produced a case of fine French claret from I don't know where, and regaled us with a lecture about how fine and desirable it was. Even to my uneducated palette it cast the Israeli table wine that was familiar to me, into deep shade. I sipped, looked up and there was Maria transformed from kitchen maid to the honored house guest, beautifully turned out, and thankfully, assigned to sit next to me - her doing of course.

Thankfully I say because I'd been feeling a little out of my depth in this company which talked of art, wine, medicine and much else. Honestly, back home in Tel Aviv conversation always turned to anxieties about ever simmering border tensions, the West Bank, the Palestinian Authority, and so on. It crowded out all else from news and people's thoughts beyond family and making a living. Oh, maybe I exaggerate. My Dad, how I miss him, always had a stupid flat joke to divert our attentions. Then I caught a whiff of Maria's perfume next to me that brought back to me memories of our first intimacies. I turned my head to her sitting beside me and as I reached on the table to pick up a napkin, she placed her hand gently on mine.

She turned her head towards me, her deep blue eyes seemed to laugh in tune with her smile. But it was not without empathy. She sensed my discomfort which I could not explain to myself. She was wearing a black dress strangely similar to Hadassah's, simple, demure, and fitting well her body type that was slightly fuller than Hadassah's. I smiled to myself as I thought I could not say such a thing out loud, but it was neither criticism nor compliment. She looked just fine to me. Around her neck she wore a white gold necklace that was in her words: 'a classic solitaire sapphire pendant', the color of which complimented her eyes and drew my gaze.

Of course, my smile had to be noticed by Hadassah sitting opposite me. She caught my eye, smiled thinly back, then refocused her attention on Marty and Atsuko sitting on her left with whom she was conversing and joking. Wilson who sat on her right was engaged in conversation with Hadassah's mother. Drinks, salads, raw carrot sticks were

201

consumed chaotically in among the rolling conversations until the oven timer signaled the shepherd's pie was ready. Avril looked at Moishe in such a way that, understanding it, he scampered to the oven with what seemed like indecent haste to extricate himself from persistent questions from Dr. John Cardozo about the gallery owner, Salander.

It was a gigantic pie which Moishe set upon the work then raised his voice to ask the guests: "If you could bring your plates when you're ready, perhaps I could serve you some pie?" He greeted each recipient with a serving spoonful and a conversational pleasantry fueled by wine and happiness which reminded me of my dad. I sat mute and rigid until Maria told me to pick up my plate, took my arm and led me to Moishe's serving spoon. "Ahh, my dear Maria, what a site you are, whoops, I mean that in a good way, and how good of you to bring to the pie poor shy Ari, who needs to, needs to," his wine-fueled babble paused while he corralled his escaping thoughts, - "fill his belly with good Yorkshire food and French wine before he will, no doubt, shine his conversational glow on this gathering."

Avril was not slow to shut him up. "Obviously it's the wine talking. Don't be ridiculous Moishe, leave the lad alone." Then adding after a pause: "In any case Yorkshire is not the only place where shepherd's pie is eaten, and California wine is stacked on the table next to the French booze for all to see."

"Just a turn of phrase," he mumbled, "no offense meant my boy

"None taken." I replied.

I was not shocked by Moishe's babble, I was used to worse from my dad after he'd had a few glasses of wine. I felt it was unlikely that I would join in the dinner conversations if that's what Moishe wanted. The shepherd's pie with gravy was truly excellent. I felt self-conscious that my silence was being noticed while everybody else seemed to be talking happily, but I didn't want to be perceived as sulking. Avril announced that dessert would be served in about ten minutes. After that a game of charades was on the cards followed by a trivia quiz, the thought of which gave me a knot in my stomach.

Maria guided me towards Marty, whom she knew well, of course, and Atsuko who was naturally garrulous, fun loving and easy to talk to but sticking close to Marty in unfamiliar surroundings.

Marty asked me about my studies at NYU and about the job that I'd had and lost. I asked him in turn about public relations at Catholic Charities where he worked with Maria, Atsuko good naturedly making fun of him in our group of four. I was a little surprised to see Hadassah followed by Wilson joining us, such that the dinner party was divided now on generational lines. I began to feel much more at ease in our little group, even with Hadassah there, who was quite interested in the different world Maria inhabited, her job and career, although this quickly switched to movie and music likes and dislikes. She was intrigued by Maria's love of opera, not something that Hadassah knew anything about beyond deprecative clichés.

Avril announced dessert, apple crumble with custard, again from a large pie dish on the countertop and again served by babbling Moishe. She followed the announcement by turning on some 80's disco music with a mesmerizing rhythm which diverted attention from Moishe and set heads nodding and toes tapping in a space that had been discretely cleared earlier.

"He's had a couple of stressful weeks," explained Avril, referring to Moishe. "He's just letting off steam. A parade of critics and reviewers have been streaming through his exhibits, over-analyzing, looking for quotes and filler for column inches." She looked at him solicitously saying: "Moishe dear, you're among friends. You can say what you like about your paintings. Nothing said here will get into print or on somebody's web site."

"In that case I will dance without inhibition," he replied. And so he did, wildly flailing his arms in the air and gyrating his hips.

"C'mon John," he yelled, "let's rock. The Hell with the bastard Salander!" At which the dignified uptight Dr. John Cardozo threw off his jacket and tie and rushed to Moishe's side imitating the former's movements singing along with the female disco singer. Avril rushed in after him followed by Gillian, Atsuko and soon all the party yelling and singing and stamping and trilling. Me too.

I joined in where I could, letting myself go. 'Home at last, home at last' I whispered to myself, 'in my new spiritual home, undefined, indefinable, nebulous, but rock solid in its own terms.'

The evening gave way to coffee with charades. There were six competing teams which were couples pre-chosen by Avril on the basis of - I really don't know, but she usually had her reasons. The team of Maria and Hadassah won. That's right, Avril worked personality matches on the two people that, I flattered myself, could have been rivals for my attention and unable to cooperate. An unexpected side of Hadassah's personality revealed itself as did the couple's superior concentration and determination. I was paired with Marty which turned into a failure matching the success of the former. We couldn't get away from our dreary business techy talk.

The following day Maria told me Gillian Mendez had invited her to share a cab with the Cardozo/Mendez family after the party ended. On the ride home she and Hadassah had exchanged phone numbers and had chatted about the party. She said her mom, Gillian, was mad at her dad, John, for bugging Moishe about Salander and whether he should buy a picture from a Salander-O'Reilly Gallery.

"So, what else did you talk about?" I asked Maria.

"Well," she answered, "Dr. John protested that he wasn't bugging Moishe, he was just asking if he thought Salander had sold the same painting to two different customers, the first having lent a valuable painting back to Salander's gallery."

"So what was Moishe's advice?" I asked.

"That if he did buy a picture from that source he should insist on possession, i.e., take it home, insure it for a very large sum, and not loan it back to the gallery."

"OK, that's all very interesting," I said to Maria, "but what else did Hadassah have to say?"

"Oh, just girl talk," she answered. "You don't think we were talking about you, do you?" she laughed. "Oh, and I told her we're going to Cyprus. She was quite envious but wished us luck."

Chapter 19 - Maria at the Party and After It - Maria

ello again, this is Maria. Ari's version of what went on at Moishe's birthday party is sort of OK, but there are some salient details which will set the record straight.

From our first meeting Avril and I had gotten along well. We liked each other and we both liked Ari, from different perspectives, of course. We both felt protective towards him although, as you know by now, my feelings for him went further and deeper. Knowing that Ari would be at Moishe's party I was certain to attend if asked, and I was asked. There was no direct subway or bus to Moishe and Avril's place, so I packed more formal party clothes in my backpack and walked there through quite a storm. Avril helped me get ready, ironed my dress, and lent me a lab coat for when we prepared the food.

I half expected some coldness or hostility from Hadassah at the party but felt none. She was quiet and agreeable, but I gathered from her mother's comments that this was not typical. The most noticeable thing about her was how she stuck like glue to Wilson who spoke to her for much of the time so quietly that it was inaudible to anyone else. You could see her wordless warm smiles and nods in her responses to him. You could see Hadassah's mother, Gillian, unable to keep her eyes from them.

Hadassah became more animated in the game of charades. At first the game was played according to conventional rules in which teams take turns to mutely act out a word or phrase to be guessed by the others, competitively. Moishe had invented a spoken version which he called "persuade me". In each team of two, one played a parent and the other a child. For example, the child may want an ice cream and the parent refuses to buy one, but each must make five arguments in turn to support their case. The other teams award points to the most original or amusing arguments.

When Hadassah and I discussed how to act out a parent persuading a child to get ready for the first day of school, I acted as the mother and she as the child. She had a serious inventory of creative childish protests and procrastinations which drew laughter from all, and astonishment from her father. I, acting as the mother, alternated between sympathetic, reassuring and ultimately firm. It was difficult keeping a straight parental face dealing with her boiling tantrums some of which may have had a dark side. They appeared to be made in fictitious response to long remembered overbearing coercion which I, as the mother, had supposedly brought to bear. I wondered if I was the only one who noticed, and if Dr. Gillian was feeling any embarrassment at putative insinuations directed at her parenting. Or was it just inventive and funny?

Moishe was paired with Dr. Gillian with mixed results. He had made himself incoherent with wine, enjoying himself immensely, and funny in spite of himself. Although she disguised it well enough, Gillian, whom I believe from observing her, has a competitive nature, had difficulty controlling her exasperation with him. After this I saw her go over to Avril. The two of them appeared for a while to be in a deep discussion. I couldn't hear them on account of the dance music, but she told me what was said the following evening when I came over to help with planning the Cyprus trip. It went something like:

Dr. Gillian: "Hadassah told me that Ari now has an American Catholic girlfriend. That must be her, Maria, that's talking to him now? Nice girl."

Avril: "I would say just 'girlfriend,' the 'Catholic' part of the relationship doesn't really come into it."

Dr. Gillian: "What about for him, Ari, is he comfortable with it?

Avril: "I don't think he's given it a moment's thought."

Dr. Gillian: "Don't you think he should?"

Avril: "Why?"

Dr. Gillian: "Because long term it might get in the way of things.

Avril: "That's for them to figure out."

Dr. Gillian: "Perhaps you could help them?"

Avril: "How?" "Help them do what exactly?"

Dr. Gillian: "Point out to them that if they had children together, they would need to make a choice about whether they were Catholic or something else."

Avril: "Something else?"

Dr. Gillian: "Well, you know, whatever Ari is, or turns out to be.

Avril: "You're not making sense."

Dr. Gillian: "Do I have to spell it out?"

Avril: "Yes. Spell it out."

At that moment there was a call to identify the next charade word and the conversation was hastily dropped. The next day at work Avril and Gillian had lunch together. Gillian had warm words and thanks for the "delightful" party and the shepherd's pie and the apple crumble with custard. Then she asked Avril if she'd thought any more about the future of the Maria and Ari relationship.

Avril was confused by the question. "I can't believe you're asking me this. Just what do you mean? What do you think I should say to Maria or Ari?"

Dr. Gillian: "Well, let me put it this way, we both have children, I know yours are a little older than mine and have left home but the same applies. In both our cases, our children grew up in communities familiar to them; they had an emotional and cultural home, so to speak. If, for argument's sake, Ari and Maria do have children, where will their spiritual home be? You know the Catholic church has quite explicit demands that children born to mixed couples are required to grow up Catholic."

Avril: (spoken with real passion) "There's no law about that. In the first place you're getting way ahead of yourself. In the second place, if they do decide at some point in the future to have children together, it doesn't matter a rat's ass that their children will have no 'spiritual' home. There's community enough these days for decent caring people of all backgrounds."

After taking a breath she continued: "I think that what you're really getting around to telling me is that Ari has no cultural or religious home. Now that the cat's out of the bag you think he's not really Jewish, descended from Jews, from out of the mists of Talmudic legend. He might, you imagine, horror of horrors, turn into a closet Muslim or even some time in the future turn into a vocal Muslim. He might make contact with his biological family, internalize their cause and politics, and go screaming to the media about Israeli crimes real and imagined. Isn't that it? Isn't that your worry? Isn't that why you 'advised' your Hadassah that a relationship with Ari had no future in your snooty Sephardic community?"

Dr. Gillian: "Well, ...er yes, partly, to a certain extent. You must admit there may be some truth in it. In any case I told Hadassah that if she persuaded Ari to convert to Judaism a relationship with him may have my blessing. It seems Ari doesn't want to convert. What does that tell you about him? I would say he doesn't have sufficiently strong feelings for my Hadassah, and that she's well rid of him. And look how quickly he moved on to someone else."

Avril let out a long sigh, calmed herself, leaned back in her chair, took a sip of her coffee and continued: "I dunno Gillian, we're friends and I'd like to keep it that way, but

211

we're not alike. You and I, we grew up on different planets. I get the feeling your advice to Hadassah was somewhat stronger than mere advice. I'm no stranger to 'different' in a relationship, look at me and Moishe.

"Moishe was born in London's East End near the docks and grew up in a working-class neighborhood in an Orthodox Jewish family. That's right, there were many working-class Jews in East London who worked at manual laboring jobs of all kinds. Not your stereo-typical kind of Jewish occupation. However, for most of his adult life he has lived and worked in Israel."

Dr. Gillian: "So what? That's his background. You're not so different.

Avril: "Er, well, even by your lights yes we are. I was born two hundred miles north of him into a medical family. My father was a doctor. And, oh yes, we were Church of England, that is to say, in our parlance, we attended an Anglican church and involved ourselves in that community, and given my father's profession we were prosperous upper middle class, (I hate that expression,) by any standards. I didn't know any Jews while I was growing up and I know very few now. I've travelled widely in my first career as a news photographer, but I've never been to Israel. Moishe and I are both English born, but culturally we couldn't be more different. Our backgrounds and acculturations have never been the slightest hindrance to our relationship, which is, by my confident reckoning, as loving and caring as any.

Dr. Gillian: "Ah yes well er..., I guess I just assumed you were Jewish too. But anyway, you're older now and don't face the same pressures.

Avril: "Pressures? From people like you, you mean? My son has an African American girlfriend and she's lovely."

Dr. Gillian: "I only want what's best for them. I've been around in this world for longer. I can give them advice from experience. So could you if you'd wake up to the problems your son may have later."

Avril: "My former husband was Anglican like me, from a prosperous family local to ours. Now we're divorced. He's still in Yorkshire and he would probably feel the same way as you do about our son's African American girlfriend. Anyway, more to the point, I'm not going to tell my ex. My son can if and when he feels ready. It's his choice not mine. Moishe is a breath of fresh air. He doesn't care about ethnicity or religion. He sees it for what it is, suffocating!"

While Dr. Gillian stared speechless at her, she spoke a little softer, almost to herself. "Although he understands the sense of community and mutual help it can bring." She mused a little more adding: "He loves much of the religious music canon and spends hours looking at religious paintings by the great masters."

Dr. Gillian: "Well that's all very interesting but we're never going to see eye to eye on this, I need to get back to work. By the way, I refuse to be paired with Moishe in any future game of charades."

Avril laughed. "And one thing more, she added as Gillian got up from her seat, "I saw your Hadassah was close with Wilson at the party. Where will their spiritual harmony come from if that relationship prospers?"

She waved a quick bye bye to her friend, who yelled back at her as she walked away, "that's different."

"How so?" Avril yelled back. She sat and thought for a few minutes, then went back to work.

That evening before going to Moishe and Avril's place (I'm going to call it the "atelier" from now on for the sake of brevity), I stopped in to see my mom and dad after work. My mom asked me about my life, of course, which is code for "how are your relationships progressing." "Now let me think," said my mom, "his name is er… yes, I know, that nice young man that works with you at the Charities, Marty? That's right isn't it dear?

"Actually mom, if you must know, if there's a relationship with anybody it would be the young man called Ari that you met briefly when you stopped in at my place the other week."

"Oh yes," she answered, "I think I remember now, sort of. There was one smartly dressed gentleman and another one that was very quiet, wasn't he?"

"That's right mom, it's the quiet one. He'd been having a rough time recently, that's why he was quiet."

"Are things going better for him now? It wasn't a 'rough time' with the police or anything like that he was going through, was it?"

"No mom, it was a crisis of an entirely different nature."

"A romantic crisis?"

"No, not that either, just drop it mom, it's complicated, he's had some misfortune in his life but he's getting over it slowly. I'll tell you the whole story sometime.

I just wanted to give you a heads up that I'm going to Cyprus on vacation in a couple of weeks. I wanted to know if you could take care of my cat?"

"Of course dear, we love Beelzebub. We go way back to when he was a kitten, it will be a pleasure. Your dad's quite the expert cleaning his litter. But Cyprus? Where's that? Why would you want to go there?"

"Get the atlas down, I'll show you on a map. Look here, a lovely place. The south of the island is Greek, and the north is Turkish. We'll be going to the Greek area."

"Well I'm happy for you dear, but I must say it's a long way to go for something Greek. You could go to Tarpon Springs in Florida. Most of the folks there are Greek, and some of them still speak Greek.

"Not really the same thing Mom." I answered, finding the conversation hard work, but she wasn't quite finished.

"Your Aunt Mavis went there last year," she persisted, "she told me that there are lots of little picturesque boats. They're owned by divers who harvest sponges, like, from the seabed just a few miles out offshore, just like they do in Greece. Some of the divers will take you out with them to show you what goes on. And there are lots of lovely restaurants by the docks serving real Greek food."

I was about to lose my cool, but my dad stepped into the conversation. "That will do dear," he said to my mom. Foreign places are always much different and exciting for young people. You know that dear. I know you're anxious about our daughter being so far from home. There are no wars going on in Cyprus to my knowledge, or anything like it. It will be a great experience. She has my total blessing, and she needs yours too, provided of course, that she calls to tell us that she's arrived safely, and she sends us a postcard when she has a few minutes to spare.

I smiled, nodded in agreement with my dad, stood up and put on my jacket in great haste before my mom could dream up any more awkward questions or dumb suggestions. As always, when visiting my mom and dad, it was such a relief to get back out to the sidewalk. There was a spring in my step as I pushed through a stiff damp breeze on my way to see Avril. She was on her own there, busy on the computer looking at Cyprus hotels and rental villas around Paphos.

I told Avril that I'd exchanged phone numbers with Hadassah and that we were on friendly terms. She had walked with me to my apartment door while her parents waited for her in the cab that we shared after Moishe's party. Then she called me later to say how she absolutely loved playing charades with me. She found that acting the part of a rebellious child cathartic, and that my gentle persuasiveness cajoling was a perfect foil for her suppressed anger. She said that if her mother had played that part the Charade turn may have come close to violent.

Then she went on to apologize about the scene she made in a Brooklyn restaurant a while back where she first saw Ari and me talking. She said she'd just come from a screaming clash with her mother who insisted she should not associate with Ari under any circumstances unless he converted to Judaism, and he had to be explicit and unequivocal about his beliefs. Also, he had to renounce any intention of contacting or associating with his biological parents or any biological family members.

She told me that she'd had a crush on Ari when he attended a Rosh Hashanah party at their home in September. It cooled when he showed no interest confirming or even stating he was Jewish. She interpreted that as lack of interest in her but admitted her understanding of his position may have been narrow. She said she liked Wilson who seemed smart and ethnically uncomplicated, and more difficult for her mother to find fault with. In some indiscernible way, though, he was less exciting than Ari. She asked me somewhat mournfully if I thought she was shallow for not standing up to her mother.

"How did you answer her?" asked Avril.

"Well I told her:" 'I can't judge you, I'm not in your position. I don't live with my parents anymore and I don't have to make compromises any more about the way I act and think. I'm a little older than you, my university days are behind me, and I have reasonably paid employment which makes independent living possible, but only just, given the cost of an apartment here in Brooklyn. No, I'm exaggerating. I. we, can afford it OK'

"OK, Let's get on with this," said Avril, "time's a-wastin," and the two of us immersed ourselves in finding and choosing a villa for about two weeks. I'd found some really nice two- and three-bedroom places online. When I showed it to her she asked if I would prefer a room of my own or to share one with Ari?"

217

"You need to ask him." I answered. She looked at me quizzically trying not to laugh which was infectious. "No you don't." I added sharing her laughter. She brushed aside my suggested two- and three-bedroom suggestions and showed me some five- and six-bedroom villas instead. "They're only a little more expensive," she said, "and Moishe and I can cover the extra cost, actually all the cost. This is our gift and Moishe agrees. I asked him and he said as long as he can take his easel and paints with him, he's fine with it."

"OK, five bedrooms if you're paying, but why? You can get a smaller place with all the same luxuries."

"I talked it over with Moshe," she replied. "And any way you look at it, we'll have a lot more space and a private garage to park the car.

"You're losing me." I told her. "What's the point of that?"

"Oh, I'm sorry she said, there have been some developments you don't know about. Ari kept trying to call Anwar, the most communicative of his 'cousins' and after about a week of trying he answered. He said he was in Paphos trying to uncover what had happened."

I stared at Avril while I digested this bit of news. She paused then continued:

"Ari had been missing his family. At my suggestion he emailed his dad then called them and asked them if they would like to come to Cyprus and meet up. They answered with an enthusiastic 'yes'. He spoke to his little sister Hannah. She was crying, he said, but so was Ari. Tears were running down his face. It was really quite moving, he's such a lovely boy, but you know that don't you?"

I nodded silently as tears welled up in me in answer then said: "They would need two rooms max so that makes four. Why five bedrooms?"

"Six." She answered followed by another silence. "Well you keep interrupting me." She continued, in affected irritation at my curiosity, then continued":

"You've heard of the journalist, Shona?" she asked.

"Remind me," I replied, I sort of remembered Wilson had told me about her but at first I couldn't recall in what context. "Oh wait, is she the Israeli journalist that bust open the whole baby mix up and, if truth be told, the creator of this whole big mess. Yes, yes, now I remember who she is. I need to thank her. I never would have met Ari without her."

"Right, she's the one." Avril continued. Ari called her too. He got her phone number from his mom."

"I got the impression his mom didn't like her very much." I said, "but I guess that's understandable. Anyway, go on, what about her?"

"Well Shona is the one person Ari knew, and could trust to contact Nadeem's, that is his Palestinian counterpart's, family."

"And…." I said, but I'd guessed what was coming.

"Cyprus is one of the few places, if not the only place, that's quite close to the whole Middle East mess that people can travel to, from both sides of the endless conflict.

"OK, just give me the short version, you invited his birth mother and she's coming too? Right?

"Right, as is his father and sister," she added."

"And they can get entry visas and all that bureaucratic stuff done in time?"

"That's right too," she continued, "All done, they had help, they have contacts, and since word got out that Nadeem disappeared and might have died, the Islamists have left them alone."

"It's going to be quite a party," I said slowly and thoughtfully.

Chapter 20 - The Journey - Maria

OK, this is me, Maria, I still have lectern, so to speak. Ari's a nervous wreck about the whole Cyprus thing. Moishe has been subdued although Avril suspects he's been thinking a lot about the journey. She says he's going to see his oldest and closest friend after a long separation and is also stressing about what paints and canvasses to take. Avril is cool and organized. She told him to take his paints with him but to buy canvases and any other supplies that he needs when he gets there. On the day of departure I took a cab to Avril and Moishe's place at about three PM, and the four of us took a car together to JFK Airport. There were no direct flights to Cyprus; the first leg of the journey was to London Heathrow and the second, about twenty-three hours later from London Gatwick to Paphos. Avril had reserved two small hotel rooms near Gatwick and a rental car to get us to our villa in Paphos and for subsequent travels for the duration of our stay.

Ari and I were excited about our first visit to London. Avril and Moishe were excited to return to a place they both knew well and loved, which made our one-day visit to the town pretty smooth. I always find clearing customs and immigration exhausting and stressful, and this time was no different. Thankfully there were no complications. We caught the Airport Express train from Heathrow to Paddington, where we switched to the Underground Bakerloo line for a connection to Waterloo station. There we dumped our baggage into lockers, found a Prêt-à-Manger café and the four of us relaxed for the first time after landing. Avril insisted on paying for everything saying she had some British pounds left over from a previous visit that she wanted to spend.

The sense of purpose that the four of us had invested in this journey had no power to speed us on our way. So, in the twenty-three-hour stopover in London we succumbed to the inevitable and relaxed. Since Ari and I had no clue how to fill our time in London we left the planning of it entirely to Avril and Moishe. It is a very busy city, as busy as New York, but there the similarity ends. The streets are not as wide and are, to my eyes at least, chaotically arranged. They're not on a grid, something that my brain after a sleepless night had difficulty in coping with.

Ari and I just followed Moishe who was perfectly relaxed. Avril linked arms with him. The tired New Yorker in me wanted the streets to go North-South and East-West at right angles to one another. But they were like spaghetti on a dish and the buildings as sauce slithering into winding sidewalks which widened and narrowed around ancient walls. We walked beneath a few railway bridges under which market stalls appeared out of nowhere, and suddenly a panorama of the River Thames opened up before us.

"We're on the "South Bank," Moishe said. "We can have a quick look at what's going on here, then catch a boat down the river to Greenwich." We strolled among the crowds along a broad riverside pathway and paused to watch acrobats, buskers, and a variety of performers. It felt like a vacation that would have been better if it had been longer, but the little we did in London was quite memorable.

"This place rocks!" Ari told me as we retraced our steps beside the vast vertical wheel that is the London Eye, crossed Westminster Bridge with the iconic Houses of Parliament building in full view then descended some steps on the other side of the river to embark upon a small tour boat to Greenwich. The commentary on the boat ride was a mix of comedy and history. I couldn't be sure where one ended and the other began. Ari told me his enjoyment of the city was enhanced by the crazy conspicuous diversity of its inhabitants. In that regard it is New York's twin.

At Greenwich Ari became animated at the Cutty Sark museum, the restored fast sailing ship that raced from India to Britain in record time carrying cargoes of tea. Of course! Where else does tea have such urgency? After walking up the hill through Greenwich Park he was further animated at the old brass strip inserted into the cobbles which marked the position of the Prime Meridian outside the Royal Observatory Museum. I hadn't previously experienced this bubbling enthusiasm in him. The museum hilltop afforded views of distant profiles of the city's historical landmarks and of the nearer modern towers Illuminated by the mid-afternoon sun, low in the October sky of this northern latitude.

The love affair with Greenwich continued with a late pub lunch in which Ari hand-pumped a glass of unpressurized beer. He did it from behind the counter at the invitation of a friendly waiter trying to deal with Ari's questions about how the beer was manually pumped from oak cask in the cool cellar to glass with such antiquated equipment. And how could it be so good?

I figured this delightful mood change in Ari must be, at least in part, attributable to the approaching reunion with his family. It was infectious too as Moishe and Avril, brandishing their cameras, enthused about the "quality of the light In London" and joined in nerdy conversations about Coordinated Universal Time for navigation, GMT's successor Avril explained. Knowing London's reputation, I guessed we were fortunate with the weather.

There was, however, one more treat in store, namely, the Greenwich Foot Tunnel, the entrance being right next to the Cutty Sark beneath an iron and glass dome. We eschewed the elevator descending one of the helical staircases to walk for about a quarter mile fifty feet under the River Thames, then about the same again on the Isle of Dogs to Mudchute Station where we caught a train on the Docklands Light Railway. The train wound its elevated way among the towers of the Financial District until we changed to a subway train, called the Underground in London, which in turn connected to Waterloo Station. Here we picked up our suitcases from their lockers and took the train out to Gatwick followed by a short shuttle ride to our hotel.

Having had little sleep the previous night it came easily for me after such a busy and surprisingly pleasant day. Embarkation and the flight out to Paphos was thankfully uneventful. The weather remained clear and Moishe was eager to point out some of the Italian coast and what he believed to be Mount Etna in Sicily, identified by its caldera belching a smokey plume. He also identified the Peloponnese region and several Greek Islands which had the effect of sending Avril to sleep, followed by me, while he and Ari enthused over them.

Passport control at Paphos, I think, was a little worrying for Ari who had withdrawn into himself when the four of us presented ourselves to the official who saw in our party four different names, three American passports but one Israeli passport. He kept looking down at them then looking up at the four of us.

"What is the purpose of your visit?" he asked, looking at Moishe

"I'm here for the most part to paint, and secondly to take a vacation," he answered.

"Is that your profession? A painter I mean, that's how you earn your living?" he asked.

"Yes, I'm an artist, it says so on my passport and there are my paints," he replied pointing to a paint splattered holdall which contained his paints and brushes and a folded easel and stool.

225

Without handing back the passport he turned to Avril and said: "It says here on your passport that you are a physician, is that correct? What kind of physician? Do you specialize?"

"I'm a doctor at New York Presbyterian Brooklyn Methodist Hospital" she answered and would have continued but was cut off by the official saying:

"Thank you" and handed back passports to Moishe and Avril.

Then he looked at me and down again at my passport photo and back again at my face. By this time, I was feeling irritated by his inscrutable mannerisms a few degrees short of being polite but his attention had already turned to Ari.

"The address in your passport says you live in Israel and yet you have travelled here from the United States?" He asked him, then turned back to me and asked:

"You're traveling together?" I nodded and was about to speak when Avril interrupted.

"He lives in New York with us and has done so for nine months. He is attending New York University and we will arrange to have his home address changed when we get back. Now if you don't mind, please give them back their passports so that we can get on with our holiday."

But he wasn't quite finished. He asked where we were staying and for how long but there seemed to be something going on his head. "Welcome to Cyprus," he said with a blank expression as he handed back Ari's and my passport.

"Do you like New York?" he said directly to Ari.

"Yes, I love it. I love the university and my friends and my hosts. I think I will stay there forever," he answered.

"That was all very peculiar." I said as we shuffled past customs control with all our baggage. Thankfully we were not stopped there; two officers seemed to be sharing a joke.

As we made our way to the car rental office I said to Ari, smiling: "You went a bit overboard about New York didn't you?" I could see he was really freaked out and quiet following the passport control experience.

"I think he wanted to hear me speaking English. I hadn't spoken a word until his question. It's just another check. He could have been looking for someone traveling on a fake passport. He was told I was attending NYU, in which case I had to know English well. That's why I said more than I normally would have. I guess my army experience at checkpoints makes me oversensitive to them"

"He was just doing his job." I told him. "Maybe he just wanted to know if you could speak at all," I teased. "I hope you're going to cheer up soon. You were like a different person in London and again when we were flying over Greece."

We found a bank branch within the airport terminal where Moishe and Avril bought Euros. Ari and I followed them; I bought $300 worth and Ari the same. It hadn't occurred to me before then to change money for the local currency.

Once again Moishe and Avril engaged each other in esoteric conversation about the "quality of the light" of the

Eastern Mediterranean. To me it was just bright afternoon sunshine and light breezes wafting the palms and evergreens. There was no ambient urgent buzz of a gigantic metropolis, but a calmer gentler welcome. The car which Avril had reserved turned out to be a Mercedes E350 station wagon and was nice. Really nice in fact, with plenty of room for Moishe's painting gear and all our luggage.

Moishe had found the address of the villa on a map he bought at the airport. I think Google maps was around back then, but he was an old time map and compass man, and I must say quite good at it. Avril drove and he navigated in a smooth operation. It turns out they drive on the left-hand side of the road in Cyprus which didn't seem to present any problems for Avril. Subconsciously I feared a head-on crash and wanted to say move over until I got used to the cars passing one another. Ari reminded me that they drive on the left in London where we'd just been, but I'd hardly noticed. We'd used public transit all the time there.

The key to the villa was in a lock box beside the back door, as described in the rental agreement. It was unbelievably nice. It was situated on a slope which steepened on the driveway side, but on its garden side swooped gently downwards past orchards and vineyards. Other white and pastel-colored villas and bungalows with red tiled roofs nestled among the palms and citrus trees that covered all the lower part of the hill. There was a pool in the well-tended back yard, or garden as they called it, there too were citrus and all manner of flowering trees. A narrow meandering distant beach defined an edge of blue Mediterranean bay, clearly visible beyond palm lined streets and a larger distant freeway, the hum of the traffic being just about audible but not intrusive. Inside there was an enormous kitchen and even larger area for dining and relaxing with a TV. There was no computer, but there was Wi-Fi. Ari and Avril had brought laptop computers with them. I didn't have one and Moishe deliberately left his at home.

Avril didn't hesitate to choose the master bedroom for herself and Moishe, then asked me which one I wanted, meaning which one we, me and Ari wanted. I chose one with a view of the Mediterranean.

A three-ring binder on the kitchen counter was full of useful information which I consulted immediately to find a food store. I was starving as were the others. We departed the villa to get food barely fifteen minutes after arriving. It seems banal to talk about food shopping but really, I was quite taken with it. There was a wide selection of fresh vegetables, locally grown we were told. There were familiar and unfamiliar food brands on the shelves and noticeably more Greek and British brands that others. There was wine a-plenty, most of which was local Cyprus produced and recommended heartily by a helpful store employee whose English was only slightly accented.

Preparation of our evening meal started out happy and social, I felt. It was a smorgasbord, salad, nuts, cheeses, bread, hummus etc., "Something for everybody," Avril explained. Ari was mostly quiet but he joined in preparing salad and seemed, while doing it, content to be bossed around by Avril, his apparent substitute mom. I wondered how he would react to having his real mom, or should I say two real moms in the house to boss him around? And then a more serious thought struck me as I prepared some fruit salad. What would any of our expected visitors think about Ari and me sharing a room?

Moishe attended to drinks. He opened a couple of bottles of recommended Cyprus wine, sniffing and fussing, self-absorbed and ridiculous, then placing glasses and bottles on a smallish table in what I figured was a breakfast nook. Given his sweet nature his eccentricity was easily forgiven, I'd grown used to it. The table was big enough for the four of us to eat in, and oblique to the sun, which was setting over the darkened sea, visible without glare, illuminating the pinkened space, as if inviting conversation in a calm evening ambience.

"Get us some water too, please, Moishe dear," said Avril, "we may need a choice of how we quench our thirst," she added in a gently sardonic way that characterized much of how she addressed Moishe, without appearing to give any offense at all. I'd brought in some highly colored twigs of bougainvillea from the yard and placed them in a glass to decorate the table.

Moishe was the first to comment on the noticeably different flavor of the pie. "British ingredients," he said. Avril nodded in response. It was good. Not better or worse, just different. There was a brief silence while we subconsciously savored and absorbed the flavor. Then I asked out of the blue:

"Ari, I know you're looking forward to seeing your family again but what do you think about meeting your biological family?"

"It's a funny thing," he answered, appearing to make light of it. Then he continued slowly: "I and they, I mean we, would always be curious about each other. I guess it may not go well but it has to happen. I'm finding it difficult to get my head around them being so foreign. I'm moderately competent in their language but not totally so. Equally I must be so foreign to them. Shona told me that my bio dad speaks some Hebrew but not very well. My mom hardly at all and my bio little sister, good grief! I don't even know her name, but I'm guessing her Hebrew might be quite good."

"Do you think they'll be shocked by us sharing a room?" I asked him.

"Guess so," he whispered looking down on his dinner plate and his barely touched pie. "I wouldn't care about my Israeli family, I know they'd get used to it pretty quickly, they'd have to, and anyway they're not Orthodox and they're broad minded about such things. But the Palestinians, they're so different culturally. I met a lot of them during my army service. You remember what Nadeem said in his texts about surreptitiously meeting his girlfriend, just meeting. Just meeting without permission was proscribed. What was her name? er...Hiba, that's it. Jesus Christ! oh, I didn't mean that, not sure why I said it, not something I should be saying in my position."

"Listen my boy, Ari," Moishe said suddenly and softly from behind his wine glass, "firstly, we'll stand behind you, whatever happens. Secondly, all of the people who will arrive here the day after tomorrow have lost something. Let's make sure we have a large dollop of forgiveness to dispense for anyone that's steps out of our perceived norm. And thirdly, a young man your age, exactly your age, and the natural son of your own mother has disappeared and may have lost his life, and if so, possibly at the hands of bigots of some kind."

"We can hope for the best but can't realistically expect anything better than knowing just what happened to him, and in the worst case where his remains are buried. If we find anything that sheds light on his disappearance the police will need to know and so will the rest of the world. Wilson's journalist friend Shona may be able to help there."

Avril put her hand affectionately on Moshe's.

Ari and I slept together that night savoring and enjoying our union. It had already become implicit from the dinnertime conversation that to avoid offending our expected visitors, we would not be able to be together like that for a week at least. Not a tragedy, I thought, but why hide such a thing? I smiled to myself when I remembered that my own Catholic religion would not condone our sharing a bed.

Ari would have his own room. Each of the two sets of parents would have a room of their own and the children that came with them could share a room. I couldn't help thinking that Avril realized this but said nothing when she first booked the villa insisting on six bedrooms. She left me to work out why. I smiled again to myself when I thought that Ari would never have worked that one out, for all his genius and nerdiness in other fields.

Moishe asked at the grocery store and Ari looked on the internet the following morning for an artist supply store in Paphos for blank canvases for Moishe's paintings. The nearest suitable store, it appeared, was in Limassol to where Avril said she and Moishe would drive, and Ari and I were welcome to go with them. We had the time to visit there and in Avril's words "an excellent cover, if needed, for whatever else we felt like investigating on the way."

Of course we would go with them, but the first stop was going to be at the District Administration Office in Paphos. If Nadeem had died in Cyprus, and his body had been found, there would be a death certificate. If he had been identified it would be filed under his name.

The four of us arrived at the counter, where a helpful official printed a pdf application for a death certificate copy. Five Euros was the fee for the certificate itself. The official's English was fluent but the questions on the form were all in Greek. He helpfully printed a second blank form where he wrote the questions translated into English in their respective answer boxes. Then he advised that since the clerk who would do the search was out, to come back tomorrow having completed the form in English.

Blank forms in hand, Moishe passed them to Avril and sat himself in the driver's seat. "The A6 highway will take us directly all the way to Limassol to get my art supplies," he said. "On the way we could stop into a cafe to get lunch. First we have to find the A6 highway though."

"You're lost aren't you dear?" said Avril. "That's the second time I've seen that church, and pretty as it is, we don't need to see it a third time. Never mind the A6, let's eat."

"But we're not out of Paphos yet," he replied, sounding a little frustrated. "Oh well, no worries, we can stop anywhere. Look, there's a cafe over there with outdoor seating, near the church."

Avril had brought the map with her and spread it out on the only available table. "We are out of Paphos," she said to Moishe. "We're in Geroskipou, and the beautiful little church over there is called Agia Paraskevi."

"It is beautiful, isn't it?" said a voice on a table near us, "we love it here."

"I can see why," I said, joining the conversation. "I didn't see a sign or any indication that we'd left Paphos and are now in a different town?"

"You can't tell going from one to the other." said the voice "It's like all one town but the locals identify strongly with either Paphos or Geroskipou," said the voice, as its owner reached out to shake my hand. We mutually introduced the four of us to the four at the neighboring table who turned out to be two retired couples. One couple was originally Cypriot and local, but had lived and worked in England for many years and the other, English. All four of them were garrulous and inquisitive and noticeably intoxicated. Spiros, the Cypriot guy, saw Avril was holding a form with Greek writing and asked her if she speaks Greek, and if not, what use is the form to her?

She showed him the form with the questions, hand written in English, to which he asserted that it was normal for the desk clerk to know English, however, the clerk dealing with the forms in the back office may not, and there could be a delay in processing a request for a death certificate. He offered to translate the answers that we gave him into Greek, and write it in the forms.

"All we know is his name and that he disappeared recently in this area." Avril told him. "We don't even know that he died, but if he had it would be quite recent, only two to three weeks ago. Except for his name most if not all the answer boxes will be blank."

"In that case you certainly need my help." Spiros answered

"Forgive me," said Avril, "but just how do you propose to help us? Wouldn't the officials at the office simply do a document search on the name for the original certificate, if it exists, and then give us a copy?" When our gyros and salads arrived the conversation reverted to food for a while. Moishe refused an offer of wine on account of needing to drive after lunch.

"I know the officials here." Spiros said. "It's not like England. Oh, er you sound English by the way, but... this young lady...er Maria does not, American or Canadian I presume? Anyway, I grew up with some of these officials' parents. If you don't have a lot of time, like six or eight weeks, and you don't have all the information to hand about the death, then, certainly you need help, especially if you cannot prove the presumed deceased is related to any one of you. Is he or she related to one of you?"

"We accept," butted in Moishe, but can we continue this conversation tomorrow? I must get to Limassol to get my art supplies. I think the store closes at five. I'm an artist by trade, you see, and I have a limited time here to paint."

"Certainly," answered Spiros, glad to help.

"Can we meet here at, say, 10:00AM tomorrow? Asked Avril.

"Look forward to it." He answered. "Could you give me the guy's name now by any chance? I might go over there and do a bit of preliminary digging."

While Ari looked down at his phone, Avril Moishe and I looked at each other spontaneously. Since none of us thought of a reason he shouldn't, all three of us answered in unison: "Nadeem Mohammed." Out of respect for the subject of the conversation Spiros was expressionless but flinched slightly and raised his eyebrows.

With Moishe in the driver's seat and Avril's assiduous navigating through this impossible antique maze of a town we found the A6 highway without a problem, and drove East towards Limassol through rocky hills, vineyards, orchards, and goat pastures, and near ancient ruins, now tourist destinations. The highway also passed through the UK sovereign territory of Akrotiri. The value of the enclave now to the Brits is the location of a large RAF base, close to the Middle East cauldron where they need to deploy from time to time." He paused then added, "Not that I approve of that, or the Empire from which it descends." Avril made a rasping fart-like sound which I was at pains to interpret as Moishe rambled on: "We're passing the ruins of Kourion, an ancient city state with a Roman Amphitheater," he commented, "I was thinking I might bring my painting stuff here."

After leaving Akrotiri she was soon navigating the maze of ancient and modern streets of Limassol to find the artist supply store where Moishe bought four 16 X 20-inch unbleached pre-primed canvases, pre-stretched onto frames and back stapled to allow for keying or re-stretching.

We took a short drive around part of the town before heading back to the A6 highway. My brief impression of the place was of a divinely romantic but rapidly modernizing city which may seem incongruous, but that's what I saw. Apartment homes near the waterfront were stepped back from the beach by a palm filled linear park about a hundred yards wide which suggested, to me at least, some beguiled planning. I could not help thinking of Ari and me strolling carefree, hand in hand, among the palms in the pink glow of sunset. But there he was sitting next to me, rigid and nervous and silent, a mere hundred and fifty miles from his weird tumultuous birthplace.

Chapter 21 - The Death Certificate - Maria

It's still me, Maria talking. Ari's in a funk which he bursts out of from time to time. He's worse than unsure what to think about meeting his biological family. He told me he used to believe in his country, his ancestors, and the culmination of their determination to survive in beautiful triumphant permanent Israel. Now every time he remembers who his biological mother is, the ground beneath his feet feels unstable and his patronage, parentage and identity are slipping away. When he thinks of her as a real person and how much she must have suffered his heart melts and he wants to cry for her. How could he possibly meet their expectations? On some level, he and they are in enemy camps which have no empathy for one another. It was gratifying for me though, that through his misery, his affection for me shone, never letting his mood reflect anger.

We kept our appointment with Spiros the following morning, who, through local connections, had already obtained a copy of Nadeem's death certificate. "I just had to pay the five euros," he said gravely. Moishe reached for his wallet but Spiros waved away the offer. "No, no you don't have to pay me," he said. It was my pleasure, it's the least I can do."

"In which case let me buy you coffee," answered Moishe as the waiter arrived."

"That would be most welcome, especially accompanied by a croissant," answered Spiros. Moishe ordered a bowl full of croissants and butter and preserves to go with our coffees and I secretly gave thanks to my Catholic God that the French had supplanted the British when it came to breakfasts in this part of the world. Not all croissants are the same.

The sun was peeking out of an azure sky over bulbous domes of the byzantine church across the street at an angle that defeated the shade umbrellas and sparkled in a reflection of Spiros's sunglasses. He handed to Moishe the completed form with its macabre details in Greek, translated by Spiros, frustratingly vague and dreadfully simple. Cause of Death: Drowning. Place of Death: Offshore South West Cyprus and written in: 'precise location unknown'. Date of Death: Estimated first week of November 2004, followed by a similar addendum: 'precise time and date unknown.'

Gloom descended upon us as the last fading hope of finding him alive evaporated. Spiros turned the palms of his hands skywards and opened his arms and said: "I am so sorry. I knew about this yesterday when you told me his name. I thought it would be best for you to wait to see an official document rather than to take me at my word, complete stranger that I am."

Among us Avril was first to speak. "Is there anything else you can tell us?" she asked. "Do you know where he's buried?"

"Oh, right, yes I do," he answered, "it was something of a local news event. I and about thirty other people went to his funeral in sympathy for the poor lonely fellow whose body was unclaimed. We knew his name and the college he attended from a very faded student ID card the police found in the back pocket of his jeans. He had no wallet and no passport on him. The name of the college was in English alongside other Arabic script. The police found a phone number online and followed up by calling the college where he was studying in East Jerusalem."

"You suspected when you met us yesterday that we were in some way connected to this news story?" asked Moishe. "I see now why you were willing to help us."

"Well yes," answered Spiros. "This caught the attention of our quiet little town. There was a lot of sympathy for the poor fellow."

"And a lot of curiosity, to put it gently I might add?" suggested Moishe.

"Never mind all that" interrupted Avril. "What did the college tell them?"

"Nothing at first. The police, who spoke in English to a college official, told the local press that the college was very suspicious and very cautious, citing their privacy policy and other 'unspecified security issues'".

"At first?" prompted Avril intoning a question to Spiros.

"The college was persuaded to send a messenger to Nadeem's home with a request that someone call the Paphos police. The college didn't know that Nadeem's father had a phone."

"And then?" she asked.

"Nadeem's father called the Paphos number, as requested, which was answered by a desk sergeant who did not know a word of Arabic, and nor, unfortunately, did Nadeem's father know barely a word of English and certainly not any Greek. It was deeply frustrating."

We stared at Spiros in silence.

"The following day," Spiros continued after a pause, "I remember from the report…" he said very slowly, trying to remember, that a man identifying himself in English as the dead man's cousin, called the same Paphos police number but his English was terrible. The police told him to call again tomorrow, by which time the police would have found an Arabic speaker to take his call. He seemed to understand that and agreed."

"Do you remember his name?" Avril continued her interrogation.

"It's in the press report, You could maybe get back copies of the newspaper but unless one of you knows some Greek it may not be much use to you. Anyway, I think his name began with an A, something like, Andrew or Anthony."

"Anwar?" I asked.

"Yes, I believe that could be it. What of it?" answered Spiros. "The guy called again the following day, as agreed,

241

and a really weird thing happened. The two so-called Arabic speaking guys at each end of the phone call couldn't understand one another.

"I know him, the Palestinian Arab guy that called." I said, "and so does Ari." Ari looked up from his phone and nodded in agreement.

"So where is he buried?" asked Ari, finally joining the conversation.

"Right here in Geroskipou," Spiros answered. "You know, here in Cyprus you have to pay for a burial plot, you have to - sort of - rent it. We had a collection in the town to pay for the plot and a small modest headstone, but eventually the cemetery may want more money."

"Never mind all that for now," said Avril, "just take us there."

Spiros drove to the cemetery and we followed him in our rental car. Many of the gravesites were expensive looking family tombs, decorated with a variety of Greek and Byzantine crosses, carvings, and insignia. Spiros walked past them along a deeply shaded footpath beneath trees that had rich oily-looking green leaves a bit like a magnolia but not so tall. When we came out of the shade into a smallish rectangle of modest Christian graves, there, standing next to a bare headstone was a small man, slim and wiry with a dark complexion further darkened by the sun, black-brown eyes and dark hair. His clothes looked dirty and worn. He had about a week's beard growth. His wavy hair was disheveled, and he looked like he needed a shower.

At the bottom of the headstone was a note in a zipped plastic bag staked into the ground. On it were the deceased's name and a request to call the police phone number if anyone had information. I saw Ari's jaw drop as he mouthed in surprise: "Anwar, what are you doing here?

Anwar was just as surprised as we were and stared at us, unable to speak. "Do you know him? Spiros asked him in Greek, not waiting for an introduction. "We learned from his student ID that he's Palestinian so we knew he could be Christian or Muslim, but we didn't know which. As you see, all the other graves have crosses." It was easy to see Anwar didn't understand a word, so Spiros repeated the question in English

"Spiros," I said, momentarily forgetting that only Ari and I had ever met him, though Moishe and Avril knew about him. "He speaks no Greek and very little English. You'd better tell us what you asked him so Ari can repeat it in Arabic." He did, and Ari did, and all shook hands.

Anwar, who had, like us, arrived at Paphos and Geroskipou too late for the funeral, was plainly upset. He asked in broken English why Nadeem, a Moslem, had been buried in a Christian grave. At this point Ari stepped in again, explaining in Arabic what had happened. Anwar was visibly touched when told of the community involvement in his funeral.

"Do you know how Nadeem died?" asked Moishe.

He began in faltering English and then continued in Arabic, pausing for Ari's translation.

"Wait," said Moishe after just a few seconds. "Do the police know what you're telling us? In any case we want all the details. Come and have lunch with us."

243

"Ok if I come along too?" asked Spiros. Five of us loaded into the Mercedes station wagon and drove back to our villa, stopping at the grocery store on the way. It would have been convenient to go to a restaurant but we didn't want to be overheard. Spiros followed in his car, came into the grocery store too and made some helpful suggestions about lunch, including and especially which wine to buy.

As soon as we were home inside the villa Avril told Ari to get Anwar and take him to one of the unoccupied bedrooms. Avril followed. There she threw Moishe's robe on the bed and told Ari to explain to Anwar, who was plainly embarrassed about his appearance, to take a shower. Also, she told Ari, if he wants to shave, lend him your razor. When finished, tell him to return to the kitchen in Moishe's robe. His clothes will be clean and ready in about an hour and a half. She enlisted me to wash his clothes, which I did without a word, feeling slightly intimidated by her doctor's take-control demeanor and grossed out by Anwar's icky clothes.

"We want to know what he knows," she explained. "You catch more flies with honey than with vinegar."

Anwar emerged after about half an hour, clean shaven, his hair combed flat and Moishe's robe wrapped around him almost twice and dragging on the floor. We somehow remembered not to offer him an alcoholic drink and a Coca Cola with ice was accepted with gratitude. It was Ari's turn now to step up, "lose your sulky mood," I told him, "and charm this guy," since he was the only one of us who could communicate anything more complicated than asking for the time. I hoped that was not too crudely expressed but treating my dear Ari with kid gloves all the time can get

244

tiresome. In any case Ari needed no prompting. Judging by his mannerisms and a rediscovered smile, he asked Anwar something like: "Feeling better now?" The two of them continued happily in Arabic with only the occasional place name recognizable to our English-familiar ears.

Lunch by consensus was another help-yourself affair. Several pairs of hands laid out various salads, vegetables, hummus, corn and potato chips, set out on the kitchen counter. What's going on, Ari?" Avril asked. What does Anwar know about Nadeem?"

"He says thank you very much for the food and that Moishe's robe is too long," Ari replied.

"What else"? She asked.

"When will his clothes be ready?"

"In about twenty minutes, what else?"

"He wants to borrow a toothbrush."

"OK, take mine," she answered as Moishe shook his head at her, "Wash it carefully and pour mouthwash over it. It's the yellow one in my bathroom cabinet. There's toothpaste there too."

The two of them disappeared again in the direction of the bedroom. Then Ari reappeared.

"OK funny man, spill the beans." I said to Ari.

"What?" he said holding up the palms of his hands. Irritating though it was, in another way his lighter mood was a relief. Then he continued: "He said he travelled to Cyprus on an Israeli passport which has been stolen."

"Who travelled to Cyprus on an Israeli passport, Nadeem or Anwar?"

"Both of them, but Anwar came here a few weeks after Nadeem, of course. He said Nadeem's killers stole Nadeem's passport before he (Anwar) arrived in Cyprus. And when Anwar caught up with them, Nadeem had already disappeared."

"Did he tell the police?" asked Spiros.

"Slow down, no he didn't tell the police," answered Ari. There's a lot of ground to cover and I don't know all of it yet. He says the two guys that came to New York with him that we called Big-beard and little-beard, they tricked Nadeem."

"How does he know all this?" Asked Avril, "If Nadeem had already disappeared when Anwar arrived in Cyprus."

"OK, let's be clear. Nadeem disappeared twice. First from his home in East Jerusalem when the Jihadi guys went looking for him, tricking Anwar to help them, and a second time after he was located in Cyprus. The beard guys thought he'd gone to America at first and could find him through me, even suspecting he may be living at my place. Inadvertently I did help them because I was texting and emailing him in Cyprus by that time and I was quite open about what was going on."

"The day they left my apartment they'd gone out to the airline office to switch their return destination to Cyprus. This cost them, of course, but they were not as hard up for cash as they'd claimed. They dumped Anwar at this point who could not afford to alter his round-trip ticket and who ended up back in East Jerusalem. It took him a couple of weeks to scrape together a loan for an airline ticket to Cyprus."

Getting back to Nadeem though, at first he lived rough in Cyprus. He stopped calling his father a day or two after his arrival since he had nowhere to charge his phone. He resumed contact when he had a place to stay. To get Nadeem's address from his father the Jihadi beards used threats concerning Nadeem's family members, insisting all the while that they did not mean to hurt Nadeem, to the contrary they meant to welcome him back to his community and assist him in his journey there, whatever that meant."

"Interesting, dear Ari," I said, "what kind of treatment would you have received from these people if you'd gone with them to Cyprus or Jerusalem? If they could threaten Nadeem why not you?"

"Oh, good grief," answered Ari with a slight smile of adolescent bravado creeping into his expression at everybody's confusion. That didn't happen, so let's just get back to Anwar's phone call to the Paphos police. The question is, 'why couldn't the two Arabic speakers understand one another?' "Well, this is the difficult bit," he continued, suppressing a laugh at this desperately sad situation. "It seems like the Arabic spoken in Cyprus now is unintelligible to other Arabic speakers. I believe it's called Maronite Arabic and frankly I'd never heard of it and very few people speak it anymore. The young Greek policeman dealing with it at Paphos was not aware that it was different from any other Arabic."

There was another silence in the room which Anwar walked back into at that moment, flashing his freshly brushed regular teeth.

"Your brush by sink." He said to Avril.

"Maria dear," said Avril, "would you mind getting Anwar's clothes for him. I think they're finished in the dryer."

I surprised myself in how willingly I could follow orders from Avril. It was quite contrary to my nature. I brought back Anwar's clothes from the tumble dryer which he accepted gratefully and disappeared into another room to dress. When he reappeared with Moishe's robe over his arm he asked, via Ari, if there was anything in the house that he could use to clean his dusty shoes which he'd left with footwear outside the door. I stared back at Ari in response which was enough to send him and Anwar diving into closets looking for shoe cleaning tackle. We talked over what we had just heard until Ari came back, then I picked up my questioning where I had left off:

"So…," I said, "You told us Anwar had just found Nadeem's apartment above the restaurant with two Jihadi guys inside it, what then?"

Chapter 22 - Kidnap - Maria

I looked at Ari, now sitting next to Anwar. He seemed to have been numbed into silence, so I said to him, again: "Anwar had just found Nadeem's apartment above the restaurant. There were two guys inside it, the ones he'd travelled to New York with a few weeks earlier, and by this time must have figured their goals may be not entirely in Nadeem's interest. What did he do?"

Anwar looked at me as if he understood me, but Ari translated anyway, as he did with the replies. The going was slow but it was clear. Anwar talked thoughtfully as if trying to get the details right and Ari did the same with the translated version as he looked back at me. Spiros, Avril and Moishe listened intently too when Ari began in English: "Well," he said, "Anwar asked them what happened to Nadeem, of course, and what were they doing in his apartment, and how was he even able to afford an apartment? It wasn't luxurious by any means, but it was modestly comfortable. He said the two Jihadists there were reasonably friendly. The first thing they told him was that they were leaving before dawn next morning. They were not coming back; he could have the apartment, (which belonged to Nadeem's employer,) if he wanted it, as if it were theirs to give.

Anwar asked them why they were leaving so early? They answered that they had done what they came to accomplish and thought the Mossad might be after them.

"Oh Jesus Christ!" interrupted Moishe with a rhetorical question as Anwar walked back into the room, "What could they, the effing Mossad want out of this?"

Thus the question - translation - answer - translation session continued with Anwar who seemed ready to trust us after all our friendly treatment of him. I wasn't sure what the Mossad was so Ari explained that it was Israel's version of the CIA, their security service. The startling revelation that they might be chasing the two guys installed in Nadeem's apartment led to a repeat of Moishe's question, this time in non-rhetorical form: "Why did these Jihadi guys think the Mossad was interested in them?"

Anwar replied: "The Mossad got a tip from one of their informers in East Jerusalem that Nadeem was targeted by the Jihadists for ransom. The Jihadists in turn realized that their intentions might have leaked because of all the buzz that Nadeem's case was generating in their community. Quite simply, too many people knew about it. If the ransom was refused by the Israeli government or his newly discovered Israeli family he would, they admitted, likely be killed. Their commitment or fanaticism or whatever you want to call it could not let them leave Nadeem to find a new life in Cyprus. Israel, on the other hand, may have let him be, except it would do all it could to prevent his assassination.

His limited foreign language skills notwithstanding, I was impressed with Anwar's sophisticated narrative. And listening to Ari translating my next question I reflected briefly on my own limited foreign language skills. Then I asked him how did Nadeem get himself an apartment? He can't have had much money.

Anwar replied: "The Jihadi guys told me they talked a lot with Nadeem in an effort to get him back to East Jerusalem or the West Bank voluntarily. They were quite open in their objectives. They thought I would understand and sympathize with them, talking to me as if I was a collaborator. They were, at some level, simply naive. In the course of coaxing Nadeem to return to Palestine they learnt a lot about his stay in Cyprus and relayed it to me conversationally. They told me (Anwar) that Nadeem knew English well and talked himself into casual jobs doing yard work and fruit picking for a few weeks while living rough.

"He did not have a work or residence permit but figured he could maybe get one in time, after learning how to apply for one. One of his jobs was working for a restaurant owner, weeding his herb garden and clearing some dead olive tree branches to chop and store for winter firewood. When the olive grove was cleaned up the restaurant owner offered Nadeem a job washing dishes at his restaurant and paid him a large part of his wages in lieu of rent for the empty apartment above the restaurant.

"How did the Jihadists attempt to persuade him to return?" I asked.

Anwar replied: "They were not explicit in their methods. They told me the outline and I made some guesses to fill in the gaps. They had sharply contrasting personalities. One of them, slight, bearded and slim, remember him? Guess not, you had other things on your mind. He appeared gentle in his demeanor, an academic or professor, well spoken, devoid of slang and profanities in his speech, and deeply religious. The other was tall and stooped. He was also bearded with long shaggy hair, unclipped nose hair and an outward slant in his brown-green eyes so you could not tell exactly where he was looking, and he didn't speak much. He had a gold Rolex on his black-haired left wrist which he kept looking at, more to admire the watch than to know the time. When he did speak it was to emphasize something that had already been said by the other."

"OK, but how did they attempt to persuade him?" I persisted, "and obviously they didn't succeed because he's six feet under, isn't he?" I added trying not to be annoyed at the slow progress.

Anwar: "Well actually they did, partly, succeed." He paused to gather his thoughts. "The arguments were dark and I'm embarrassed to repeat them."

"Go on," I said, "we weren't born yesterday."

Anwar replied: "They told him that every time Israeli settlers stole another hilltop from villagers, every time a Palestinian was stopped at a checkpoint in their own country, every time the Israeli army took away another young freedom fighter and imprisoned him forever, every time an Israeli tank rumbled down a village street breaking the paving stones and belching acrid diesel fumes into modest kitchens, every time a jet screamed overhead and seconds later a bomb exploded hitting a Palestinian target..."

"That's enough 'every time,'" I interrupted, "then what?"

Anwar replied: "Well - then some of our people would wonder where his loyalties lay. Then, our people, knowing about his Jewish birth, some of them would wonder if he had informed on some brave fighter that was fleeing from the Israelis. Then If he did well financially they would wonder if his money came from Israel. Then if he married his girlfriend some of her people, some of her own family even, would disown her too, and their children. It would never end. Never. If he ever got a job in the West Bank he would have a problem keeping it. Not even if there would be peace. Because it would be a cold peace. And in any case, there hadn't been any real lasting peace in Palestine for a hundred years, and there might never be."

"But Anwar!" I almost screamed, "you're making the argument that he should not go back to East Jerusalem or Palestine."

Anwar: "No, I'm making the argument that they, the Jihadists made, that he should submit to capture by the Jihadists and subsequent ransom. It would have advantages for him. First some of the ransom money would go to his family. Second, rough treatment by the Jihadists would stoke sympathy in Israel for him, and it would be implicit that payment should be made to bring him home to his own people. His own people, meaning Israeli people, would see a greater need for him to be rescued, than if he were to just

253

show up somewhere in the heart of Israel, telling all he had changed sides and wished to be accepted into his mother country. They would be suspicious of that."

"Is that it?" I asked.

Anwar replied: "No, that's just half of it.

"And the other half?" I asked.

Anwar replied: "The other half is that he would never find the peace and security he craved in Cyprus. The Jihadists would always want him. If this attempt failed there would be another one, and for each attempt that failed he would still be regarded as cash in the bank, to be withdrawn when the need arose. If the finances of the Jihadist movement were particularly strained they would make more desperate and dangerous attempts to kidnap him."

"Is that it?" I asked again.

Anwar replied: "Not quite. The scholarly one insinuated that by reason of his natural birth mother and father, he was racially incapable of being a true Muslim. Being Jewish is a racial thing to some people, and something deep within his soul would always pull him to Israel and his fellow Jews, just as he, the Jihadi guy had an immutable Muslim soul that would follow the great prophet Mohammed, no matter how his conscious intellect informed his actions."

"That's a lot of twaddle!" I couldn't help saying. I watched Ari hesitate before translating that for Anwar. I watched Anwar's face for a reaction, but he'd understood me before Ari spoke and sighed deeply before the translation ended.

254

Anwar continued: "Look, we Palestinians don't all think like the Jihadists, maybe one in ten of us thinks like them, but one in ten is enough to poison the well of peace. The Jihadists are constantly helped in their case by Israeli provocations. It must be, in fact I know it is exactly the same dynamic in Israel. Most Israelis want peace, I know they do, I have friends among them. But when thousands of Iranian-built rockets fall on Sderot, for example, even though most of us hate the idea, it's easy for Jewish fanatics to demonize all Palestinians. Think for a moment why we're all here. It's all about a Jihadist atrocity twenty some years ago when Nadeem's and Ari's mothers were injured by a Jihadi bomb planted on a bus. And every time the matter is brought up by an Israeli news bulletin it stokes hatred and distrust again and again and again forever."

There was a heavy silence in the room again. Anwar was an articulate and gentle man. I recalled the hostility and suspicion I felt for him the first time I met him in New York but now I was filled with admiration for him. To look at him you would believe he earned his living as a farm laborer. I wondered if that was true but refrained from asking him. Ari's continuous translations were amazing.

Moishe and Spiros were sipping silently on their wine watching and listening. Avril was listening too, hanging on every word.

I broke the silence by asking Anwar if he'd had enough to eat. He nodded and said thank you. Ari pointed out some hummus and flatbread and salads that would be familiar to him and got him a glass of ice water from the spigot on the fridge.

"So," I said, "I gather the Jihadi guys persuaded Nadeem to go with them after all that?"

Anwar replied: "That's right, but they had to work out how they were going to get back to Palestine. Although they were minor operatives, the two Jihadi guys were known to Israeli security services. They believed the risk of the three of them on the same flight was too great. Nor could they travel separately, fearing Nadeem would change his mind mid journey or on re-entry to Israel. Alternative return flight destinations could have included a Lebanese or Syrian airport, but they had security issues of their own and the same issue that Nadeem might tell a different story on landing.

What followed was Anwar's monologue, carefully and slowly translated by Ari with only the bare details, but my imagination filled in the scenes of Nadeem's terrifying last day and night. It had been casually narrated to Anwar, mostly by Little-beard, as they waited for nightfall having nothing more to do than talk to Anwar. Little-beard admitted all to Anwar, frankly and shamelessly, confident of the righteousness of his cause, regarding Anwar as a sympathizer, or at least not hostile to their cause.

Here's Anwar's story from my notes:

They had planned to steal a boat and had a vague plan to beach the boat somewhere in South Lebanon and then make contact with local Jihadists to help them get back to the West Bank. They would not allow Nadeem to return to Jerusalem. Stealing a boat that could make the one-hundred-and-fifty-mile passage was not an easy task, nor for that matter was the passage. They made Nadeem negotiate with his landlord the temporary stay of his two guests in his room above the restaurant. He had no choice; they would have been discovered anyway coming and going and he risked losing his job if he attempted to deceive his landlord. The smart Jihadi, Little-beard, had some knowledge of small boat equipment and an idea about how to navigate the passage, but first they had to get a boat. Then they had a stroke of luck.

While dreaming up a plan gazing out of Nadeem's upstairs window, they happened to notice a family of five board an airport taxi right outside an expensive looking home. They also noticed a large pleasure boat on a trailer half hidden in the home's leafy driveway. They guessed correctly that the family would be away for a while and there was likely to be a capable towing vehicle in the triple door garage. They broke into the home that same night, found a set of keys which included a vehicle key, but they did not take the vehicle, yet. They figured that if they drove it around the neighborhood in daylight, local people might recognize that it was not being driven by its owners, and raise the alarm.

With money they 'borrowed' from Nadeem they rented a scooter. They had to pay a large deposit because they didn't use a credit card. Then they bought several five-gallon gas cans from a local hardware store. The big guy drove and the little guy rode pillion carrying the cans whose handles were tied together with string, to a local gas station where they filled them. Then they did the same, again and again but each time at different gas stations, until the closet space under the stairs at Nadeem's apartment where they stored them, was full.

In midafternoon the same day while Nadeem was out at work downstairs at the restaurant, they went through all his belongings. They found and took his passport and all bits of paper or anything that Nadeem might have used to identify himself. Then they departed on their scooter to reconnoiter the coastline East of Paphos to find a suitable boat launch-ramp. After finding one they went to a nearby beach and made a bonfire of Nadeem's passport and all else they had found among his meager possessions. Then they went back to the apartment and waited.

Immediately after dark Little-beard drove the scooter up to the house and, as expected, found a large SUV equipped with a trailer hitch. He returned to the restaurant in it, loaded the fuel that he'd previously stored under the stairs into it, then returned to the boat and loaded the fuel under the boat's weather cover. Out of an abundance of caution he used the scooter to return once again to Nadeem's apartment above the restaurant.

Then they waited for Nadeem to finish his shift at the restaurant. On account of having a busy day the two Jihadists had not had time to eat since the morning, and their moods were dark when Nadeem came up the stairs after work. He was tired, but he had at least eaten well, courtesy of the kindly restaurant owner. He went to his room to rest and saw his few disturbed possessions. Then he looked some more and saw his passport had gone. The Jihadists, sitting at the small kitchen table, explained that they had burned any identifying documents to 'protect' him, because on their return journey they would be passing through territory where people would be hostile to Israel. It would be safer to not carry documents that identified him as Israeli.

Anwar asked them what Nadeem had thought about them burning his passport and Little-beard admitted that he didn't like it very much. He challenged them carefully for the first time, knowing He might be dealing with dangerous people, suggesting that Nadeem's feelings may have been a little stronger than 'not liking it very much'. The big stupid one, Big-beard, admitted that Nadeem screamed at him and wouldn't stop screaming. To shut him up, so nobody would come to investigate, he hit him, but not too hard, just enough to shut him up. And it worked. He was quiet after that.

The Jihadists told Nadeem that they were going to take a luxury cruise back to Palestine on a friend's yacht that night, but first they had to eat, and Nadeem must return to the restaurant to bring some food back for them. Nadeem explained that he could not because the restaurant had closed now for the night and was locked up. Big-beard said they're going to try the back door anyway, just in case it wasn't locked and made threatening gestures to Nadeem to force him to go with him because he knew where the best food there could be found. Not to belabor the incident, Big-beard broke several panes of glass until Nadeem could reach in to force open a deadlock, open a door, and collect a stash of food into a plastic bag, enough to eat then, and more for the journey.

Nadeem felt sick about stealing from his kind and trusting employer. Little-beard told him he had more important things to feel sick about.

That same evening, Little-beard left on the scooter leaving Big-beard to guard Nadeem. He returned twenty minutes later, driving the large sport utility vehicle, towing behind the fuel-laden boat and trailer, having abandoned the scooter at the house where he stole the boat. The three of them threw their small cases and backpacks into the boat and took off to the launch site. To their relief the boat ramp was deserted but paid no attention as to why that must be.

Little-beard started the engine; Big-beard got his feet wet shoving it out. After splashing and panting mightily through a few yards of deepening water he grabbed the boat and threw himself over the side, landing face first on the deck, wet and cursing. Little-beard steered the boat out to sea, adhering to the line of buoys through the shallows, and out into the black water and sparse light of a gibbous moon, helped only slightly by the stars, a dim cabin light and a softly glowing compass on a gimbal. No external lights were showing, and communication equipment was switched off.

Nadeem's cell phone, which had been in his pocket all the while he was working, had not been thrown out with his other possessions. He took it out now to call his father before he would lose land-based cell service. The lights on shore were getting dimmer, the breeze stronger and the swell and roll of the boat told him they were in deep water. The two Jihadi guys were busy with high fives and a crude victory dance when the Big-beard turned and saw the glow of the phone's screen.

Violent wrestling resulted. Big-beard went to grab the phone. Nadeem held on to it and fought back, and in the struggle fell overboard. He may have been pushed as Big-beard fought to separate him from his phone. In a fit of triumphant rage Big-beard threw the phone into the water after him so that he could 'finish his call'.

Controlling his anger, Little-beard told him to get the boat light and find him as he turned the boat around. He reminded Big-beard that without him, dead or alive, they had failed and had used precious resources of the 'movement' without even a body to show that they'd done anything more than having a vacation. They yelled and searched for hours but could not find Nadeem.

Avril pierced the shocked silence with the comment: "What banal pathetic way to lose a precious human life!" We mumbled and grunted in stunned agreement. I felt a tear on my cheek and saw Ari's and Moishe's eyes were watery too.

"What happened then... and how do you know all this?" I asked, and the account continued.

For the first half hour they were yelling his name. They found a powerful lamp inside the cabin and switched on the boat lights hoping Nadeem would see the boat and swim towards it, but the wind was rising and the sea was getting rough. What little light there had been from the moon and stars was now obscured by clouds and after about three hours they gave up, exhausted. But what to do now?

Little-beard switched on the boat radio and tuned in to a marine weather station broadcasting in English from the British base at Akrotiri about thirty miles to the east. The Big-beard asked him why he hadn't checked the weather report earlier. Little-beard told him to shut up and pray to which Big-beard answered how could he do both at the same time?

From the weather report the two Jihadists learned there was going to be a storm that night. Little-beard realized that not only had their kidnap plan failed, but it was too dangerous to continue the journey on account of the storm. They had no choice but to turn back. The boat was by then pointing east again having changed directions several times when searching for Nadeem, and now the sea was getting seriously rough. Little-beard dialed up the speed and timed a one hundred and eighty degree turn from just over the brow of the next wave during a slight easing of the wind. For a brief moment when the boat was square to the swell it tipped so steeply and precariously that water almost came over the side and the stack of full fuel cans tumbled into a messy heap. After completing the turn he steered the boat in direction of shore lights from where they'd come. Big-beard puked over the side then prayed aloud for himself alone.

Little-beard figured the boat might have drifted while they searched for Nadeem. He reversed the compass bearing that he'd set earlier in the evening and wove the boat towards the littoral in pattern twenty degrees either side of the bearing. 'Puke all you want but find the buoys!' he yelled as the boat crashed over each steepening roller, 'or we'll smash on the rocks and die.' The tactics worked. They did indeed find the buoys and cruised eventually into calmer water and back to the boat launch. Unsurprisingly there was still nobody around there. With great difficulty on account of the waves crashing on the ramp, they winched the boat back onto the trailer and towed it back to the suburban home from which they had stolen it.

After helping themselves to food in the refrigerator and a pantry the two of them slept in the empty home for a few hours and arose at dawn without a plan. The storm had abated somewhat but a check on the radio weather station told them it would resume immediately and continue for about thirty-six hours in the northeast Mediterranean. Big-beard, who'd been severely seasick, refused to travel in the boat again for the passage home and the other could not crew it alone. Throwing caution to the wind they used the house telephone to call the airlines which served routes to Lebanon, Syria, and Israel but there were no seats available on any flight until evening.

They knew that if they stayed in the house during the day, they could be seen by someone calling at the house, a cleaner, a neighbor, a friend to water the plants, a relative, anybody. If somebody called the police they'd be sunk. The restaurant was out of the question because as soon as the broken windows and missing food were seen, and Nadeem, not having turned up for work, they'd be discovered.

Then they had another stroke of luck. They rode the scooter to the restaurant before it opened and found that today was the only day of the week that the restaurant did not open. The owner and staff would not be around, so they hauled their storm-wet belongings out of the boat and, the two men sitting on the scooter, absurdly loaded with two suitcases and two backpacks left the suburban home, the boat and towing vehicle innocently parked in the driveway, and sneaked back to Nadeem's restaurant apartment. There, they hid the scooter and themselves, confident they would not be discovered until they departed for the Airport in a taxi at 3:00PM.

"And this is where I found them at about 8:00AM," said Anwar. "I hollered up the stairs, 'Nadeem, are you there?'"

"The two beards were truly astonished to see me. They knew me of course, and surmised when I spoke to them in our local dialect, and just by just looking at me that they had nothing to fear. They greeted me almost like a friend. I suppose they'd been pretty tense, and seeing me and not the restaurant owner or a policeman was a relief. They gave me food for which, not knowing its source, I was most grateful. And, of course, I asked them: 'Where's Nadeem?'

"They couldn't go out and had about six or seven hours to kill, which they did, mostly by talking to me. And that answers your earlier question about 'how do I know all this?' At first, they were coy about talking of events of the last few days. But, while talking, Little-beard had developed a narrative which, in his mind, justified all their actions as patriotic, heroic even. I didn't argue that point. For most of the time I was with them I felt anxious. They were so callous and unfeeling about Nadeem, if I uttered one wrong word of disgust or protest, they might turn on me."

"I nodded in agreement the whole time, even when the big guy said if Nadeem hadn't been so foolish trying to make a phone call and fighting him on the boat, he might still have been alive. They also believed strongly in their own humanity insofar as they searched for so long for Nadeem in

264

the gathering storm. But from all they told me I had a very faint hope that he could still be alive. I complimented them on the brilliance of their actions and their courage."

"At 2:45PM they went downstairs to the restaurant phone to call a taxi and that was the last I saw of them."

"But Anwar," said Avril, "you couldn't stay in the apartment either, you'd be accused of breaking in and burglary and responsibility in some way for Nadeem's disappearance."

"Yes, he replied, that's why I left too, I've been living rough for a while."

"Where?" I asked.

"Oh, nowhere in particular, there are a few bridges where I find shelter. There are ancient ruined buildings all over the countryside, I hid a few of my things in one of them."

"How long have you been living rough and what have you been eating?"

"Twenty-two days, I scratched some marks on a wall to keep count. If I could only speak some Greek or some English I might be able to earn a little money. At least enough to get home. There are a lot of fruits and vegetables ripe in the orchards and fields. It's a good time of year to live rough in the countryside here. But I'm scared. If I go to the police to turn myself in they'll suspect me of robbing the restaurant and killing Nadeem."

Avril took over the conversation like the doctor in charge. She told Moishe to take Anwar, with Ari to translate, to pick up his hidden possessions from his hiding places.

Before they left, though, she asked Anwar, via Ari what the staples of a Palestinian diet were, and took notes. Implicit in this was that Anwar would move into our villa. She didn't ask him, and he didn't protest. She told me to find a suitable corner of the considerable living area, haul a sleep-able couch there and find bedding for it. Then she even organized Spiros to take her in his car to go food shopping in anticipation of the arrival of Nadeem's family tomorrow for whom they'd also need Palestinian food. She would need to pick up food for Ari's family too, who would be arriving the day after. Spiros was very willing. I guessed all this action had spiced up his retirement days somewhat.

Chapter 23 - Arrivals - Maria

It would be more authentic if Ari had written this chapter. He said his heart was "too heavy" to express himself in writing. Then he said, "there are no words, I just want to let it happen and accept my biological parents and love them and hope they will do the same for me." The question "what if" was churning inside him. His life could have been so different in a thousand ways. I have to say that if his heart was too heavy to write this, mine was too light. How could I ever find that depth of empathy to express it, when my life experience has been so different from his? I'm just going to tell you what he told me, what I saw and heard, and leave the rest to you.

On the morning Ari's biological family arrived we decided that, to leave enough space in the car for the newcomers, only Avril and Ari should drive to the airport to pick them up. I regretted that I would not be there to give Ari emotional support since he would be meeting his natural biological family for the first time. He had made a cardboard sign to hold up at the arrivals gate on which he wrote in Arabic script: "Welcome Nadeem Mohammed family to Cyprus."

The flight from Ben-Gurion Airport in Israel arrived on time and they cleared customs and immigration at Paphos airport without incident. Ari told me the family just seemed to appear out of nowhere, standing speechless in front of the sign, staring at him and Avril while he was still looking at the distant line of people filing through the entry gate. A handsome middle-aged lady in a mauve minimal headscarf which carefully reigned in dark brown wavy curls stood in front of him. She was wearing a lightweight matching summer coat and addressed him in accented English: "Excuse me," she said, simply. Ari snapped out his reverie to welcome the party of three, man, woman, and ten-year-old girl in Arabic. He introduced Avril as a friend of the family, 'the family' being a somewhat vague term in the circumstances.

As expected, the first meeting was pregnant with unexpressed and conflicting anxieties. Ari silently took a suitcase from his real natural mother as they peered at one another for the first time. The father, Rafik, wanted to be sure that accommodation was arranged and not an inconvenience, trying to say something normal as his voice croaked with emotion. Ari assured him that everything was arranged, and they would be very welcome and very comfortable. He felt most peculiar when he spoke, conscious that his Palestinian Arab parents were looking and listening to him for the first time, mindful of his own fluent but accented Arabic.

The three new arrivals looked around them at the unfamiliar town as they walked slowly to the rental car in the airport parking lot, stepping back in surprise at the curbside as a car drove past on the left-hand side of the street. Ari carried his mother's suitcase for her, to which she silently consented with a look of approval. "You are so like Nadeem," she said, speaking to him a second time, and in English, he guessed out of respect for Avril, not wanting to leave her out of the conversation. He had no answer. He was thinking of Nadeem who these people had raised and loved was tragically no longer with them. He felt like an imposter. There was no hugging or tears of relief, but restrained tension. Further attempts at conversation failed in the overwrought near silence which pervaded the journey back to the villa as their Mercedes purred effortlessly in rush hour traffic.

Ari's biological mother, Mrs. Mohammed, told Avril, who was sitting next to her, to call her Saarah, and thanked her formally for coming to the airport to pick them up, saying what a relief that had been.

When they reached the villa Ari said Daanya, his ten year old natural sister, spoke for the first time since her arrival: "You seem nice and a bit like my brother, but I would like to have my real brother back," she said as they were getting out of the car and staring at him so intently that she backed into her mother who overheard and flinched in surprise, then said something calming to her daughter to sooth her embarrassment.

Ari patted her gently on the shoulder and said: "So would I Daanya, so would I." Daanya may have been a little overdressed, perhaps a little formal in tights and a heavy looking dark dress and cardigan but in other respects looked like a western child with her straight dark shoulder length hair. She kept close to her mother, but her eyes wandered, resting momentarily on each one of us, then the house, then the car again, and said no more for the time being as if trying to be not noticed and may have succeeded had it not been for her alert pretty face.

Mr. Mohammed, Rafik was his name, wore a brown suit and color coordinated tie with a 1950's look. His brown shoes were polished and had a look of high quality. I think somewhere in our conversations I'd heard he was a shoemaker by trade. His complexion and eyes and a full head of wavy hair were like Ari's as was his unmistakable though more wrinkled mature face, and stockier trunk.

There was no easy way to reaffirm to Nadeem's parents what they'd already been told - that there was very little doubt that the body buried at Geroskipou cemetery was Nadeem's. He had been identified initially by his student card with a photo ID that was found in his back pocket. His employer, the owner of the restaurant where he worked had identified him formally.

Complying with a request from the Mohammed parents to see his grave as soon as possible, seven of us, Ari, me, Moishe, Avril and the Mohammed family drove there immediately after unloading suitcases at the villa.

The car had two rear-facing fold-out third row seats where Ari and Daanya sat. Moishe drove and Avril sat in the

270

front with him. I sat next to Saarah. When I told her I was Ari's friend she looked at me very closely, reading me, I could tell by her expression. She replied simply, "yes," then thought to say: "I'm Saarah, Nadeem's mother, this is Rafik, my husband, his father. I saw scars on the backs of her hands. When I turned to look at her face to acknowledge her reply I saw more scars on her neck and cheek and the lower part of her chin on one side. Rafik reached over to shake my hand, but he didn't know English and hadn't read me like his wife had. His expression was blank but there must have been a lot going on inside his head.

Daanya, the ten-year-old sister, wept out loud at the graveside; the parents too could not contain their grief. Rafik muttered a prayer while the family threesome hugged and we stood aside respectfully, with bowed heads.

After returning to the villa the Mohammed family were surprised to meet Anwar whom they hadn't seen on their arrival earlier, on account of their eagerness to see Nadeem's grave. A familiar face of a well-loved nephew helped to put them at ease in our shared deluxe accommodation. As usual Avril weighed up the changing dynamic to best advantage. She told Ari to tell Anwar to show the family their rooms, and figure out what the newly arrived guests would like to eat and drink for a late lunch. Anwar was already deep into conversation with the family who answered the food question via Ari, that anything they had in the fridge was fine with them, and added, "as long as it meets basic halal standards - er - just no pork, please, they

271

say." We put out a smorgasbord from the contents of the fridge.

Anwar talked with them for hours, telling them all that he had told us the previous day. Spiros, who had arrived sometime during the morning was at last introduced to them. He helped update the Mohammed family by explaining his dealings with the Cyprus government agencies. They took to him immediately, plying him with questions which, for a while, tied up Ari who translated for them. When Daanya became restless, Ari offered to show her the garden which was a welcome escape for her. I tagged along, eager to get to know her. Standing by the pool Ari asked her if she could swim. She answered no, and then in English she said to me: "I don't have a swimming."

Returning to the house from the garden Ari and Daanya went looking for games and toys in a myriad of closets and cupboards. Avril was reading and Moishe was setting up his easel and paints in the garden. As I feigned reading a Greek language fashion magazine I could make out our names in Anwar's otherwise incomprehensible endless monologue which drew nods, slight smiles and glances at me and others from the listeners. After all, our kindly treatment of Anwar should have given a good impression of all of us, and most importantly of Ari.

Anwar needed no help showing them their rooms. When questioned about the relative modesty of his own corner with a couch, he informed them that Ari's Israeli family would be arriving the following day. The Israeli parents would occupy the one still-vacant room. Daanya would share with Ari's Israeli sister Hannah, who was about the same age. The Mohammed parents greeted the information thoughtfully and without comment.

As dusk approached Moishe brought inside his half-finished, and determinedly uncontroversial landscape painting, along with the familiar Brooklyn atelier aroma of linseed oil and turpentine. Avril had insisted that all human forms in his paintings must be fully dressed for as long as there were guests in the villa.

Ari and Daanya discovered a wealth of board and electronic games which helped to advance their friendship under the watchful and curious eyes of the Mohammed parents who attempted very little conversation with anybody for the rest of the day except with Anwar. Their grief was palpable. They retired early, neglecting to send Daanya to bed nor advising us when she should go. She played electronic games on the TV with Ari. In the silence that followed switching off the TV for the night, Saarah could be heard sobbing behind the closed doors, followed by quiet spells, then Rafik was heard, then both of them sobbing and eventually there was quiet.

Chapter 24 - More Arrivals - Maria

The following morning four of us, Avril, Moishe, Ari and I went to the airport again to meet Ari's Israeli family. Neither Avril nor I had ever met them and weren't to be deprived of excited airport greetings and introductions. We'd been assured by Ari that although they would still be suffering shock from losing their natural born son, nothing could stop them from being overjoyed at seeing himself and Moishe again. And so it was. Little Hannah, Ari's sister leapt into his arms. He spun around joyfully stumbling over a dropped suitcase, followed by hugs and tears of joy by his Israeli parents. After the initial excitement there was a more somber mood on the drive back to the villa. "I had a son who I never met and never will," said Ari's mother without warning, unable to hold back the tears when Ari was telling them that the Mohammed family were waiting at the villa.

Introductions at the villa were brief in a mood that was polite but inescapably gloomy. As if in a rerun of the previous day's visit to Nadeem's grave, now Ari's Tel Aviv family wished to visit there without delay. At the graveside

Hanna was silent about the brother she had never met until she heard and saw her parents weeping. She went to Ari and told him she wanted to know all about Nadeem and was sure she would have loved him just as she loved Ari if she'd ever had the chance. Ari told her that Daanya, Nadeem's sister, would tell her all about him if she asked, but maybe not to ask her immediately. She should make friends first, remembering Daanya would still be very sad about losing him.

Back at the villa Moishe set up his easel in some shade on the patio and got back to work on his painting. Hannah went first to the back yard, saw the pool she shrieked with delight before rushing upstairs to put on her swimsuit. When I saw the saddened look on Daanya's face I asked her mother for permission to take her shopping for one. She agreed, and asked to come with us, followed by Hannah who wanted to come too as did her mother, Ayelet, whose hand she was clutching tightly as if to emphasize her enthusiasm for the shopping trip. Avril agreed to drive us. I would have volunteered to do that but, New York City girl that I am, I had never learned to drive. Altogether on the shopping excursion there were six of us, four women and two nine-year-old girls.

As we found out earlier, Daanya and Nadeem's mother Saarah knew some English. The girls, who had both been learning English at school from an early age were drawn to speaking it to one another, having made a pact to use it as much as they could because it would, in their words, be an "equalizer." This had the advantage of pleasing Saarah whose English was functional but less than fluent and her Hebrew even less so. Daanya was competent in Hebrew, but Hannah knew very little Arabic and said with mature gravitas that she would not force her own culture on her new "sister". The friendship was sealed. Daanya translated the English conversation into Arabic for her mother when necessary, and her mother's replies into English for Avril, Ayelet and me.

Shopping over, Avril pulled into a parking space by the restaurant in the square where we'd first met Spiros. A waitress helped us pull two umbrella-tables together. We ordered ice-creams for the children which they begged for, and a variety of drinks for the rest of us. The girls proudly chipped in with helpful translations as the adults struggled in three languages with their ordering decisions.

The two mothers had not yet conversed with one another beyond brief everyday sentences but appearing to have a shared curiosity about me, asked Avril if I was her daughter, even though I had recently been introduced to them as another "friend of the family". She answered that she had an adult son whose father she was no longer married to. I thought she was playing for time, thinking what to say, as she explained her own relationship with Moishe. "You're right," she said to Ayelet, "Moishe is my husband. We were married about six months ago. It is a common law marriage, you see, and need not be solemnized by religious or civil authorities. We are both of independent means and our commitment is to each other alone."

I listened with astonishment. She hadn't answered the question and didn't talk about me at all. I wondered if by implication, she was trying to make it seem normal that Ari and I might be bound by a similar understanding, and if so, what was our level of intimacy? It seems convoluted, but having discussed this when planning the trip, we didn't want to be regarded as having lax morals by people whose views on such matters were formed by lifetimes within a much more conservative culture. By simply pretending to misunderstand the question she had deflected attention from me. I don't think the mothers were fooled but they dropped the subject.

We wanted the occasion to be sympathetically focused on their loss and not our own behavior. We couldn't really know what their attitudes would be, and we were trying our best to avoid a culture clash. I figured Anwar had done a good job representing us in a favorable light yesterday. The conversation returned to the perfect weather, the coffee, the ice cream and beautiful friendly Cyprus, but I had a strong feeling that there was lingering curiosity about me and my relationship with Ari. The two girls were laughing and joking, enjoying their ice creams having abandoned the solemn airs pervading the conversation of the adults.

When we returned to the villa, Spiros was there and the guys were all deep in conversation dipping into English, Hebrew and Arabic, a truly bizarre cacophony when heard from a distance, as trilingual Ari at the center of it switched languages like a professional. Spiros had reminded them that Nadeem's burial arrangements in Geroskipou may not be permanent, and they were working on a plan to have him reinterred in neutral ground, permanent and accessible to both families. "Good luck with that one," said Avril with a hint of irony in her voice, "I really have no idea how they will find a solution to satisfy all, given the families' different religions and nationalities."

The girls put on their swimsuits and rushed outside to the pool. Hannah could swim but Daanya could not, but was determined to learn. Hannah was just as determined to teach her. I seized the opportunity to put on my own swimsuit to join them, and was followed by Avril. Together we coached Daanya who was naturally athletic and already had an idea of how she needed to move her arms and legs. We explained how to breathe and when to breathe out and hold your breath under water. She practiced with wild resolve. I turned my head and saw that the girls' mothers were sitting on the patio under shade umbrellas talking and watching us.

The next time I looked I saw that they'd gone inside to the kitchen and were preparing food, still visible to me at the other side of tall sliding glass doors as they talked. How must they feel right now I asked myself? How does anybody cope with such loss? The fathers were subsuming their grief while planning a re-burial for their inadvertently shared son. I asked myself, had the mothers resented one another when they learned they had each other's babies and raised them in cultures anathema to each? How much did they bond out of a shared loss and shared suffering from injuries in the same outrage? How much could the remaining son, Ari, be consolation for the loss of the other?

I looked again at the mothers who were now engaged tugging bits of clothing aside in different parts of their bodies to show each other ancient scars beneath. Could you call them fortunate that their faces were mostly spared the disfigurement and scarring that their necks, breasts, limbs and torsos suffered from that crazy terrible bomb twenty-some years ago?

Multiple visits to government offices occupied the next few days for Moishe, Spiros, Ari and Rafik. Moishe was the chauffeur, Spiros the facilitator and translator of Greek to English, Ari the Arabic to English translator and Rafik had to be present as the father of the deceased to sign all official documents. Time was short, all had to return to jobs or studies.

The first journey that the four made, however, was to a re-started ancient monastery about fifty miles away in the mountains. With the support of the Greek Orthodox church, seven monks had restored a small derelict nave, living quarters and rooms for contemplation and prayer. Partial self-sufficiency in food came from a kitchen garden supplemented by income from and six rentable vacation cabins with plans for more. Steep rocky terrain made conventional farming impossible.

The four men had a proposal. It helped their negotiating position that one of the monks was an old friend of Spiros and that the monastery's very survival was precarious. They, the four men, sought to buy a plot of land for a nominal price, twenty feet by ten feet, from the monastery in a patch of forest that was otherwise unusable.

Firstly, they made a powerful moral case for a lost soul suspended permanently homeless between the final resting places of two religions. How better to validate the monastery's bedrock Christian principles than to give refuge to this soul? The owners of the plot would be both sets of parents.

The monks knew the story of Nadeem's death from the Paphos newspaper and how its burial at Geroskipou was made possible by community support. Accepting the body, Spiros submitted, would be a follow-on story and would attract much needed support from the public and the diocese. It would be sympathetically written as was the initial story.

Lastly Moishe explained that he was an artist of some repute in New York City and urged the monks to verify this assertion for themselves using whatever resources they wished. He offered in payment to donate a signed painting of the monastery, the image of which could be printed on postcards, or prints of it could be made and displayed for sale to visitors to the monastery, or even at tourist retail outlets at Paphos and Geroskipou.

In short, the offer was accepted after much discussion and celebrated with bread and wine produced by the monastery. Rafik could not accept the wine, of course, but was well content with fruit juice

Chapter 25 - The Funeral - Maria

Ari takes copious notes, gives them to me, which I copy and enhance into a reality perceived by me. He claims he's so busy translating the negotiations and permits for exhumation and reburial that he had to, reluctantly, hand responsibility for the written account to me. I don't think he was all that reluctant. As much as I loved Cyprus it became evident that it is still a male-dominated society. Thus, for practical reasons Avril and I left the dealings with officialdom to the guys who were capable enough, though in my opinion none reaching the prowess of Avril in that department.

As befitted a former territory of Byzantium, the next day and a half obtaining permits for exhumation and reburial of the body at Geroskipou, plus conveyancing of the title of a thirty-by-ten plot was truly byzantine. It taxed Spiros' negotiating skills to the fullest. The monks promised to clear the plot and dig a grave even before the land title was exchanged, and permits granted.

The guys used Spiros' car for their errands leaving the beautiful Mercedes station wagon to us females in their absence. We used the time to explore some tourist sites, and the delights of outdoor dining, which incidentally abound on this island. In case you were wondering, nobody paid me to say that. A visit to only one tourist site is apropos to this story. It was late on Thursday afternoon that the guys caught up with us at the beach by Petra tou Romiou, also known as Aphrodite's Rock. Greek mythology tells us that those who swim around it will be blessed with eternal beauty, and also other things from mythology that involve gore and violence, and which we preferred not to share with the children at the time.

The girls and I were skimming flat pebbles across the water competing to see who could make them skip most times. When Ari joined us he soon demonstrated superior skill which delighted the children. They made a game of challenging him to make more and more skips with pebbles that they were finding and feeding to him. I watched them loose themselves, carefree in the diversion which morphed into chasing and splashing in and out of the waves. In a calmer moment they stopped to examine some small object that had washed up in the foam. They moved up close to Ari, one on each side to hold a hand. What a picture, they just seemed to gravitate towards him.

"I think that is Nadeem's shoe," said Daanya. The briefly lightened mood became instantly solemn. The parents recognized the shoe too. We put it in a plastic bag, which I must say was too easily found on the beach. The girls carried the shoe to the car as if handling a fragile treasure and we brought it away with us, for what purpose we could not say. The memory of the two children paddling in bare feet with their backs to us, reflexively holding Ari's hands, lingered in my mind in hideous contrast to finding the shoe. If there was any more room for me to melt to him that little moment took it.

Back at the villa Avril told the girls to keep the shoe outside and wash it thoroughly with the garden hose. When finished they placed it outside by the door with some others. While the older adults were preparing an evening meal and I was rummaging absently through another Greek fashion magazine Daaniya came up to me followed by Hannah and asked: "Are you going to marry Ari? We know you love him."

"How could you know a thing like that?" I answered, playing for time, but I could not help smiling in response. They were too polite to press the question, but I wondered how I'd been so obvious about it. The pair came back about half an hour later with another question. This time it was Hannah that did the talking.

"We know Ari's natural parents are Arab Muslims and that the family he grew up with, and the religion he knows and practices, is Judaism. Are you a Muslim or are you Jewish? and if you were to marry Ari which religion would you choose?"

After I'd thought for a few seconds, I decided that these kids were too smart to bare dissimulation. Only honesty would do. I hoped that when my views were inadvertently shared with the parents they would not meet

283

with disapproval or worse, excite their ire. "I am neither a Muslim nor a Jew, I said, "and the only people I know that belong to either of those religions are here with us in the villa. I am a Roman Catholic, as is my family and just about everybody else I know. If Ari and I did decide to get married my commitment to him would override any rules other people might try to make us follow. To put it another way, I do care about the people who believe, but less so about how their beliefs are expressed in religious form. They are my people and his people, and it may always be like that. All I ask is that they accept me as I am, and us as we are."

I was surprised at Daanya's follow on question: "Does that mean you're a Christian?" she asked.

"Yes," I replied, thinking as I answered that everybody in New York knows that Catholics are Christians, and we're comfortable with our solipsistic ways, until we travel, I should add.

Daanya gasped and put her hand over her mouth, but Hannah's reaction was more muted as if such sentiments were not so foreign to her. The pair left me in the direction of their room, I guess to talk over what they'd just heard and to escape the curious glare of Daanya's mother.

On the day of the funeral there was no hearse in the three-vehicle cortege waiting outside the cemetery in Geroskipou. When told of the destination all the undertakers in the town had refused us the use of one. While they waited in late morning sunshine, passengers fussed discreetly The children wriggled in discomfort from the rising heat in the crowded vehicles. They were waiting for Moishe, Rafik and three cemetery workers.

After tipping them generously, Moishe directed the cemetery workers to place the modest whitewood casket they were carrying in the back of the Mercedes wagon, which had its rear seats folded down flat, and the enlarged rear area covered in dark blue velvet. Rafik placed flowers from the families and well-wishers on and around it. Then Moishe disappeared again with the cemetery workers along the shady trail in the direction of the gravesite from which Nadeem's body had just been removed. They reappeared carrying a small, polished headstone which they placed carefully in the back of the third vehicle in line, a rented three-row VW people mover.

With Rafik in the passenger seat beside Moishe in the driver's seat in our makeshift hearse we were finally ready to move. The cortege pulled away from the cemetery and out of Geroskipou at a slow dignified speed. With lights still flashing we turned on to the A6 highway and travelled East for a few miles. Then we pulled off onto a minor road, traveling North toward green lush, forested hills, then off again onto a yet smaller road which turned into a dirt road half a mile later. We zig zagged our way over hills and up a mountain side on the most appalling rutted dirt road, thankfully dust free on account of a light shower earlier in the day. So steep were some of the inclines and so deep some of the potholes that it was all Avril could do in the driver's seat, to keep the large overloaded VW van on the track and moving.

After about half an hour toiling uphill, we were relieved to see a small cluster of buildings appear before us on an oblong level area of about an acre in size. Stepping out of the vehicle and looking back through the clear mountain air over steep forested ridges and plunging valleys you could just see a patch of blue Mediterranean which darkened to a brief horizon line. Above that a brighter blue sky arched its broadening way back to us over the hills. Here in the forest clearing, stepped down on its west side was a small flat area, cleared of trees and brushwood. There was a newly dug grave in the middle of it and sufficient room around it for a gathering of about thirty people.

About ten people, some dressed in traditional black habits, others in jeans and t-shirts sauntered out towards us from the larger church-like building at the center of the cluster. One among them, the Abbot I presumed, walked up to Moishe, shook hands and spoke to him in perfect English. He was more formerly dressed, wearing a golden cross on his chest hanging from a gold chain. On his head he wore a black hat with a flat top, a bit like a stovepipe hat without a rim - not quite so tall maybe. In keeping with the somber event, he spoke respectfully and with calming authority directing us to the building from which he'd just emerged. Cool water, fresh baked flatbread and fruit were set out to welcome us.

A few Greek words from him had the effect of a command to the others in the group that had approached us on our arrival. They carefully removed the casket from the back of the Mercedes, cooperating with each other as if by telepathy, their feet skidding a little down the steep embankment to the graveside. There they placed the casket on two hand hewn logs and threaded straps beneath it at each end, in readiness to lower it into the ground.

Aware of the circumstances of Nadeem's death, the Abbot, with Ari translating into Arabic, (Ari's Israeli parents understood English,) was especially gracious talking to the two sets of parents. He explained to them that pathways around the grave and along the site remained rights of way while the freehold to the grave was theirs alone. They could, and should decorate the headstone with symbols and scripts of their choosing. One of the monks was a stonemason and could help with that. In addition, a resident of the abbey, i.e., a monk who was also a carpenter, would build a bench and plant flowers to turn the small space into a garden setting for relaxation and contemplation.

Wearing shoes that were not ideal for the unfinished terrain, the ladies were helped down the embankment to the graveside, by the group of monks who had miraculously shed their working clothes. They were now dressed in the customary black habits of their order. In just about a minute, we were all assembled ready. For what? I didn't know, but things moved along as if choreographed. Four of the monks positioned themselves, picking up the end of a strap and clutching it in readiness.

The abbot looked at Moishe who nodded in approval. The casket was lowered smoothly into the ground. On cue from Moshe, Rafik began to speak, his clear Arabic piercing a silence disturbed only by a slight rustling of the surrounding forest. He waited after each phrase for Ari to translate it, maintaining his dignified tone:

"In our care for the first twenty-three years of his life, we now commit Nadeem to the ground. He was a loyal and loving son and brother, a dear friend to those who knew him, a bright student and diligent worker. While freely acknowledging his Jewish natural parentage and their evident goodness and love of our own natural born son, we wish to apprise all, that Nadeem was a faithful servant of Allah to whom we commend his soul in confidence that it will find rest and redemption in Heaven."

He paused for a few seconds while several around the grave wept openly, then continued:

"To our friendly hosts we say that, though you worship differently from us, we commend to Allah your protection, prosperity and success in your endeavors."

Then David followed in Hebrew, and as before, Ari translated each phrase into English for his Israeli father, which some people present strained to understand, but the sentiment was clear enough:

"This son of Israel was raised by our Palestinian Muslim neighbors with love and care. We have learned that this love was rewarded by returned love and respect. And now this knowledge warms our hearts; our hearts that had been frozen by thoughts of regret that Ayelet, my wife, his natural mother, and I David, his natural father, had never met him. To the man and woman that raised him we give our thanks without reservation or limit. May the God of Israel care for his soul."

The Abbot then stepped forward to say: "Our small community will preserve this site as a reminder of the folly that sometimes divides humanity, and of the goodness that sometimes overcomes it to redeem us. Our hospitality awaits the frequent return of both families to celebrate the all-too-brief life of this dear departed son. To the one God that unites us all we commend his soul to everlasting life, tranquility, and peace. Amen."

And as if rehearsed all the diverse religions present whispered "Amen" in unity. It was the shortest funeral I'd ever attended and as moving as any. The Abbot invited us back into the church for more snacks and to rest and relax before our departure. The monks joined us, eager to get to know us and assure us of a welcome if and when we returned. The relief that it was over was palpable but hardly joyous.

Spiros introduced a journalist intern to the Abbott. She had ridden to the funeral in his car to write a story for the Paphos newspaper. Spiros was motivated to help his friend at the abbey who had listened to his suggestion to find a gravesite in the grounds. The plan was that additional visitors to the monastery, local and foreign, could provide additional income, and more so when Moishe's painting that he'd already started work on could be leveraged into postcard and print sales. She tried speaking to Rafik but was met with a blank stare, as she was by David, too, who could have answered some of her questions in English. I might have embarrassed her when I told her gently, that it may not be appropriate to talk to close family on this day, but I and Avril and Moishe may be able to help. And so we did. She got her story.

The two mothers, Saarah and Ayelet, tearfully embraced each other. They talked about the friendship they had formed while convalescing years ago and how they regretted that it had lapsed in their separate worlds. Ayelet's pride in Ari's competence and maturity was shared with Saarah as they watched the two children gravitate to him and his easy warm responses to their questions about monks. I don't think he knew as much as he pretended to know but when I saw the girls challenge him on an issue the three of them went to the Abbot to check the answer.

The mothers brooded on the distance of Ari's new home from his Middle East roots but were cheered, they said, by his relationship with me! Really? How could they know? And what if it didn't work out. But they knew, better even than I knew.

You could not say that the families had found "closure" from the visit shared, and from the funeral. Such loss I'm told is never really "closed", but you might say the families had turned a page.

The warm relief of finding a permanent resting place for Nadeem's remains was chilled by a shared frustration that the people responsible for Nadeem's death had not been held to account. Anwar felt it as deeply as anyone and wished to make amends if possible, by making a statement to the police. We thought this might be hazardous for him since it was possible that he could be arrested as a suspect. But he was willing to take that chance.

With regard to our own safety, we were mindful too of what Anwar had told us earlier, that Nadeem's murderers had departed, ostensibly for the airport, but we could not be sure that they had left Cyprus. Then there was the odd complication that someone from the Mossad might show up.

There were two days left before the Palestinian family was due to leave, three for the Israelis, several more for us New Yorkers, and an unknown number for Anwar.

Chapter 26 - The Police and the Palestinian Family's Last Day in Cyprus - Maria

With a lingering anxiety that the Mossad would show up in pursuit of the Jihadists and mistake him for one of them, Anwar was now resolved to go to the police to make a statement. More than that, he felt he was in danger of being arrested at the airport anyway as a suspect, in some way connected to Nadeem's death. To make his statement he would need the assistance of Ari to translate and Spiros to navigate the bureaucracy. In our muted celebration dinner, Spiros, of course, was with us again and had brought along his bilingual - Greek and English - wife who wanted to meet us. She was curious about her husband's prolonged absences the previous week.

As the most accomplished typist, I assisted in the written preparation of the English version of Anwar's statement using Avril's computer. After making an appointment at the police station Anwar, Spiros, Ari, and I crowded into the small bland interview room as two additional chairs were brought in. The junior of the two interviewing policemen took a copy of the statement on a flash drive from Avril's computer which I had brought with me. He returned a few minutes later with a printed version after the slow moving, translated-while-you-go interview had already started. The senior of the policemen, a captain, I think, but I'm no expert in police ranks, his name, something '...opolos', was quite eager to get to the bottom of what had happened. His English was fluent, and silence prevailed as he started to read the statement. The expression of his face moved from bland, to wrinkled, to surprised, as his pursed lips vanished behind an ample mustache. With a hand-over-mouth intake of breath he stopped, at which point only the hum and swish of the ceiling fan was audible.

Then he said something in Greek, and in a tone that sounded urgent. His junior colleague left the room in a hurry, leaving the door open. We overheard some more urgent yelling that sounded like orders. Captain ...opolos, if I may call him that, dislodged his ornate Greek headgear to scratch his balding pate, put down the half-read statement and looked up at each one of us while considering what to say.

"You see," he started, "these two guys who you so helpfully describe in detail, match the description of two guys we released only late yesterday afternoon. We strongly suspected they might have been involved with your cousin's death," he continued, while looking at Anwar, "but we had no concrete evidence and no witnesses. From fingerprints, we knew that they had been in the flat above the restaurant, the owner having called us to report the break-in but the only fingerprints we could identify with the break-in were Nadeem's. My sergeant left the room a few moments ago to convey my orders to re-apprehend the two suspects. I believe that we now have a key witness. I'm afraid, Anwar, I have to insist that you do not leave Cyprus for the time being."

Anwar's expression moved from worried to thoughtful as he listened carefully to Ari's translation. The captain continued: "Here's my phone number if you think of anything more. It is likely I will need to speak to you all again, so please leave your addresses and phone numbers with my sergeant before you leave. In the meantime, I will be reading the rest of your statement and taking steps to corroborate as much of it as I can."

"Anwar can't stay in Cyprus, he has no money and nowhere to stay," I told the captain.

"What about the flat above the Aphrodite restaurant, the one mentioned in the statement?" replied the captain. "I know the owner, I'll call him, see if he wants a dishwasher. I can tell him he is not a suspect in any crime."

Ari translated for Anwar who nodded his approval.

"How could he give evidence in court if he doesn't know a word of Greek and very few of English?" I asked.

"We'll find a translator," he answered.

"If he's anything like the last translator you found to call Nadeem's father a few days ago you'll get nowhere," I told him.

The captain responded with a brief plangent laugh which wobbled his belly taking with it the front of his uniform shirt. After calming himself, he placed his ornate peaked cap on the table, leaned back in his chair, and said: "I heard about that. He was a Maronite and spoke some sort of antique dialect that we call Arabic." Then after an intake of breath he spoke more seriously, mournfully even: "Most of those Maronite speakers fled the Turkish invasion of the Northern part of our Island back in 1974. Their communities broke up and refugees spread out over the Southern Greek section of which we are part. Our well-meaning constable asked his neighbor, an old guy from the North to come into the station to translate. The old neighbor thought he would be translating for one of his fellow Maronites. We'll pay some guy from the University to come over. It shouldn't be a problem."

"OK, thanks," I said, remembering that Ari had figured out the problem a few days ago.

The next day was the last before the Palestinian family had to return home and wished to spend it getting to know Ari a little better. His Israeli parents and sister were not to be deprived of his company either, but in the knowledge they had an extra day with him stayed in the background. The day was spent around the villa where the one constant was Moishe painting, hour after hour, stopping to talk to the children, giving them each a blank canvas, then resuming his work. The children, now firm friends, painted, swam, ran around the yard, jumped playfully on Ari and then on me. It was all too strange to be called bitter-sweet. Too bitter to be a celebration; too sweet to not smile at the conciliation.

Ari told me his Palestinian parents were proud when he told them of his university education, comparing it to Nadeem's. But they were confused, outraged even, but in spite of themselves impressed, when he told them about his army career, about where he worked when in the army, and about how he perfected his Arabic. They were curious about his accommodation in New York City, their parental eyes moving first to Moishe, absorbed in his painting, then to Avril who was constantly catching up with her email from work.

"What about Maria?" his Palestinian mother asked him. How does she fit in, and do your Israeli parents approve of her?"

He told them: "You'll have to ask my Israeli parents,"

At which point I said, feeling irritated: "What did you tell them about me, funny man!"

He answered with a smirk: "I told them we were just friends."

"That's all?" I said feeling even more irritated. He smiled, looked embarrassed and turned away. So I let the matter drop, for now. Later he told me he really didn't know how to answer their question about me, then added: "Cultural norms are so different for them that 'just friends' when talking in Arabic of a person of the opposite sex could be quite loaded with meaning. When I get the chance to talk to my Israeli parents I'll be more explicit."

"Good," I answered, "you can tell them in English and I'll be right there listening."

He smiled a sweet smile and said: "That's OK."

Chapter 27 - The Airport, the Mossad and the Jihadists - Maria

Seven of us loaded into our Mercedes wagon to take Ari's Palestinian family of three to the airport. In the car with them were Avril who drove and Moishe in the front seat next to her. Ari and sat on the fold-down seats at the back which we shared with the family's baggage among which was a pretty souvenir doll, dressed in Greek traditional costume which I'd bought for Daanya.

Ari walked with the family a few steps ahead of us. Daanya, holding his right hand, dragged her suitcase with her doll tied to the top of it, her mother Saarah, linked his left arm. Moishe and Avril towed the remaining luggage. Inside the terminal building the noise from the traffic and outdoor odors vanished, only to be replaced by indoor food smells and busy crowds and multilingual public address announcements. Unaware of people milling around, Saarah held Ari's cheeks between her hands, kissed him, wept, then stood aside for Rafik and Daanya to hug him, not a dry eye between them, or me, nor when I looked, between Avril and Moishe.

As they separated from Ari, we noticed Ari do a double take to look at two guys deep in conversation quite near to him. They didn't notice Ari until he spoke to them in Hebrew. I'd heard so much of it recently, I could recognize it. They looked at him in surprise and immediately engaged him in conversation, straining their necks while staring into the crowds searching near and far. Ari swiveled to return a blown last kiss and wave at Daaniya as she and her parents disappeared through the security barrier. Even as he did that he and the two guys he was talking to took off in a fast walk, almost running. to the far side of the terminal. There at the far side of the terminal were two guys, vaguely familiar to me, yes! That was it. That was their quarry, Big-beard and Little-beard. They must be the two guys I'd seen only once in Brooklyn who marched away so insistently with Ari, that horrible day weeks ago when he left me cold.

The two bearded guys realized immediately they were being pursued and took off, sprinting through the busy crowds towards the men's restroom or toilets as they're called here. One of the guys that Ari was talking to pursued them into the restroom as the other watched and Ari took out his phone to make a call. I must have been about a hundred feet away staring in his direction glued to the spot, waiting, watching an intense drama unfold while the rest of the world carried on as if nothing unusual was happening. Suddenly the two bearded guys appeared again, straightening their clothing and hair as they dashed across the terminal. In a flash they disappeared through the security barrier to the baggage check area, each carrying only a small backpack.

I had a sinking feeling that they might have escaped. "Where's Ari?" Avril asked, seeming to appear out of nowhere. "What's going on?" I told her what I'd seen, and she repeated the story to Moishe who said to her, "You wait here with Maria. I'll ask Ari if I can do anything to help." The guy standing with Ari went into the restroom to look for his partner whom he found barely conscious under the half-closed door of a stall. He dragged him out carefully and called an ambulance. Then he took off his jacket to place carefully under the dry side of the injured man's bleeding head.

Sirens of emergency services were soon audible; first came the police whom Ari had called via Captain ...'opolos, then came the ambulance. Ari had the presence of mind to ask which hospital he was being taken to. His companion took out the injured man's passport and wallet from his jacket pocket, handed the passport to the emergency workers to identify him, and made plain that he was holding on to the wallet as he accompanied the wheeled stretcher to the ambulance, stepping inside it with the injured man. Ari had slipped a piece of paper to him on which he had written his phone number and Cyprus address, then turned his attention to Captain ...'opolos, who was tugging on his sleeve. A brief conversation with him took place to confirm the identities of the attackers.

Shocked by this unhappy turn of events and with nothing more to do at the airport we walked back to the car speculating on the destination of the two Jihadi guys and whether the captain would be able to catch them before their plane took off. "By the way," said Ari, you know the guy that got hit over the head...."

"Yes," I said, "what about him?"

"He and his partner, they're with the Mossad."

"He's what?" I yelled. "The guy dumb enough to let himself be ambushed by going into the men's bathroom, alone, when he knows two violent motivated men may be waiting for him?"

"Right first time, he's the one," he answered. "These guys are trained for that sort of thing you know, physically fit, capable of looking after themselves."

"Guess he missed the lecture about how to deal with a guy that comes from behind and whacks you over the head," I answered, feeling a little too stressed to find a kinder view.

Back at the villa a recent model expensive looking car was in the driveway, a BMW I think, no definitely a BMW, it said so on the trunk. It was considerately parked in the shade under the riotously flowering bougainvillea tree allowing space for our car to stop next to it in our usual spot in the shade of a palm. I was feeling emotionally drained by the airport experience and looking forward to relaxing with a cup of coffee, as I'm sure were the others.

It was curiously silent and still as Avril opened the door. Sitting stiffly upright on the long, sectioned sofa were Ari's Israeli parents and next to them the big bearded Jihadi guy, holding Hannah on his lap with his broad left arm around her throat and a sharp butcher's knife from the kitchen in his right hand, pointing at her ribs. The four of us froze simultaneously in horror. The other Jihadist guy, Little-beard, stood a few feet away to give him a commanding view of both groups of people, four of us just inside the front door and four on the couch. In his hands and pointing at us was an Uzi automatic rifle, a staple personal weapon of the Israeli foot soldier.

Leaving only sufficient time for us to assess that Hannah was in danger for her life, he put down his weapon, turned on the safety catch and carried a pillowcase to us in which was Avril's computer and the home's Wi-Fi router. "Your phones," he said holding the pillowcase in front of each one of us in turn. We obeyed without a word. Then he picked up his gun again, released the safety catch, pointed at Ari and said to him: "Get into the front passenger seat of the BMW outside." He returned to Avril, holding the pillowcase in front of her for the second time and told her: "The keys to your Mercedes, please." Then he nodded at the Big-beard who took Hannah with him onto the rear seat of the BMW, roughly holding her arm, still clutching the kitchen knife in his right hand. Hannah was bravely silent, but her parents frantically remonstrated with the kidnappers to no avail.

Seeing Hannah and the big guy on the car rear seat, and Ari installed the passenger seat, the Little-beard, obviously the brains of the operation, placed the pillowcase containing the phones in the trunk. He then turned, pointed the Uzi directly at us while he walked back to the house, keeping the gun trained on us. "If you go into the garage you will be safe, he said, as will the child and young man that we'll be taking with us back to Palestine as insurance." Then, after a pause and sneer added, "They should feel quite at home there." He walked back into the house, slammed the door and locked us in it from the inside.

301

It was pitch black in the garage, but I'd been in it before and had a good idea where the light switch was, which I found to not work having inadvertently groped various body parts of the three people while feeling my way towards it. I shouldn't have been surprised. Writing this now it seems slightly funny, but it really wasn't at the time. David and Ayelet were beside themselves with anxiety and quite honestly, I was freaked out too.

The garage had an electric steel double door out to the driveway. It was controlled simply by pressing a button by the house door, which I found after a second groping session.

"Surely it's not going to be that easy to get out of here," said Avril.

It wasn't. I pressed the 'open' button, but nothing happened.

"Anybody know where the electrical breaker box is?" asked Moishe.

"It's inside, in the laundry room." I answered.

"Never mind," he said, plan B coming up, we'll need to release the latch on the door's screw drive and open it manually."

There was the slightest inward leak of light from around the garage door which allowed Moishe to identify the latch he was talking about after feeling around the opener hardware standing on his tiptoes.

"Damn, it's jammed," he said. There was a plank wedged above the opener drive and the drive itself was distorted to stop the slider moving along the screw. He pulled out the plank which jammed the latch then tried to heave up the door again but couldn't because the latch was badly bent and warped into the screw drive. In other words, the door was jammed shut and we were locked in the garage and out of the house.

Moishe strained some more, and David came over to help him at the manual opener handle. After heaving and emitting foreign sounding expletives they did manage to force up the door about two inches through which an amazingly bright beam of light surprised our darkness-accustomed eyes.

"Pass me those planks and those bricks," said Moishe. David caught on to what he was doing, as did I. We joined in levering the door open inch by inch, supporting a second plank with a brick and a third with another brick. The screw drive warped some more clanking and groaning and snapping until after about fifteen minutes we had the door open about two feet. It was enough for Moishe to crawl out on his belly followed by the rest of us, scraping our knees and hands while squeezing though.

We caught our breath and some shade from the mid-afternoon sun under the bougainvillea on the driveway outside the garage where the BMW had been. Avril said some soothing words to Ari's deeply shocked Israeli parents, adding, "We'll get her back, and him too, don't you worry. Just you wait here, we'll be back very soon, in just a few minutes."

"You go that way, I'll go this," she said to Moishe, c'mon Maria." There were not many houses on the street, it was not a subdivision, having just an occasional house on either side of it as it wound chaotically around old orchards and gardens up the hill. We went to the first house, where a woman screamed something at us through a glass door, at the second no answer, at the third some angry male Greek voice, but at the fourth: "Good evening, can I be of any assistance?" asked a frail stooping white haired Englishman holding a glass of red wine.

"We have an emergency; may we use your phone?" Avril asked him.

"Of course, of course, bit of an old fashioned one you know, right here in the hall."

Avril called Captain …'opolos, who said that seconds ago he'd just had a call from Moishe from a different number. He told us he'd sent a car out to our villa and another to the general area, circulating the neighborhood in search of a late model BMW.

After Avril hung up the phone she asked the old Englishman if he happened to know a good locksmith in the area.

"Indeed I do," he answered in such a way you'd think we were old friends, "Would you like me to call him for you. I know that Captain Stephanopoulos, you know - fine guy - pronounced Steph-an-o-pou-los, he said carefully articulating each syllabus."

"Most kind of you," she interrupted, cutting him off, "tell him we'll need a front door key and a Mercedes Benz key at number 33 as soon as possible."

So back we walked to the villa where the police car pulled into the driveway as we arrived. We told the two cops a brief version of our story, that a child and a young man were hostages in immediate danger, possibly held in a late model BMW. Ayelet described both her children and exactly what each was wearing while David watched and nodded. Then she broke down, staggered over to the low wall at the side of the driveway and wept aloud, unconsolably. David put his arm around her shoulder and wept too.

One of the policemen called the office. He was speaking in Greek, but we gathered he was inquiring about reports of the theft of a late model BMW. The two nodded at each other, one of them turned to Moishe and David saying, "We have a license plate number." They drove away.

A locksmith arrived after a seemingly endless half hour. He didn't have a problem with the front door key, but things seemed to get complicated trying to get a replacement Mercedes key and only smoothed out when he examined the rental contract and compared the name on it to the one on Avril's passport, which thankfully she'd hidden with tape behind a bedroom drawer, before leaving the house that morning.

Armed with a new front door key we went inside, had a bite to eat and talked about what we could do. The plan was that David and Ayelet would wait at the villa to explain to the police how to find us and take any messages if needed. Everybody's phone had been stolen. First, we'd drive to the Aphrodite restaurant to ask Anwar if he had any insights about what the Jihadists might do, then return to our own neighborhood looping around everywhere in search of the late model BMW. It wasn't much but we had to do something.

The owner of the Aphrodite led us into the kitchen where Anwar was being coached as he worked by a good humored waitress, to pronounce words in Greek, as she held up a dinner plate, then a spoon, then a wine glass. It was briefly kind of charming, trying to get Anwar's attention as he diligently mouthed a Greek word to the attentive waitress. She hurried off back to work as he turned to us. The task of explaining to Anwar what had happened and what we needed was so difficult we almost gave up.

But then something clicked in him. He said: "boat, look by boat, look at boat, look for boat."

He looked at me with an intense glare as if the penny had dropped, and I looked back at him mystified, wondering what the hell is he talking about?

Then it hit me. Of course, the Jihadist guys may have realized they could be captured at the airport, got away from there somehow, stolen a car and now they were trying the sea route home again. "Yes!" I said. "Yes," I said again as the idea began to clarify in my mind. Instinctively I held his cheeks but missed and got his ears, stooped, he was just a little guy, and I kissed him on the forehead while Avril and Moishe looked on, stupefied, Anwar beamed.

The logic was pretty simple. Avril, Moishe and I talked it over. What Anwar had suggested seemed to us the best possible approach to finding Hannah and Ari. People trying to leave the country in a boat on a trailer would need a launch site. They might have tried to hijack a boat, but given the length of their voyage they'd need extra fuel, and the only boat readily available, and pre-stocked to the gunwales with fuel, was the one in which they'd made their

306

first attempt to leave the island a few days ago. Getting that car and boat would not have taken them long. It was about, maybe an hour and a half since they locked us in the garage and presumably, they drove away immediately after that. I figured Ari would know to slow them down any way he could. Not only that, but I'd seen during the previous few days how well Ari and his sister knew and trusted each other. I was sure they'd find ways to work together.

The obvious place to launch a boat to avoid being intercepted was the closest one. To get away the Jihadists knew they would need to leave in a hurry. We had detailed maps in the car and sat in the restaurant parking lot scouring the coast nearby for launch sites. We were already near the coast and found a launch site barely three miles away. We were just about to pull out on our way, when Anwar came running after us, knocked on the car window and jumped in the back seat. He was holding a brown paper bag containing four gyros. "I think you hungry," he said, "my boss says 'you go, here take this.' I come with you."

It wasn't that long ago since we'd eaten back at the villa, but it was such a lovely gesture that we ate the gyros anyway, except for Moishe. He was driving and Avril wouldn't let him have it. "Go, go, and turn left out of the parking lot," said Avril as she wiped a spot of yogurt from her map, licked her finger and added: "Look for a lane on the right, in half a mile, maybe a mile. Slow down Moishe, don't let's miss it." The road was busy with late afternoon traffic. Moishe slowed right down, annoying a driver behind us. With four of us looking we soon found the lane to the boat launch. A car moved close behind and honked but Moshe ignored it and signaled right a few seconds later.

The dirt road wound gently downhill, around fields and orchards until it opened out onto a stony beach crossed by the road on a raised rocky embankment which let out to parking spaces on the beach at both sides. The last thirty yards was surfaced with serrated concrete forming a ramp down into the water.

Moishe turned the car into a parking space on the beach to give us a complete view of the goings on around us. A jeep like car had backed a trailer down the ramp into the water. A small boat steered towards its cushioned curved poles. Then a guy jumped out of the boat over the side into knee deep water, attached a cable to the bow and proceeded to hand winch the boat into its cradle where he secured it. The driver pulled away leaving the ramp free for a waiting sport utility vehicle with a large luxurious boat in tow. I mean to say large in terms of a boat you can pull with a car.

The sport utility vehicle pulled closer to us to line up for backing the trailer and boat down the ramp. There was nobody else at the launch site or on the beach after the jeep rig pulled away and It was now late afternoon so there would be no more launches that day unless, unless "Good grief! Good grief! That's them," I yelled. And sure enough, there was Ari, out of the car directing the driver as he quite skillfully backed the boat and trailer down the ramp. Ari's cooperation was diligent, dashing to one side, then the other signaling to the driver which way to turn the wheel and when to go and stop. Little-beard was driving the vehicle but there was no sign of the big guy. Oh wait, there he was in the back seat and there was Hannah next to him.

We had no phones, we could not call for help, there was no one left on the beach that might have had a phone we could use. Moishe backed up the car to turn it around with the intent of driving back to the restaurant to call the police. But he stopped. We really needed to see what was going on, riveted to the action on the ramp. Ari released the clamps on the boat cradle and switched on the power winch to release it down off its cradle into the water. Big-beard walked into knee-deep water with Hanna, holding her arm with one hand and the butcher's knife in the other. We saw her climb over the side and the big guy followed all the while brandishing his knife. Then Little-beard got out of the sport utility vehicle pointing his gun at Ari who walked calmly over to the boat where he waited for Little-beard to climb in first then shoved out the boat and climbed in after him. They hadn't bothered to pull the vehicle and trailer away from the ramp. For a moment Little-beard had been vulnerable as he climbed in. I wondered if Ari would act, but then, obviously, he couldn't risk Hannah being harmed.

We watched helplessly as the inboard motor hummed gently, powering the pretty pleasure boat down the shallow channel into deeper and deeper water. We could see less and less of what was happening on the boat since it was now late in the day which had turned dull and overcast.

Our hearts were sinking. "Don't worry," said Moishe, trying to cheer us up, "the coast guard or police will intercept them for sure. We've just got to tell them." But I wasn't so sure, and even if they could catch the boat there were two hostages on board whose lives meant little to their captors.

Then I saw something like a dark colored streak chute down one side of the boat and a splash, maybe? Did I really see what I thought I saw? They must be two hundred yards away and the light was fading; but the others saw it too. "Looks like Hannah dived in," said Moishe. I couldn't be sure but he might have been right. "Yes, yes," said Anwar, "I see too."

We saw the boat rock, then turn, as if to retrieve whatever had gone over the side but at that very moment we heard the stutter of a gun, multiple shots were fired. My heart went to my mouth. "Oh God, what's happening? I gasped.

Then there were more shots and pinging as if bullets were hitting something metal. Then there was another streak over the side, accompanied by a bigger splash.

The boat's diesel engine sputtered and stopped and seemed to be slightly lower in the water. "Do you think the boat's sinking?" I asked Avril, who by this time was running down the beach as she peered anxiously out into the water, as were we all.

"I think you're right," she answered, I looked again, the boat was definitely sinking. I heard a faint yell from Ari: "Hey wait for us, we're coming."

It was such a relief to hear his voice. I internalized 'wait for us' so now I knew they were both out there. They were probably two-hundred-and-fifty, maybe three hundred yards out at sea now. Even this thankfully calm water occasionally obscured their distant heads bobbing up and down between small waves. Fortunately, I was thinking,

310

although the water can be rough, there is very little tidal current in the Mediterranean, unlike the Atlantic beaches in New York and New Jersey that were familiar to me. Slowly, slowly they came. They were talking to one another. You could hear a word or two but not make out what they were saying as their heads sank momentarily between wave crests. I even caught some distant laughter.

Meanwhile the boat out there was sinking lower. We could see two stick-like figures standing on the stern platform, one taller than the other. Each was holding a circular thing; must have been those life preserver things you use for buoyancy. But they just stood there, motionless. They'd seen us, I'm sure. How could they not have? They must have seen us earlier when they were launching but felt secure as long as they had hostages.

After reminding myself a hundred times, to help calm me down, how long it takes to swim two hundred yards, suddenly Ari stood up, panting. His head and shoulders were out of the water as he turned around to take Hannah's hand to pull her shoreward until she found her own feet. We saw they'd both managed to shed all but their underwear as they scrambled the last few yards to dry land. The two of them started to shiver in the cool sea breeze, so after a quick wet group hug we walked quickly to the Mercedes. Moishe gave Hannah a piggyback. Ari took some of the weight off his feet which hurt on the sharp pebbles, putting his arm over my shoulder. I bore his arm and cold wet side stoically, but I suspect he was enjoying the moment, smirking as he made me wet.

On the drive back to the villa we stopped at the Aphrodite restaurant where Moishe called Captain Stephanoupolos who thanked him for the news and added, "We'll pick 'em up." For his part he had found the stolen BMW, complete with our phones, Avril's computer, the router, and the Mercedes keys.

I have no words to describe the relief and outpourings of emotion from Ayelet and David when they welcomed Hannah and Ari safely back at the villa. When things were a little calmer Hannah was bursting to tell us how they'd escaped. Ari nodded as if to say: "you tell it". First, she told her parents in Hebrew, then in English for Avril and me, and finally Ari translated into Arabic for Anwar. I had to marvel at her childish resilience in telling the story, as if she'd just scored the winning goal in a soccer game.

"The little guy with a beard asked me if I could swim," she said. "I shook my head, 'no,' I squeaked, and pretended to cry and then I said angrily 'I'm scared, why are you doing this to me? I want to go home, and I want my mom.' He looked at me, then told the big guy to take the life preservers to the front of the boat, out of my reach. I yelled even louder and when he was all the way at the front with the life preservers, Ari nodded at me and I slipped over the side and swam underwater as far as I could in the direction of the shore. Even under water I could hear the gun and I was scared for Ari and just kept swimming as fast as I could. A minute later I heard Ari yell: 'You OK Hannah?' I was never really scared as long as Ari was with me. He's much tougher than he pretends to be."

So our eyes redirected to Ari for his part of the story which followed in triple translation as before. "The little guy steering the boat tried to make a quick turn to look for Hannah who had just dived over the side." he said. "I thought that was really dangerous and stupid because it ran the risk of running over her. But as he turned suddenly the boat rocked alarmingly, aided by the swell from deeper water. Both these guys were momentarily thrown off balance and the big guy dropped his knife to hold the side and get his balance. The Uzi, which Little-beard had used to threaten us, and had been parked above the binnacle as he steered the boat, crashed to the floor and I made a dive for it. There was no other weapon I could have handled so deftly. I'd trained and practiced with one like this, literally for hours, as part of my military training. I rolled over twice and when I was front side up I managed to point the muzzle at the shocked pair. They heard me click off the safety catch.

"Holding the gun in my right hand, with my left hand I flipped open the engine cowl and fired multiple shots through a bare low section of the hull causing an upward fast gushing waterspout. The two guys had retreated to the far end of the boat. They knew I could re-target them at a split second's notice. They were petrified. I looked at the clip having saved a few rounds then picked up the kitchen knife from the deck that the big guy had just dropped and started sawing through the fuel line which was some kind of reinforced textile. But the knife was hardened steel and after sawing and sawing and sweating profusely it started to leak, then snapped. I started shooting some more to make another

313

hole and I hit something metallic, I don't know what, but the two guys may have thought I was trashing the motor. It made no difference, the motor stopped anyway with no easy way to restart it."

"These pleasure boats usually have buoyancy tanks so it's not going to sink all the way, but it will be completely swamped and useless to them. They had their life preservers. I don't think they can swim They may still be standing on a remaining dry spot. I had no thought of shooting anybody but they weren't to know that. I guess I might have though if they'd attacked me. I just threw the gun over the side and dived in after it. I knew Hannah was a strong swimmer, but I yelled at her to reassure myself and felt relief when I heard her reply. I had to swim as fast as I was able even to catch her. I could see you all standing on the distant beach peering out in our direction and that spurred me on too."

Captain Stephanoupolos stopped by the villa later to ask Ari and Anwar to visit the police station the following afternoon to make a statement. He told us that Little-beard succeeded in swimming to the shore but he was obviously not a strong swimmer and was staggering up the beach, completely exhausted when a police car showed up just in time to arrest him. As for Big-beard, he was not a swimmer, but he made an attempt to reach the shore holding on to a life preserver. The police had taken an inflatable launch with a searchlight along the line of buoys and found him exhausted, flailing and splashing, about a hundred yards out.

Spiros showed up while the captain was talking to us. I think it was just a social call, but he was welcome, of course, and made himself useful preparing a meal, directed, as usual by Avril. I noticed Anwar had cornered him later for an impromptu Greek lesson as he mouthed the word for spoon and meal and dish and practiced writing Greek characters.

Later Avril drove Hannah and me to a tourist souvenir store to buy a doll in Greek costume for Hannah like the one I'd bought for Daanya. I bought a postcard to send to my parents and wrote it that evening so that I could mail it the following morning when we took Ari's Israeli family to the airport. Except for tears and smiles and hugs there was little else of note which happened there. And except, oh well, it went something like this:

Ayelet hugged me affectionately and told me to look after Ari. "He's a good boy," she said, but don't take any nonsense from him, make him look after you too."

"I'm... I'm from Brooklyn, I can cope," I answered idiotically, and struggling for words, like I needed anybody to look after me. Huh! I think not. But I was not sure how to frame my conflicting emotions, and concerned that my state of mind may be reflected in facial contortions accompanied by an uninvited tear rolling down my cheek.

"I'm...," and I choked.

Her response was still and mute except for a mutual tear and her hug frozen in place for what seemed like a decade.

"I knew it," she replied, shedding a few more tears, "does he know it yet?"

I shook my head feeling a little fragile following my admission.

"That's alright my dear," she said, "just don't wait too long to tell him. Email me to tell me what's going on. I lost a son and gained a daughter, and now I don't know, perhaps perhaps?"

The End